W9-AXR-481

BY EVELYN SKYE

The Hundred Loves of Juliet

THE CROWN'S GAME SERIES
The Crown's Game
The Crown's Fate

CIRCLE OF SHADOWS SERIES
Circle of Shadows
Cloak of Night

Three Kisses, One Midnight

DAMSEL

DAMSEL

EVELYN SKYE

BASED ON A SCREENPLAY BY
DAN MAZEAU

DRAGON LANGUAGE BY REESE SKYE

RANDOM HOUSE WORLDS
NEW YORK

Damsel is a work of fiction. Names, places, and incidents either are products of the author's imagination or are used fictitiously. Any resemblance to actual events, locales, or persons, living or dead, is entirely coincidental.

2024 Random House Worlds Trade Paperback Edition

Copyright © 2023 by Netflix, Inc.

All rights reserved.

Published in the United States by Random House Worlds, an imprint of Random House, a division of Penguin Random House LLC, New York.

RANDOM HOUSE is a registered trademark, and RANDOM HOUSE WORLDS and colophon are trademarks of Penguin Random House LLC.

Originally published in hardcover in the United States by Random House Worlds, an imprint of Random House, a division of Penguin Random House LLC, in 2023.

Based on a screenplay written by Dan Mazeau

Directed by Juan Carlos Fresnadillo

LIBRARY OF CONGRESS CATALOGING-IN-PUBLICATION DATA
Names: Skye, Evelyn, author.
Title: Damsel / Evelyn Skye.
Description: First edition. | New York: Random House Worlds, 2023
Identifiers: LCCN 2022055290 (print) | LCCN 2022055291 (ebook) |
ISBN 9780593599426 (paperback) | ISBN 9780593599419 (ebook)
Subjects: LCGFT: Fantasy fiction. | Novels.
Classification: LCC PS3619.K935 D36 2023 (print) |
LCC PS3619.K935 (ebook) | DDC 813/.6—dc23/eng/20221122
LC record available at https://lccn.loc.gov/2022055290
LC ebook record available at https://lccn.loc.gov/2022055291

PRINTED IN THE UNITED STATES OF AMERICA ON ACID-FREE PAPER

randomhousebooks.com

1 3 5 7 9 8 6 4 2

Book design by Elizabeth Rendfleisch
Title page art by tetyanatr/stock.adobe.com
Ornament by migfoto/stock.adobe.com

To all the brave souls who dare to remake the world

DAMSEL

ELODIE

I NOPHE WAS THE sort of place for which the globe moved backward. While the rest of the world progressed, barren Inophe slid further and further into the past. Seventy years of drought had reduced the duchy's meager croplands to endless sand dunes. The people harvested their gardens of cacti for water, and they existed in a system of bartering—a length of homespun cloth in exchange for the chore of mending a fence; a dozen eggs for a tincture to ease a toothache; and on special occasions, a goat in exchange for a small sack of precious imported flour.

"It's a beautiful place, despite everything," Duke Richard Bayford said as he rode his horse to the edge of a plateau that overlooked the soft brown landscape, broken up here and there by the lean branches of ironwood trees and the yellow flowers of acacias. He was a tall and wiry man, his face wrinkled by four and a half decades under the relentless sun.

"It's a beautiful place *because* of everything," his daughter Elodie chided gently as she rode up beside him. At twenty, she'd been helping him with the Duchy of Inophe for as long as she could remember, and she'd one day inherit the role as its steward.

Lord Bayford chuckled. "You're right as usual, my dove. Inophe is beautiful *because* of everything it is."

Elodie smiled. Below their plateau, a long-eared fox sprang from the shade of a desert willow and chased something—probably a gerbil or lizard—around a boulder. To the east, undulating dunes rose and fell, mountains of sand cascading toward a glittering sea. Even the dry heat on Elodie's skin felt like the welcome embrace of an old friend.

There was a rustle in the scrub behind them.

"Pardon me, Lord Bayford." A man emerged, carrying a staff. A moment later, his herd of bearded gray desert goats followed, indiscriminately biting off the heads of spiny flowers and their thorned stems and swallowing them whole. If only the people of Inophe had such gums and stomachs of iron, they'd be able to survive much better in this harsh clime.

"Good day, Lady Elodie." The shepherd swept off his tattered hat and dipped his head as the duke and Elodie dismounted.

"How may we be of service, Immanuel?" Lord Bayford asked.

"Er, your lordship . . . My oldest son, Sergio, is about to be married, and he'll be needing a new cottage for his family. I was hoping that, uh, you might be able to . . ."

Before the pause could grow awkward, Lord Bayford jumped in. "You need building materials?"

Immanuel fiddled with his staff but then nodded. Inophean tradition held that fathers gifted their sons with new homes on their wedding day, and mothers gifted their daughters with handmade gowns. But decades of impoverishment meant it was harder and harder for the old ways to continue.

"It would be an honor to provide the materials for Sergio's

cottage," Lord Bayford said. "Do you need assistance with its construction? Elodie is particularly good with rigging solar stills."

"True," she said. "I'm also good at digging latrines, which Sergio and his wife can use after they've drunk the water they collected in the solar stills."

Immanuel's eyes widened as he stared at her.

Elodie cursed herself under her breath. She had, unfortunately, a gift for saying the wrong thing at the wrong time. When faced with social interaction, especially the expectation that *she* say something, Elodie seized up—her shoulders tightened and her throat went dry, and her once coherent ideas tumbled on top of one another like books from an upended shelf. Then she'd end up blurting out whatever thought had landed at the top of that pile, and it would inevitably be inappropriate.

That wasn't to say she was unappreciated. The people respected her devotion to Inophe. Elodie rode several days every week under the scalding sun from tenancy to tenancy, checking on what the families needed. She helped with everything from building rat traps around henhouses to reading tales of princesses and dragons to children, and Elodie loved every moment of it. She had been raised for this. As her mother used to say, giving yourself to others is the noblest sacrifice.

"What Elodie means," Lord Bayford said smoothly, "is that she doesn't mind getting her hands dirty."

Thank goodness Father is still in charge, Elodie thought. One day she would be duchess of these lands. But for now, it was a relief that the duchy had the charismatic Richard Bayford at its helm.

Elodie kept an ear on the conversation as Immanuel detailed how much wood and how many nails he would need, but she turned her body so she could look past the dusty landscape to the open water beyond. Ever since she was a child, the sea had soothed her, and as she focused on the waves shimmering under the sun, some of the sting of her latrine faux pas faded, and her shoulders began to release some of their tension.

She sighed in relief.

Perhaps, in a past life, she'd been a sailor. Or a seagull. Or maybe even the wind. For although Elodie devoted her days to the work of Inophe, she spent her evenings dreaming of being out on the ocean. She liked sitting in the local taverns, listening to stories the seamen brought from abroad—what festivals and customs other kingdoms celebrated. What their lands looked like, how the weather was. How they lived and loved and even how they died. Elodie collected sailors' yarns like a crow hoards shiny buttons; every tale was a rare treasure.

Once the list of requirements for Sergio's new home was finished and Immanuel and his goats had departed, Lord Bayford rejoined Elodie at the edge of the plateau. As they gazed out at the horizon, a small speck sailed into view.

Elodie tilted her head, perplexed. "What do you suppose that is?" It was not yet the season for Inophe's trading vessels to return from abroad with much-needed grain, fruit, and cotton.

"There's one way to find out," Lord Bayford said, climbing onto his horse and winking at Elodie. "Whoever arrives at the harbor last has to dig Sergio's latrines!"

"Father, I'm not racing—"

But he and his horse were already charging down the plateau.

"You're a cheater!" she called after him as she leapt onto her own horse.

"It's the only way I have a fighting chance of winning," he shouted over his shoulder.

And Elodie laughed as she took off after him, because she knew it was true.

THE SHIP'S FLAGS bore the colors of wealth, a rich crimson with gilded edges, and the gold dragon on its prow gleamed proudly. The officers on board wore uniforms of velvet with fine golden embroidery around each button and cuff, and even the ordinary sailors sported berets of deep red decorated with a jaunty gold tassel.

In contrast, the Inophean harbor stood hunched like a wizened old man, splintered and gray, its docks weather-beaten by both salt and sun. The posts were composed of more barnacles than wood; they creaked noisily with every wave, the ancient bones complaining of the wind and the damp.

The port was a sizable one, for Inophe depended on trade to feed its population. The duchy produced two natural resources— gum from acacia trees and slabs of guano, dried bird excrement used as fertilizer—and in exchange, Inophe received just enough barley, corn, and cotton to get its people by.

Elodie had spent as much of her life in the dry plains inland as she had here on the piers, tallying export and import receipts and picking up bits and pieces of new languages from the traders. But this ship's colors were unfamiliar to her, as was their coat of arms: a gold dragon clutching a sheaf of wheat in one claw and a cluster of what looked like grapes or berries in another. When Elodie reached its dock, Lord Bayford was already there.

She exhaled. "All right, you win. It's a good thing I was planning on digging Sergio's latrines anyway."

He waved away her concession. "There are more important things at stake now. Elodie, I would like you to meet Alexandra

Ravella, royal envoy of the Kingdom of Aurea." Her father gestured to a trim woman in her fifties, wearing a gold tricorn and a
crimson velvet uniform. "And Lieutenant Ravella, may I present
the older of my daughters, Lady Elodie Bayford of the Duchy of
Inophe."

"The pleasure is mine," Lieutenant Ravella said in perfect Ingleterr, one of the common languages used in international
trade and also the official language of Inophe. She removed her
hat, revealing silver hair tied back in a neat knot, and bowed
deeply.

But Elodie frowned. "I'm afraid I don't follow. Father, what's
going on?"

"Only the very best of news, my dove." Lord Bayford
wrapped his arm around her shoulders. "Forgive me for keeping
secrets from you, but I confess I have met Lieutenant Ravella
before, several months ago. When we negotiated your engagement."

"My what?" Elodie froze beneath the weight of her father's
arm. She must have misheard. He wouldn't do such a thing without consulting her—

"Your betrothal, my lady," Lieutenant Ravella said with an-
other low bow. "You shall, if you agree, marry Crown Prince
Henry and become the next princess of the golden kingdom of
Aurea."

ELODIE

EIGHT MONTHS LATER

N EVER LET IT be said that women's fashion is merely shallow decoration. Although old Captain Croat was steering the ship, Elodie was currently double-checking the ship's navigation through the nighttime fog, using a mother-of-pearl hairpin and a reed pen as a makeshift sextant. In her years of running the imports and exports at the Inophean harbor, Elodie had devoured any information she could come by from the sailors so she could sail the seas at night in her dreams. And now, by an improbable turn of events, this was actually her reality.

"*Cóm visteù*, Lady Elodie?" Gaumiot, one of the crew, sauntered up beside her. He, like the rest of the Inophean crew, spoke a polyglot vernacular, a mishmash of words acquired here and there from their travels and cobbled together into a freeform language. Elodie had heard it often enough at the harbor that she could understand it, and after two months at sea, she'd now begun to speak some of their language, too.

How does it look? Gaumiot had asked.

"Ugh, *emâsia nebline gruëo*," she said. The fog was much too thick to see clearly. She sighed as she tucked the hairpin back into her chestnut locks.

"A destination we can't see." Gaumiot grunted as he turned away to go back to work. "It's *malseùr.*"

Bad luck. Elodie smiled to herself. The sailors were a superstitious lot. But the most superstitious people always had the best tall tales and legends to tell, and she'd enjoyed the crew's company immensely during this voyage. Sailors didn't mind her awkwardness; those who lived and died at the mercy of the sea had bigger things to worry about than unvarnished conversation.

Unlike Gaumiot, though, Elodie was eager to see Aurea. In the eight months following the offer of betrothal, Elodie and Prince Henry had exchanged several letters. Aurean vessels were much swifter than Inophean ships, and they were able to make the journey between Aurea and Inophe in weeks rather than months. Henry's letters were written in neat, angular script and told tales of the beauty and abundance of the isle on which he lived. Elodie's letters were full of stories about her people and their tireless pride in their work. And of course, she also wrote about her favorite person in the world, her sister. Floria's current obsession was the intricate mazes Elodie created for her, always interestingly shaped—a beehive, a coyote, a birthday cake on the day Flor turned thirteen.

In fact, it was at her sister's prodding that Elodie had drawn a heart-shaped maze for Henry and included it in her final letter, the one accepting his engagement proposal and informing him they would set sail for Aurea in time for the September harvest. Of course, being Elodie, she hadn't sketched just any heart. She'd drawn an anatomically correct one.

In hindsight, it *might* have been a bit off-putting. Elodie hoped Henry would be as willing to overlook her social gaffes as the sailors were.

She still wasn't sure what Aurea was getting out of the marriage contract, but Elodie knew full well what Inophe was getting out of it: more than she could have offered if she'd stayed behind, even if she'd given every ounce of sweat and every piece of her soul. One could not feed an entire country on sheer will alone.

The damp fog kissed her cheek, as if soothing her. She was doing the right thing, being on this ship. Soon they would arrive in Aurea, and the deal would be done. As for the whole idea of marriage, she would make it work. Her feelings on the subject didn't really matter. She would serve the people of Inophe.

Lieutenant Ravella strolled over and bowed to her. As royal envoy, she was accompanying Elodie and her family to Aurea.

"You know, I could ask Captain Croat for a proper sextant if you'd like." The lieutenant gestured at Elodie's hairpin. She must have been nearby when Elodie tried using it.

"It's fine, mine's better," Elodie said, realizing a split second after the words came out how rude that sounded. "I'm sorry, what I meant to say is, I know how my makeshift sextant works so, uh, no need to trouble yourself. I can't see the stars much anyway. But thank you."

"I'm impressed that you can chart the night sky, given that you've never been at sea."

"I never even thought I'd leave Inophe."

"No?" Lieutenant Ravella cocked her head. "Then why learn to navigate by the stars or study the languages of those who came to your harbor, if not for plans to travel the world? Most people don't learn the intricacies of grammar and syntax without a greater goal in mind."

Elodie shifted her feet uncomfortably on the deck. It felt like a betrayal of Inophe to have ever wanted something more than her life there. And yet, Lieutenant Ravella was right. Elodie may have started out studying the languages of the traders in order to better run Inophe's harbor, but at some point, she'd begun learning for herself, too.

"I love Inophe and would do anything for my people, even if that meant never leaving its shores," she said. "But I must admit I *have* dreamed of experiencing the sailors' tales for myself someday. And thanks to you, I can now do my duty to my country *and* expand the boundaries of what I thought my life would be."

The lieutenant winced. Or so it seemed, but then the expression was gone, replaced by a distant smile, the type Elodie knew well from merchant ship traders when they didn't agree to her terms but were thinking about how to pivot the conversation.

Or perhaps it was Elodie who had committed some social faux pas. That was as likely as any other explanation. "Forgive me if I said something that offended you. It was not my intention but sometimes I, um—"

Lieutenant Ravella shook her head. "No, my lady. I suppose I was only thinking of the obligations that await you as princess." The envoy's expression remained formal, a marked change from the easy conversation they'd had for most of their time at sea.

"I understand duty well," Elodie said. "Please do not worry about that on my behalf. I assure you that whatever Aurea expects of me as their princess, I shall deliver. As long as it's not charming speeches."

But her attempt at levity fell flat.

"Of course, my lady," Lieutenant Ravella said with another tight smile. "Now, if you'll excuse me, I just remembered something I need to attend to before we make landfall." She bowed quickly and hurried belowdecks to the cabins.

Elodie sighed. Once she arrived on Aurea, she should probably say as little as possible. At least until the wedding was official.

That way Prince Henry wouldn't change his mind and instead decide to find a wife who could actually speak without tripping over her own tongue.

A minute later, Floria burst onto the deck from the cabins below. At thirteen, she was all black braids and unrestrained exuberance, bounding to Elodie. "I solved the maze you made me!" she shouted, waving the piece of paper Elodie had given her just that morning. "Those decoy exits didn't fool me."

Elodie plucked the maze from her sister's hand to check her work. Floria had, indeed, found the correct path out of the ship-shaped maze.

Their stepmother, Lady Lucinda Bayford, laced up tightly in a gray wool kirtle with a high neck, ascended from below and joined them on deck. She was the type of woman who was beautiful in a bronze statue kind of way, and with the personality of a statue, too—dignified and polished, but inflexible.

"Is this horrid odyssey almost over?" she said. "We have been on this ship for sixty-three days, and I am damp to my bones."

"My dear," Lord Bayford called as he climbed up the stairs. "I brought you your extra cloak." He emerged on deck and wrapped her in a thick silver cape lined with the fur of sand foxes.

"We are all going to catch our death before we make it to Aurea," Lady Bayford grumbled.

Suddenly, a beam of moonlight cut through the fog. Elodie gasped as she caught sight of the stars. *"Merdú!"*

Lady Bayford flinched at yet another of the "uncouth" phrases Elodie had picked up from the sailors. But now was not the time to worry about her stepmother's sensibilities. Because if Elodie's calculations were correct . . .

"What is it?" Floria asked.

Elodie didn't respond, only rushed for the ropes and scurried up the netting.

"Come down immediately!" Lady Bayford shouted. "You can't swim! You'll fall and die!"

Elodie wouldn't fall. She'd been climbing towering eucalyptus trees her entire life.

"And the sailors will see up your skirts!" Lady Bayford added, as if decorum were equally as important as Elodie's life.

"She *is* wearing breeches under her chemise," Floria said.

Elodie laughed. As if *that* would alleviate the scandal of a woman letting everyone peek up her gown. But that was also not Elodie's concern right now. What was important was—

"*Pari u navio!*" she shouted to the sailors as she reached the top of the ropes. "Stop the ship *now!*"

Old Captain Croat, who'd been lazing behind the wheel, jumped to attention. "You heard the lady!" he snapped at the sailors. "Slow our course!"

The ship creaked as the sails loosened, the canvas luffing in the wind, momentum easing. The moonbeam had disappeared back into the fog, and the ship drifted blindly. The silence on deck was as thick as the mist, all breath held in anticipation of whatever Elodie knew was coming.

And then two looming shadows appeared, silhouettes in the near distance. The sailors craned their necks.

Hungry, razor-toothed jaws towered over them.

"Stone dragons," Elodie murmured in awe. Lieutenant Ravella had told her about them, the markers of the outer boundaries of Aurea. Dew glistened on the etched scales, topaz eyes glinted in the moonlight that now broke through the fog, and water gushed through the open maws like fountains, sprinkling the ship with droplets of rain.

"Malseùr," Gaumiot and some of the other sailors whispered, touching their hands to their hearts to protect them from ill luck.

But Elodie smiled. Dragons weren't real, only fantasy. This was no bad omen. If anything, it was a symbol of the extraordinary to come.

From her place high up on the ropes, she held her arms straight out, and the wind puffed open the long sleeves of her dress. For a brief moment, she felt as if she could fly. Two decades in small Inophe. Two decades wondering what else was out in the world. A lifetime of accepting that she'd only get to hear stories and never experience them for herself.

But now, this . . . Elodie filled her lungs with briny air. She was doing it. She was saving her people while also soaring high.

Even the most predictable life can gift you with the unexpected.

Captain Croat maneuvered the ship around the stone sentinels.

"I don't like them," Lady Bayford shuddered.

"I think they're beautiful," Elodie said as she slid down the ropes, back onto the deck.

As soon as the ship sailed between the two dragon statues, the fog burned away completely, and everything that lay before them was softly illuminated like it was dawn, as if this place was so different from the rest of the world that it somehow defied nighttime.

A sapphire lagoon revealed itself, with a verdant island at the center of the horizon. Next to Elodie, Floria's jaw dropped. "I-is that it? Is that where we're going?"

On the eastern side, deep green orchards and gentle fields of grain stretched as far as the eye could see. On the western side, a majestic violet-gray mountain reigned, its head crowned by clouds and stars. A golden palace sparkled under the adoring light of the moon.

Lord Bayford wrapped his arms around his two daughters. "Welcome, my doves, to the Isle of Aurea."

LIEUTENANT RAVELLA DISEMBARKED first and rode ahead to inform the palace of their arrival. Elodie still wondered why the royal envoy's demeanor had changed as they neared Aurea, but soon Elodie was distracted because a gold carriage arrived to whisk her and her family from the harbor.

They began their journey into the isle, and Floria held tightly on to Elodie's hand, squeezing every time something delighted her.

"Look at those orchards," Floria gushed, pointing at rows and rows of trees laden with the famed Aurean silver pears Henry had mentioned in his letters, and hedgerows of blood-red sangberries, coveted the world over for their juicy sweetness and healing properties. The fruit was so richly colored, it shone like jewels under the preternaturally bright light of the Aurean moon.

"There's so much . . . green," Lady Bayford said, gaping. "How do they have enough water to grow it all?"

"The Isle of Aurea is not parched like our own poor duchy," Lord Bayford said. "Elodie's marriage to Prince Henry allows us to cease worrying about drought. With this alliance, the In-ophean people will never go hungry again. Our storehouses will be full this winter, and every winter forevermore." He reached across the carriage and squeezed Elodie's knee. "Thank you."

Elodie bit her lip but nodded. Not because she didn't want to marry Henry—from their correspondence, he seemed like a thoughtful man who enjoyed her intelligence and who would one day be an honorable king. It was actually because she *did* want to marry him that she felt so unsettled. Elodie had long resigned herself to a hard life on Inophe. But everything about Aurea seemed like a dream—from the prosperity of the beautiful island to Henry's eagerness to wed her—and Elodie worried it might all disappear if she thought about it too hard. Perhaps she'd wake up and discover it had all been a figment of her imagination.

Besides, why would the future king of Aurea—one of the richest countries in the world—want to marry the daughter of a minor lord from a drought-ridden duchy with no natural resources (other than guano) or military might or other political capital to offer? With this union, Inophe would be guaranteed food and financial support. But what was Aurea getting out of the bargain?

Her father and Lieutenant Ravella had assured her that Aurea was thrilled to have a well-educated lady like Elodie as their future princess, especially one with practical experience in overseeing people and land.

The compliments were flattering, Elodie had to admit, and yet . . . they still did not add up. She picked at a loose thread on her sleeve. The yellow silk was the nicest fabric ever to touch her skin, and yet it now seemed rough-hewn and dull next to the splendor of Aurea.

"Oooh, look at the little lambs," Floria cooed as the carriage rolled past pastures dotted with herds of fluffy sheep. Their wool was supposedly softer than any other, and these sheep lived only on Aurea. Another reason for the island's wealth.

Elodie leaned out the carriage window to admire the lambs. They had big black eyes and cute button noses, like illustrations in a children's book come to life.

"Can you believe you get to live here?" Floria asked. "It's incredible, and if anyone deserves to be princess of a paradise, it's you."

Lady Bayford snorted. "No one is more worthy than another," she muttered under her breath.

Elodie fought the urge to roll her eyes. From the moment their stepmother had walked into their lives, Lady Bayford had been insecure about the love Lord Bayford had for his daughters. And how ridiculous! A grown woman, worried about sharing his attentions with two children.

Or maybe it was because Elodie so resembled her mother, and every time Lady Bayford looked at Elodie, she was reminded that Lord Bayford had loved—*still* loved—another before her.

The carriage wove through villages of windmills and quaint, thatch-roofed cottages where people poked their heads out of windows and bowed as the coach passed. They looked so different from the people on Inophe. Both were suntanned and strong, but the Aureans' cheeks were filled out from being well nourished, and their easy smiles suggested a life of bounty rather than survival. Elodie waved but couldn't smile back, for her thoughts were on the Inopheans who had never had the opportunity to be so carefree.

But maybe now they will, she thought. After all, that was the impetus for accepting Prince Henry's proposal. Elodie's marriage would ensure the well-being of her people.

For *that,* she could smile.

As the road wound higher, out of the fertile valley and onto the base of the mountain, the royal palace came into view. Although Elodie had seen the glimmering walls from afar on their ship, the sight of the castle this close was almost too much to behold.

The palace made of pure gold rose from purple-gray granite

like a vision from a fairy tale. The castle stood three stories tall with shield-shaped parapets at the top, and seven perfectly cylindrical towers soared above those, each one wrapped in vines of golden roses that scented the air with honeyed perfume. Gold-tasseled crimson banners bearing Aurea's coat of arms—a dragon clasping what Elodie now knew was a sheaf of aurum wheat in one claw and sangberries in another—hung with dignity around the drawbridge, and flags with the same heraldic bearings fluttered in the warm, gentle breeze.

This place is going to be my home? Elodie thought.

But what she actually said aloud was, "This place must be . . . quite difficult to keep clean."

Lady Bayford let out a worried groan. "Please do not say things like that when you meet the royal family."

As the carriage passed over the drawbridge and into the main courtyard, though, it was Elodie's turn to frown.

There was no one waiting to greet them.

Elodie looked around, confused. Lieutenant Ravella had ridden well ahead of them. Yet in the middle of the courtyard, a silver fountain of a pear tree burbled, but that was literally the only sound. How could a castle be so silent? And where had Lieutenant Ravella disappeared to?

"Um, is it me or is this a little strange?" Flor asked.

Their father forced a smile onto his face, trying to look as if this was part of the plan. "I am sure they are merely caught off guard. According to Captain Croat's calculations, we are actually a day early . . ."

As if on cue, a handful of liveried servants spilled out of the palace and into the courtyard. The castle chamberlain bowed as the breeze carried in the faint hints of a melody in the distance.

"My lord, my ladies, we are honored by your presence in Aurea."

"You have a lackadaisical way of showing it," Lady Bayford said as a footman helped her out of the carriage.

The chamberlain hesitated, as if carefully considering his words before answering. "My apologies, my lady. It is just that you, er . . . you were not expected today."

Lord Bayford laughed in the gentle manner of his that always set people at ease. The same laugh that had helped Elodie get through the death of her mother, even though her father had been just as distraught at the loss of his wife. "Our ship was favored by an excellent wind," Lord Bayford said. "I do hope our early arrival is not an inconvenience."

"Not at all," the chamberlain said, although something about the way he said it made Elodie uneasy. Perhaps it was the overly fawning way he kept bowing. Or the fact that his smiles never quite reached his eyes.

"Your arrival is no trouble in the slightest," the chamberlain was saying. "Your rooms are quite ready, if you will follow me."

Elodie furrowed her brow. "Are we not to be received by the king and queen? And Prince Henry?" Elodie might be a minor aristocrat from a backwater country, but she was also marrying the heir to Aurea.

The chamberlain bowed yet again. "Utmost apologies, but the royal family is at prayer. Word has been sent of your arrival."

With that, he ushered them into the gold palace. But instead of the main entryway, he led them through a sequence of winding, narrow hallways.

"What are these, servants' corridors?" Lady Bayford's eyes bugged out.

Floria wrinkled her nose. "It certainly doesn't seem like a welcome fit for a future princess."

No, it doesn't, Elodie thought. And there was no outwardly good reason for it. Yet from her experience at the helm of her father's lands, she knew well that exteriors could easily belie what lay within.

Still . . .

But she hated to spoil Floria's excitement at being in Aurea, so she took her sister's arm and linked it through her own. "We ought to be flattered, Flor. It's the outsiders who are kept to a castle's public spaces. But only those who are most trusted get to see the inner workings of a royal family's home."

At that, Floria relaxed. "You're probably right. And as the future princess, you'll soon know all of Aurea's secrets."

ELODIE

THE CHAMBERLAIN LED the way up a dim spiral staircase, higher and higher, and Elodie realized they must be inside one of the golden towers.

By the time they reached the upper landing ten flights later, everyone from Lord Bayford's attendants to Floria was sweating and huffing and puffing. Everyone other than Elodie, who had routinely spent her days hiking Inophe's dunes. The only thing she didn't like about the stairwell was how close the walls seemed. As a child, she'd slipped and gotten trapped deep inside a crevice in a plateau, and no one had looked for her for hours because they assumed she was simply out exploring or playing, as Elodie always was. It wasn't until she failed to turn up for supper that her parents realized something was amiss.

Elodie had never quite overcome her claustrophobia, the suffocating feeling of being trapped and possibly abandoned forever in a narrow wedge of rock. So when the chamberlain opened the door at the top of the spiraling steps, Elodie burst through it to escape the stairwell's confines.

She blinked at the brightness, the moonlight shockingly intense after the stairwell.

But then she realized it wasn't just the moon. It was the entire room. The walls were made of polished gold. The furniture was, too. The mirrors and windowsills were gilded, the bedspread and tapestries and rugs were golden, and even the quills on the desk were dipped in gold.

"I pray these chambers are to your liking," the chamberlain said.

"Uh, yes . . . they'll do," Elodie said, still in shock. Never in her life had she seen so much gold. And although it was flattering that it was all here for her, her stomach turned with the knowledge that she and her people had suffered for so long, while others were living like *this*.

But Floria squealed and ran past Elodie, throwing herself onto the bed. A puff of gold dust rose like glitter and sprinkled back down on her.

Even Lady Bayford thawed at the sight, running her hands over the intricate gold scrollwork on the doorframe.

"My staff will see to your needs," the chamberlain said to Elodie. "A bath is being drawn as we speak, and supper shall be brought thereafter." He picked up a gold bell from the bedside table. "Ring this should there be anything else you desire. Otherwise, I shall return at first light to convey you."

Elodie frowned. "Convey me to what?"

"Why, to meet your prince, of course." The chamberlain rang the bell once, merely a gentle tinkle, and servants came streaming in bearing bouquets of flowers unlike any Elodie had ever known. They looked like bundles of crystals in different jewel tones—ruby red, citrine yellow, amethyst purple. She reached out to touch one.

"Oh, do be careful, my lady," a servant girl said, stepping back so that Elodie's fingers missed. "Anthodite is pretty but very sharp. You must be careful around it."

Like certain people I know, Elodie thought wryly, casting a glance at her prickly but beautiful stepmother.

Lord Bayford, having finally caught his breath after the long trek up the stairs, squeezed Elodie's shoulder. "Well, what do you think?"

"I hope my life here will consist of more than beautiful rooms and flowers."

Her father arched an amused brow.

"That came out wrong!" Elodie said in a rush. "I'm not un-grateful. The opposite, really. But I hope that Henry—"

"Is handsome!" Floria said, saving Elodie from herself. Flor slid off the bed and twirled in bliss at this golden tower room.

Elodie laughed. "Yes, handsome would be a nice bonus."

Their father chuckled. "All right, let us grant Elodie some privacy and time to settle in, shall we? We could use a good washing and supper, as well. I am looking forward to a bath and a hot meal on solid land, no offense to our excellent ship's cook, of course. Chamberlain, if you will show us the way?"

Lady Bayford took one last look around Elodie's room and sniffed. "Let us hope that our accommodations are equally golden."

Floria made a face, but only so Elodie would see. Elodie winked at her and kissed her sweet sister on the top of her head. "See you in the morning?"

"I cannot wait!" Flor said as she skipped out of the room after their father and stepmother.

With everyone, including the servants, gone, Elodie exhaled, relieved to have a quiet moment for the first time since they set out to sea two months ago. She walked around her chambers, taking in this new world. The anthodite flowers filled the room with a heavenly floral scent, and the moonlight glittered prettily off the crystal-like petals, casting pale prismatic rainbows on the gold walls. A small plate of Inophean shortbread sat on her bedside table, as if the royal kitchen had wanted to greet her with a little token from home. Perhaps this marriage would be not only fine, but *more* than fine.

A large wrapped box sat on the desk beneath the picture window. It was tied with a grand golden bow, and a gold card read:

To my future wife,
May this gift delight you on your first night in Aurea.

"That's thoughtful," Elodie said as she untied the ribbon. She folded it neatly and set it down in the corner of the desk, then proceeded to very carefully unwrap the box, making sure the gold paper didn't tear. It was thick and expensive; she would save it so they could use it again.

"Oh, Henry," she gasped when she saw the gift itself.

It was a gold-framed map of the stars, as they would be seen from Aurea three evenings from now—their wedding night.

A smile spread across Elodie's face. She traced the golden dots representing the stars and the silver lines that connected the constellations. "If these are the types of gifts you're going to give me, it's an auspicious start to our partnership."

She explored the room some more and discovered another smaller box awaiting her on the vanity. As Elodie unwrapped it, though, her chest tightened with the guilt of all this extravagance, when right at this moment, the people of Inophe were still starving.

The box was covered in gold velvet and lined with crimson silk. Inside lay a pair of gold hair combs decorated with a mosaic pattern of tiny shield shapes. It reminded Elodie of the tail of the mermaid that was carved onto the prow of Captain Croat's ship.

Another card with Henry's angular handwriting read:

*I hope you will do me the honor of wearing these
in your hair on our wedding day.*

Elodie's hands shook as she picked up a comb and felt its weight in her fingers. Just one of these combs could feed all the families in Inophe for an entire winter, perhaps more. And to Henry and Aurea, they were mere trinkets.

But she also wanted to tuck them into her hair, badly. Never had she had such beautiful things. Never had she been spoiled in life.

In the distant royal gardens, faint music began to play, distracting Elodie from her conflicted thoughts. Then, in the tower opposite Elodie's, a woman stepped from the drapes into the moonlight.

She looked to be in her early twenties like Elodie, but with waist-length platinum hair braided with blue ribbons, and pale, freckled skin. She wore a pretty blue gown, the color of a shallow lagoon, and her jeweled earrings sparkled in the night.

Who was she? A lady-in-waiting? A future sister-in-law?

The woman was looking at the gathering in the royal gardens, but she appeared . . . sad. Her eyes were downcast and her shoulders slumped.

Why was she reacting that way to whatever was happening in the gardens?

"Hello?" Elodie called out.

No response. Perhaps she didn't understand Ingleterr.

"*Scuzimme? Hayo?*" Elodie tried two other greetings she'd learned from traders.

The woman looked up.

Elodie waved and smiled.

But as soon as the woman saw her, her eyes widened. She shook her head at Elodie, then jerked her curtains shut.

What the—?

"Well, that was rude," Elodie muttered.

A swallow landed on the windowsill and chirped, as if in agreement.

Elodie couldn't help but smirk. "I know. I didn't want to be her friend anyway."

The swallow tilted its head at Elodie, then danced over to a gold hourglass on the sill.

She had noticed it before but not paid it much attention. Now she saw that its sand was a crimson color, and the wooden frame was shaped like two ornate V's, their points meeting at the center. Elodie picked it up and turned it upside down, and the dark red sand poured slowly through the gold V on this side of the hourglass.

Together, Elodie and the swallow watched time trickle past. She'd never known a bird to have such patience, to be able to stand still and focus on a single thing for so long.

But as soon as the last grain of sand fell through the V, the swallow let out a sharp screech, then darted away.

"Um, all right. Goodbye then." She hoped everyone else in Aurea wasn't as abrupt as the swallow and the woman in the other tower.

Elodie picked up the hourglass, intending to turn it upside down again. But this time, she noticed a dark reddish-brown stain on the point of one of the gold V's. It was the color of old blood. She reached out and touched it.

Suddenly—

A flash of intense green eyes.

Red hair.

The reflection of fire in the polished surface of a crown.

Elodie jolted away from the hourglass and slammed against the back of the chair, her heart pounding in her chest. The momentum knocked the hourglass off the windowsill, and it shattered ten stories below.

What in hells just happened?

She gasped, gulping air as if she'd nearly drowned.

But once she caught her breath, she started laughing.

Oh my goodness, I'm so tired that I'm dreaming while still awake, and I'm judging the people of an entire island based on the personality of a bird.

Elodie really was exhausted, from both the monthslong journey at sea and the excitement of being here in Aurea. *And* she'd be meeting her future husband first thing in the morning. It was no wonder her mind was a little unsettled.

She leaned over the windowsill and looked down below.

The broken hourglass was just a small pile of splintered wood and glass, nothing more.

Elodie rolled her eyes at her overactive imagination and laughed at herself again as she retreated back into her room.

EVEN AFTER A warm bath and a filling meal of rich oxtail stew and buttered noodles, it was impossible to sleep, knowing she'd get to meet Henry in a few hours. Elodie tossed and turned. She took the covers off, then put them back on. She tried counting desert goats, the gray, tuft-bearded kind that roamed the mesas back home. And when that didn't work, she tried relaxing her muscles, focusing first on her toes, then calves, then the muscles of her thighs, strong from years of hiking and climbing. Her stomach, then her chest, then the lean, strong muscles in her arms. Her neck. Her head. Even her ears.

Still awake.

Elodie sighed and gave up. To give her mind something to do other than fixating on her inability to sleep, she began rehearsing what she would say upon meeting King Rodrick and Queen Isabelle, and especially what she'd say to Henry. She could not afford clumsy ad libs or tactless blurting tomorrow. Elodie needed a script to make sure she got it right.

"Your Majesties, it is a great honor to meet you."

"Your Majesties, it is my great honor to be in your presence."

"Your Majesties, it is your great honor to be in my—gah! I mean, I am honorable to—no! Your Majestics—Your *Majesties* it is my great honor to be in your presence."

Heavens help me.

To concentrate better, Elodie stared straight up at the dark ceiling, focusing solely on her words.

Until the ceiling began to move.

"What is going on with this place?" She yelped, suddenly thinking again of the hourglass hallucination. Elodie scrambled upright and fumbled to light the lamp on the bedside table.

The soft flicker of the lamp revealed a gold ceiling decorated with the same mosaic as the hair combs, except these shieldlike shapes curled in a fractal pattern, starting in the center of the room and spiraling out to the edges. Elodie stared at it, covers clutched to her tightly as if they were armor, daring the ceiling to move again, but hoping that it was just shadows playing tricks on her tired mind.

There it was again! Almost like the mosaic was slithering . . .

But thankfully, logic kicked in. *The ceiling can't move. Therefore, there must be another explanation.*

At least, she hoped so.

Elodie watched the ceiling for a few more seconds.

The mosaic did *not*, in fact, move. It had only seemed to because the light cast on it was flickering, glimmering off one shield-shaped tile and then another. Like with the hourglass, it was only her tired mind playing tricks on her.

The light wasn't from her bedside lamp, though. It was coming from outside.

Elodie slipped out of bed and hurried to the window, eager to dispel the last, irrational traces of panic about the ceiling.

Thick fog made it pitch black at this time of night, except for an eerie glow on the mountainside.

Torches. An entire procession of them.

"What's happening out there?"

But the way the tower window was angled made it hard to see, for the opposite tower—the one belonging to the blond woman—obscured part of the view. Elodie grabbed a cloak and padded down the staircase.

Two-thirds of the way down, she pushed on the stairwell door and stepped out onto the battlements of the castle. A few yards away, the palace wall arced. She could get a much better view of the torches from there.

Elodie yelped when she rounded the bend and ran into Floria, who was leaning against the crenellations.

"*Merdú*, Flor, you scared me! What are you doing out here? It's three in the morning!"

Her little sister gave her a crooked grin. "Probably what you were planning to do. Getting a clearer look at whatever's happening on, what did Lieutenant Ravella say it was called? Mount Khaevis?"

"Yes, that's the name, and you did indeed beat me to getting a better look at it," Elodie said. But god, she was happy to see her sister. She threw her arms around Floria.

That's when she noticed what Flor was wearing: a silver cape lined with sand fox fur. "Is this our stepmother's favorite cloak?"

Floria burst into a full grin. "It looks better on me."

"She's going to turn *you* into a cape when she notices it's gone from her trunk. That's the nicest thing she owns."

Floria snickered.

But then their attention was stolen again by the torches, which had begun to move.

"What do you think they're doing up there?" Elodie asked.

"I was hoping *you'd* know the answer to that," Floria said.

There was something eerie about the way the little dots of light flickered in the pitch black of the night. Elodie furrowed her brow as she watched them proceeding up the mountain, the flames wavering in the wind. They gathered midway up Mount Khaevis and remained there for ten, maybe fifteen minutes.

Until suddenly, all the torches snuffed out.

The hairs on Elodie's arms stood up straight and goosebumps prickled her skin.

Floria gasped, but rather than being frightened, she clapped her hands together softly. "That was gorgeous," she said.

Was it? Elodie looked at the black mountainside and tried to see it the way her sister had.

"The synchronicity of their movements," Flor said, "and the effect of the bright flames in the darkness and fog . . ."

Elodie supposed she could understand her sister's perspective. Maybe Elodie was letting her nerves about meeting the royal family—and about how her entire life was to change—get to her. Just because a torchlit procession happened in the middle of the night didn't automatically make it alarming. Plenty of good things occurred under the moon's domain—roasting mallow candy over a fire. Charting ocean voyages by the constellations. Holding Flor's hand and watching her expression as she wished intently on shooting stars.

Floria chattered on. "It was probably an Aurean prewedding tradition!"

"Or unrelated to my wedding," Elodie said, and even though it came out a little quarrelsome, she didn't have to apologize or explain to Flor, because her sister understood her even without words. Floria would know Elodie just meant she didn't want to be the sort of person who thought everything in the whole kingdom was about her. She hugged Flor again, and Floria squeezed reassuringly back.

They stayed outside for a while longer, but the torches didn't light up again. Eventually, the cold caught up to them and they bundled into the tower stairs.

"El?" Floria said, her voice suddenly quiet.

"Yes?"

"I don't know what I'm going to do without you."

"What do you mean?" Elodie looked her sister firmly in the eye. "You're smart and strong and self-sufficient. You don't need me anymore."

"I know I don't *need* you . . . but I want you. Who will draw mazes for me to solve? Who will let me under their covers when I have nightmares? And who will laugh when I 'borrow' Stepmother's things? You've been there every second of my life. I don't want you to go." Her sister, who liked to think herself more mature than her thirteen years, suddenly looked small under Lady Bayford's blanket of a cloak, and Elodie wanted to scoop her up like she had when Flor was still little.

"Hey . . . Do you want to curl up in my bed with me tonight? Just like old times?"

Floria bit her lip and nodded. "That would be nice."

Elodie didn't have to say aloud that she needed the company, too.

They climbed up to her tower-top room together. This time, with Flor by her side, Elodie did fall asleep.

But instead of sweet dreams, her sleep was filled with stormy seas separating her from her sister, sinister processions up raven-black mountainsides, and presiding over it all was a shadow of a figure that Elodie somehow knew was Prince Henry, his eyes lit up by . . . torches.

LUCINDA

LUCINDA STOOD AT the window, in the room she and Lord Bayford shared several stories below Elodie's. The permanent creases between her brow were more prominent than usual as she scowled at the procession of torches up the mountainside.

"It is not fair, Richard," she said.

The duke came up behind her and wrapped his arms around her waist. "It is a special tradition, my dear. It will be a great honor to Elodie."

Lucinda huffed. "And would you have bestowed such an honor on *me*?"

Richard hesitated. "Our circumstances are . . . different."

She jerked away from him. "It's going to be a disaster. You think this is a good idea, this alliance between Inophe and Aurea, b-but . . ."

"My love, you always worry too much."

"And you worry too little!" But this was how it was between them. The duke existed on smiles and assurances—that's how he was so beloved by his people—while Lucinda thought of all the ways things could go wrong. Like, what would happen if an earthquake struck Inophe and the precious water towers fell and ruptured, never mind that there had never been an earthquake in the duchy's history? Or, what if Lord Bayford fell off a horse and broke his back and couldn't visit the tenants? Lucinda and Floria certainly didn't know how to take care of their needs, and Elodie would no longer be around to help—

Lucinda let out a frustrated cry. She whirled from the window, away from the sight of the torches, and stomped back to bed, throwing herself onto the covers. "What was good enough for me should have been good enough for Elodie! She should have had a *normal* wedding. Not all this gold, all this pomp and circumstance, all this *Aurean* tradition. We should have kept her in Inophe."

ELODIE

THANKFULLY, THE REAL Prince Henry's eyes were not lit by the torches of Elodie's strange dreams. From the quick glance she'd stolen as she entered the Aurean throne room—before she dipped into a deep curtsy to the royal family—Henry's eyes sparkled like the ocean that surrounded the kingdom.

Now, however, Elodie's gaze was on the gold mosaic on the floor, her head still down, her body still folded deferentially in her curtsy. The tiles were a mirror image of the fractal pattern on her bedroom ceiling, like small shields spiraling from where Elodie stood, out to the thrones before her, the courtiers at the sides of the great hall, and her father, stepmother, and Floria behind her.

"Your Majesty, King Rodrick, and Your Majesty, Queen Isabelle," Elodie said. "It is a great honor to be in your presence. I—"

"My lady," Henry said, rushing from his throne and taking her arm. "You needn't bow. Not to me. And surely not to my parents." He helped her rise.

A blush bloomed on Elodie's cheeks. Seeing her future husband this close . . . Heavens, he was striking, with the lines of his jaw like they were shorn from the mountainside, but with a smile that brought softness to his features. His hair was as golden as the castle, and his strong hands a match for hers. For a woman who'd long prepared herself for a hard and lonely life, this was more than Elodie felt she had a right to dream of, and it went a long way to assuage her anxiety from the previous night. She saw Floria out of the corner of her eye. Her little sister was swooning as discreetly as possible in a throne room, a hand over her heart. Floria mouthed, *So handsome!*

Elodie had to stifle a snort of laughter.

But then Prince Henry was speaking again, and she turned her attention back on him, keeping her posture straight enough to be worthy of a soon-to-be princess.

"My dear Elodie, I've read your letters so often, there's more ink on my fingers now than the page. I'm happy to finally meet you," Henry said.

"We *all* are," the queen said with an approving—and assessing—look at Elodie.

"Pardon me," King Rodrick said, rising abruptly from his throne. His olive skin had gone ashen, and a light sheen of sweat shone on his brow. "I—I am not well, I must retire at once." A royal attendant in a velvet uniform rushed forward to take the king's arm, and they staggered out of the throne room without the king even acknowledging Elodie.

She tried not to stare at the empty throne but couldn't help the racing thoughts in her mind. Had she made such a terrible first impression? Should she have practiced her curtsying more, as Lady Bayford had demanded? Did the king's departure mean the engagement was off?

But Queen Isabelle smiled at Elodie and continued the thread of Henry's conversation as if nothing out of the ordinary had

happened. "My son has understated our joy in your arrival. And
your father has understated your beauty."

Elodie blinked, her brain trying to catch up and find its place
in the proceedings. "I am relieved you corresponded only with
my father, and not with my stepmother. She would have pointed
out all my flaws, including that I show my petticoats to sailors."

Lady Bayford's eyes went wide.

Oh god. Elodie wanted to slap her hand over her mouth. *Why
did I say that?*

Lord Bayford rescued her with a good-natured chuckle. "My
daughter has an unorthodox kind of grace, yet it is delightful.
Inophe is a difficult place to live, and Elodie has thrived there
through her intelligence and strength. She may climb trees and
rigging, but she also understands duty and knows her place, I assure you."

Elodie bit her lip. *She knows her place?* What had gotten into
Father?

But she supposed she understood why he'd said it. Lord Bayford had had to undo whatever harm her comment about the
petticoats had done. And in truth, Elodie *did* know her place—
she had always been meant to lead others, and that meant putting herself second when necessary.

Like right now. She had to set her ego aside for the purpose
of making a good impression on Queen Isabelle and Prince
Henry. It was for Inophe's sake that this marriage go through.

"We welcome that assurance," the queen said.

Both Elodie and her father bowed their heads.

"And as such," Queen Isabelle continued, "we exhort you to
be at home in Aurea." She turned to rest her gaze on Floria in the
back of the throne room. "You, as well, dear Floria. I see even the
harsh climes of Inophe can grow the fairest of flowers."

"Your son is well grown, too!" Floria blurted.

At that, both the queen and Henry laughed jovially, and the courtiers along the sides of the hall joined in. Elodie was relieved at the passing of whatever tension her own gaffe had caused.

When the gaiety finally died down, the queen said, "I apologize that we were unavailable to receive you upon your arrival last night. How was your journey? And did the chamberlain furnish your rooms to your standards?"

"The voyage was horrid," Lady Bayford said. "As for our chambers—"

Elodie cut her off. "The rooms are *beyond* our standards, Your Majesty. Never in my life have I experienced such hospitality and generosity."

"I am glad to hear it," the queen said. "We are happy you are all here, safe and sound. We have quite a celebration planned for the nuptials and hope you shall be spoiled these next three days. The royal kitchen is at your command at any hour, there are masseurs at your beck and call, and seamstresses can assist with any finery you fancy." Queen Isabelle didn't say anything more, but she tilted her chin slightly toward Lady Bayford's simple gray kirtle.

Lady Bayford wilted, and Elodie frowned. She and her stepmother didn't always see eye to eye, but Elodie didn't enjoy seeing Lady Bayford taken down a notch.

"Now," the queen said. "I do believe Lord Bayford and I have some trivial contractual matters to finalize, which we can attend to privately. While you, Elodie and Henry, have an important task."

"We must get to know each other," Henry said.

Elodie cast a glance at the prince with his chiseled jaw and deep blue eyes.

Even though this was an arranged marriage undertaken for duty, she suspected she would enjoy the task assigned to her. Very much.

THE GARDENS SHE had seen from her tower window were even more resplendent in person and in daylight than she could have imagined. There weren't any sharp anthodite flowers, but there were roses of every hue, and lilies with tiny bells full of nectar that ruby-throated hummingbirds couldn't get enough of; the beautiful birds darted from one lily to the next, zipping around Elodie and Henry.

There were blue irises and purple violets, orange marigolds and bright pink hydrangeas bigger than Elodie's head. She saw fuzzy yellow flowers she didn't know the name of, burgundy flowers that felt like velvet, and lacy white ones that looked like ladies' handkerchiefs.

And everywhere between the flowers was lush greenery— carpets of moss, bright shiny leaves, vines that snaked up tree trunks, and an overwhelming sense of *life*. It was so different from Inophe . . .

"Lovely, isn't it?" Henry said, taking care to walk slowly to give Elodie the time she wanted to gawk. "We are fortunate on Aurea to have such resplendent plants."

"Or to have any plants at all," Elodie said. "I'm sorry, I didn't mean for that to sound rude," she added quickly. "It's just that our lands have suffered from a drought for seventy years. I'm not used to seeing such natural beauty."

"Nor am I," Henry said, openly staring at her.

Elodie restrained herself from laughing at the prince's mawk-ishness. Henry might not have been a poet (his letters had been charming, but in a straightforward rather than lyrical way), but he seemed genuine. And although Elodie dug latrines and went on long sweat-drenched hikes and all sorts of other things Lady Bayford deemed unfit for a duke's daughter, it did not preclude Elodie from also appreciating a compliment.

Nonetheless, she also had great concern for others, and she had not forgotten about the king's hasty departure from the throne room. "Your Highness, is your father all right? He left in such a—"

Henry waved off her worries. "The king is afflicted with an excess of black bile. Because of that, official duties easily overwhelm him; he does much better in the solitude of his solarium or in the kennel with his dogs. Do not concern yourself overmuch with him, however. The royal physician tends to him daily and believes my father shall live a long life, as long as he rests sufficiently."

"I am so sorry to hear that he suffers," Elodie said, both relieved that King Rodrick's departure hadn't been her fault but also slightly guilty at feeling that relief.

"I share your regret," Henry said. "But let us speak of more pleasant topics. For instance, you."

"Me?"

He gave her that heart-melting smile of his, all dimples and charm, and it was as deft a change of subject as she had ever witnessed (and she'd seen plenty, since Lord Bayford was a charmer, too). Henry would make a fine king someday. He certainly had the diplomatic charisma for it.

"You're not like other women," Prince Henry said. "Your letters—"

"You've read many other women's letters?" Elodie asked.

"N-no! I meant—"

"I was only teasing, Your Highness."

He flushed. "Oh. Thank the skies."

"'Thank the skies?" Elodie asked. She hadn't heard that phrase before.

"Ah, an Aurean saying," Henry said. "Akin to 'thank goodness.' However, more important than our colloquialisms, you don't need to call me Your Highness. I prefer Henry, if you please."

Elodie smiled. "All right, then, Henry. So tell me, why don't you think I'm like other women? Because I'm not naïve. I know a prince such as yourself could choose any wife he wanted. Why me? Why the daughter of a duke from a dusty, distant land?"

"Because there is a great deal of duty and sacrifice required to reign over Aurea, and those seem to be responsibilities you understand."

She tilted her head. "Indeed, I do."

He steered her around a bend in the garden path, leading them to a dark green lawn shaded by a willow tree, right next to a pond dotted with little white ducklings following their mother on the water. There was a gold picnic blanket laid out on the grass, with a vast spread of cakes and pastries and delicate petit fours in every pastel color imaginable.

Elodie stopped in her tracks. "Is that for us?"

"Yes, of course." Henry dipped his head and gestured for her to go first.

But she couldn't. Not because she didn't want to—she *did*, as she'd never seen so much sugar and flour in one place. But she *couldn't* move because, well, she'd never seen so much sugar and flour in one place.

"Henry . . ."

"Is something the matter?"

"I think we have different notions of sacrifice," Elodie said. "You see, in Inophe, the people are quite literally starving." It was perhaps too blunt a thing to say, but she couldn't help it. The pain of her home and the contrast to life here were too much to simply ignore.

"It won't be a problem for long," Henry said. "We are solving it, aren't we?"

"Yes, but . . ." Elodie shook her head at the bounty of sweets. "Don't you feel guilty, partaking of a picnic like this when so many others in the world suffer?"

A storm cloud passed over Henry's expression, although he quickly shook it off. "No, because the royal family of Aurea bears plenty of other burdens on its shoulders. You don't understand yet, since you've only just arrived. But you'll see . . . and I urge you to enjoy moments like these when you can. Duty shall call upon you soon after we wed, and you may regret it if you don't eat cake now."

Elodie frowned. But there was a weight in the way Henry spoke that was familiar to her, the heaviness carried by those in charge of the well-being of others. And she should not presume to understand Aurea after being here for less than a day; Elodie would balk if anyone thought they understood the intricacies and hardships of Inophean life after so short a time.

"All right," Elodie said. "If I am going to be Aurean, I shall try things your way."

Henry smiled, all his easy charm flooding back as he took her arm and led her to the picnic.

Elodie ate her fill of cake and pastry, but every bite was both pleasure and pain—relief that she could help her beloved people, but guilt that she'd left them behind in order to do so.

ELODIE

A S SOON AS Elodie returned from her garden stroll with Henry, Floria rushed into her room.

"Tell me everything!" her sister gushed. "Is he as chivalrous as he is handsome? Did he tell you how he fell in love with you? Oh, heavens, did he *kiss* you?

Elodie smiled at Floria's enthusiasm. "Let me catch my breath before the interrogation, at least!"

"You don't need to catch your breath. Those never-ending stairs don't even faze you."

"Hmm, good point," Elodie said. "Well then I suppose I *do* have to answer your questions. But first, have this." She reached into a pocket in her gown and produced something wrapped in a linen napkin.

Floria hopped up onto Elodie's bed and opened it. Her jaw dropped. "Are these petit fours? I've only ever read about them in books . . ." Flor took a dainty bite from one of the little cakes so she could savor it, although Elodie knew she was torn between slowly enjoying every morsel while in Aurea or cramming her mouth with as much as she could fit into it before she had to return to Inophe in a few days.

"Is he wonderful?" Floria asked.

"Who, Henry?" Elodie said as she undid the tight sash around her waist.

"Yes, Henry! Who else?"

Elodie laughed. Being around her sister never failed to brighten her mood. Floria, realizing she was being teased, threw a pillow at Elodie's face.

"Tsk-tsk," a woman said as she barged into the room. "Please do not injure our princess before the wedding!"

A veritable army of seamstresses followed the first into the room. One set up a trifold mirror. Another, a velvet-covered platform. Another had a cloth dressmaker's mannequin and baskets full of needles and thread, and the youngest hurried in with her arms full of yards of different fabrics.

"Uh, what's happening?" Floria asked.

"We are making the lady's wedding gown, of course," the first woman said. "I am Gerdera, the head palace seamstress."

Floria squealed. "El, you know what that means? You don't have to wear whatever awful creation Lady Bayford made!" It was Inophean tradition that the mother of the bride sewed her daughter's wedding gown and presented it as a gift on the morning of the ceremony. But of course, Elodie and Flor's mother had passed away a long time ago. And Elodie knew Floria was terribly concerned about whatever their stepmother had crafted, given Lucinda Bayford's bland taste for proper gray wool that went all the way up to her chin.

"I'm so pleased to meet you," Elodie said to the seamstress with a smile to Floria.

"Let us begin with the overall silhouette," Gerdera said.

One of the other seamstresses opened up a display of dress sketches. "We have many options for you, my lady. We are able to tailor a gown according to your preferences, whatever they may be. However, I find that showing examples to the bride is often most helpful—"

"Have you made a great many wedding dresses for future princesses?" Floria joked.

"Wh-what?" the seamstress turned an alarming shade of dark pink. "N-no, I—"

Gerdera jumped in to explain. "She meant for others in Aurea."

"Y-yes. Others in Aurea," the seamstress echoed.

"I'm sorry," Floria said. "I was only jesting. I didn't mean to unsettle you."

"Oh." She let out a nervous titter. "All right."

Elodie furrowed her brow at the exchange. But Flor saw her expression and immediately walked over and smoothed the wrinkle with her small fingers while whispering, "We're just making dresses here, not solving Inophean hunger. Relax, El. It was only a bad joke." She winked.

"You're right, sorry."

"Shall we carry on?" Gerdera asked.

"Yes, please!" Floria clapped, then scooted closer to Elodie so they could study the sketches the seamstress presented together.

"The, er, most traditional," the woman said, "is a lace chemise, worn under a heavy velvet kirtle—colored blue, of course, for chastity and purity."

Elodie made a choking sound, then started coughing.

The poor seamstress's eyes bugged, as if she thought she'd just killed the future princess.

"Just give me a minute . . ." Elodie cleared her throat several times. The thing was, she had enjoyed her freedom at home (she'd lost her virginity to a groom in the hayloft in the stables, and she'd had a few other dalliances besides), and when the seamstress began talking about chastity and purity, it had caught Elodie off guard. But she pulled her composure back together; she preferred that Floria *not* know how very inapplicable the "innocent" bride comment was.

When Elodie had stopped coughing, the seamstress continued.

She showed them a flowing green tunic with bell sleeves; a long, straight red sheath with a corset belt; and a brocaded silver kirtle accompanied by a cape. There was a brown dress with angular panels, edged in black piping; another that looked like it had been skinned off an Inophean lizard; and finally a stiff gown that seemed to be one giant corset from neck to ankle.

"I bet that's the one Lady Bayford would choose," Floria whispered, and giggled under her breath.

But Elodie wasn't enjoying the process as much as Floria was. All of Elodie's life, clothes had been utilitarian. Even the duke's daughters wore the same shades of beige and gray as commoners, because dye was a luxury they couldn't afford. The nicest dresses she and Floria had ever worn were the ones on the ship right before they arrived in Aurea, because they couldn't show up looking like paupers for a wedding to a prince. And even then, their gowns had been a dull yellow, trimmed with only a scanty bit of lace.

But here in front of them were jewel-toned chiffons and silver and gold silk; rich brocade and pastel velvet.

"Honestly, this is all a bit much," she said. "I don't need anything fancy. Perhaps I *should* just wear what Lady Bayford made. It would be such a waste of precious fabric—"

"El, no!" Floria cried. "For once in your life, let someone take care of *you*. You deserve it. Or at least do it for me, so I can see a custom-tailored Aurean wedding dress!"

Elodie sighed. "All right. For *you*."

Floria turned to the sketchbook, happy again. "Is there anything that isn't a variation on tunics and kirtles? Something more audacious, but not as colorful?"

The seamstress looked at her blankly. But Gerdera swooped in with a knowing smile. "How about this?" She flipped to the back of the sketchbook to a blank page and quickly drew the lines of something not at all structured, but rather like a waterfall of silk. "It would be in white, or cream, I think," she said as she put the finishing touches on an elegant toga, the soft fabric cascading off the shoulders and décolletage, falling in gentle folds around the ankles and trailing a hem behind it like an eddy.

"Wow," Floria said. "El, *that* is the gown you need."

Elodie was transfixed on the design, already nodding. She still felt guilty over such indulgence, but if they were going to insist, then yes. This dress was perfect—untraditional and stunning, glamorous in a subtle way.

"Very well," Gerdera said. "Let us take your measurements, and then you may select your fabrics."

Elodie stepped onto the velvet platform in front of the mirrors. Meanwhile, Floria jumped down from the bed to make way for the spools of cloth to be laid out. Her mouth dropped as she watched the young seamstress display all the different silks and laces.

"I can't believe you get to design your own wedding gown," Floria said. "Just the *sound* of these delicate fabrics against the bedspread is enough to make me feel faint."

Elodie smiled at her kindly. Then she turned to Gerdera.

"After we're finished with my dress, can we design one for my sister?"

"F-for me?" Floria's mouth hung open even wider than at the sight of the petit fours.

Gerdera dipped her head in a bow. "Of course, my lady. You are one of the honored guests at the wedding, are you not?"

"I am," Flor said softly. And with the confirmation that she was indeed part of this fairy tale, she did faint.

ELODIE

ELODIE WANTED TO know more about her future kingdom. Aurea might be a powerhouse in the world of trade, but it was both geographically and diplomatically isolated—an isle in the middle of a massive ocean and surrounded by perilous volcanic outcroppings. Little was known about it beyond its famed harvests, and that the ships that brought its fruit and grains for trade returned home to Aurea laden with chests full of gold bars, which would be smelted to produce all the grandeur she'd seen in the castle. Other than the letters from Henry and Queen Isabelle's promise that Inophe would be taken care of, Elodie knew next to nothing about the royal family or the people or culture of Aurea.

Which is how she convinced Prince Henry to take her on a tour of the farms. Their first "date" had been his choice, a slow ramble through the royal gardens and the dessert picnic. Their second date would be hers.

"You ride well," Henry said as they cantered down the dirt roads of the countryside. Back at the palace, Elodie hadn't waited for a stable hand to help her mount the horse. She rode in a normal saddle, rather than sidesaddle, wearing under her skirts the breeches Lady Bayford hated. At first, the Aurean knights who accompanied them had gone slowly to make sure Elodie could keep up. But after she goaded them to ride faster, they'd finally realized she could more than keep up. *They* would have to keep up with *her.*

"Thank you," Elodie said. "I learned from my mother. She and I always accompanied Father to check on his lands. Now that she's gone, I make sure to visit each household at least once every fortnight to ensure they have enough to eat, shoes for their children's feet, work where work can be found."

"You admire your people, despite their poverty," Henry said. "I can hear it in your voice."

"Their fortitude of spirit is a model to live by. I would do anything for them."

Henry opened his mouth as if to say something, but then shook his head. Instead, he pointed to the vast fields of golden wheat that they were approaching. "This is aurum wheat," he said proudly. "It is a perfect food; a single loaf of bread made from aurum flour contains all the nutrients a person would need for an entire day."

Elodie slowed her horse so she could reach over and touch the wheat. Its stalks bent gently in the breeze toward her, and its golden, grasslike fronds were as soft as feathers. "I am grateful for aurum wheat," she said in awe. "It will save many an In-ophean from starvation."

Her prince dipped his head in humble acknowledgment. "The farmers of Aurea take great pride in knowing the good they do for the world. Every harvest is a gift, and we know it."

"It's incredible, and I'll get to be a part of it," Elodie said. "I wish we had known a long time ago that aurum wheat existed."

"And I wish we had known Inophe was suffering so badly.

Your home is tucked quite far away from Aurea; we didn't know. We would have helped sooner."

"Thank you, I appreciate you saying so."

Elodie would have been happy just in those wheat fields, but they had only the afternoon, for there was a prewedding feast for the two families scheduled for the evening. "Are there sangberries nearby?" Elodie asked. She recalled their carriage rolling by hedges of the blood-red berries on the way from the harbor to the palace, but it was all a blur and she didn't know how far, exactly, they were.

"They are a short ride away," Henry said. "Come with me."

Elodie spent the next two hours oohing and aahing over the cornucopia that was Aurea. Between the orchards of silver pears and the fields of every vegetable known to man, she peppered Henry with questions about the kingdom.

"When was Aurea founded?"

"Eight centuries ago, by my many-times great-grandfather."

"How do you grow such miraculous crops?"

"A combination of the climate, fertilizer made from seaweed harvested from the ocean, and a special Aurean quality that words don't suffice to explain," Henry said.

"Magic?" Elodie laughed.

Henry shrugged but didn't share in her mirth. "Perhaps you could call it that."

"Hmm, very mysterious," Elodie teased.

"Is conversation with you always this active?" But he didn't seem to mind, since he gave her one of his dashing smiles. "Here, let me distract you for a moment." He plucked a silver pear off a tree. "Try this."

She bit into it and luscious juice dripped from the silver peel all over her hands. "Oh goodness . . . if you're exporting fruit like this, why don't people outside the kingdom know more about Aurea?"

Henry laughed. "I see the pear didn't deter you one bit from your questions."

For a moment, Elodie wondered if she was pushing too hard, saying too much. She knew the risks of what happened whenever she opened her mouth.

But no, this was all important information. "I'm eager to understand the country I'm about to help rule," she said.

He grew quiet for a minute. When he spoke again, the levity had left his tone. "We're a private people," Henry said, glancing at some farmers in an orchard nearby. "The citizenry has always believed their harvests spoke for themselves without needing personal details to grease the wheels of trade."

"And yet," Elodie said between more bites of pear, "I still know very little about you, even though I am here in person now. For example, I saw a blond-haired woman in the tower across from mine on the evening I arrived. Is she someone I ought to know? Your sister, perhaps?"

Henry stiffened for a moment on his saddle, but then he drew his shoulders back as if to stretch them out. "Not a sister," he said, fiddling with his reins. "The royal family has only borne sons for our eight-century rule. The only female members of the family must come from foreign lands, as my mother, the queen, did."

No sister . . . no wonder Henry had looked sad. Elodie wouldn't have been able to bear life without Floria. "Are you an only child, then?" Elodie asked gently.

Henry's mouth pressed into a grim line. "I have a brother. He is a fair bit older than I, but he left Aurea and I don't . . . get along with him. We are estranged, and I prefer it that way."

"I'm sorry."

"It's fine. It's only that, when he decided to leave the kingdom, he saddled me with all his responsibilities. But I'd rather
not talk about him, if that's all right."

"Of course." Elodie didn't regret prying, though. If she was
going to sit on the throne of Aurea someday, she needed to know
all the relevant facts.

However, she didn't have to learn *everything* today. And if, in
the future, Henry continued to insist on not speaking about his
brother, then she would let that be. Not all stories were meant to be
shared. Everyone was allowed to keep some secrets of their own.

They rode in silence for a long while. Elodie focused on the
farmers in the fields. They were beautiful in their spellbinding
rhythm, the swing of their scythes against wheat perfectly timed.
Everyone was muscled and well fed, unlike her people back
home in Inophe, and they smiled as they worked together as one.

The children who weren't old enough to cut wheat—those
ten and younger—had the job of shaking tambourines and sticks
with strips of shiny ribbon to scare away crows and other pests.
Even though they'd been in the aurum fields all day, they still
skipped and sang a song to ward off the crows.

In plains of gold we live,
With joy we harvest our barley and wheat.
To the world what treasures we give,
And at home we relax and feast.

So away, crows, fly far,
These grains are not for your covens.
The barley is destined for the brewery,
And wheat for bread and muffins.

The children's voices were light and airy, and every so often, the adults joined in for a refrain or two. Never had Elodie seen people so uniformly happy.

But right after she rode by, a trio of boys grabbed at the tambourine in a girl's hand. "Rahhh! We are dragons and you are Princess Victoria!"

"No! I don't like this game!"

"We are going to eat you, Victoria! But first, we'll trap you in our lair!" They growled again and shoved her into a gully.

She shrieked and disappeared from view.

With a cry of alarm, Elodie leapt off her horse and ran into the wheat. The bullies scattered, and she flung herself down into the gully where the girl had been thrown.

Elodie landed only a few feet below in what turned out to be a muddy trench. It had appeared a lot deeper from the road.

The girl was curled in a ball, covered in mud, weeping. She was probably eight or nine years old.

"Are you all right?" Elodie asked, crouching next to her. When Elodie returned to the palace, Lady Bayford would comment on the state of her boots and dress, but propriety be damned, this small girl was much more important than dirtied skirts and leather. "Are you all right?" Elodie repeated, touching the tiny shoulder, as fragile as a bird's bones. "Those bullies ought to know better, even at their age."

The girl looked up and gasped. "Y-you're a princess. Like Victoria."

Elodie didn't know who Victoria was, but she smiled. "I'm *almost* a princess. I will be, tomorrow."

"You saved me." Then the girl let out a whimper, like a kitten who'd been stabbed. "But who will save *you*?"

"Your Highness!" a farmer yelled from the top of the ditch.

He bowed repeatedly as he climbed down. "My apologies, my daughter, she didn't mean to say—"

"Thank you, that will do," Henry said sharply.

The farmer's eyes widened as he realized who had appeared, and he bowed deeply—hastily—then scooped up his daughter and hurried her away.

Elodie watched them disappear into the thick stalks of wheat. *Huh.* That was at odds with the behavior of the jolly farmers she'd observed before.

"Shall I carry you out of the ditch in the same manner?" Henry joked, now seemingly relaxed again.

She shook her head and gave him a small smile, then climbed out on her own. But she still spent the entire ride back to the castle thinking over what the boys and the girl had said.

Victoria. A former princess whose name began with the letter V. Had the hourglass in the tower belonged to her? Suddenly, Elodie found herself shivering over the memory of touching that bloodstain and the accompanying vision. It had only been her imagination, right?

But there was also the peasant girl's last question. *Who will save you?*

Elodie shivered again. Did it mean anything? Or was Elodie just making connections where none existed, an imagined puzzle for her anxious brain to obsess over?

Definitely the latter, she tried to tell herself.

And yet, the mystery of V and the echo of the little girl's question lingered and rattled deep into her bones.

ELODIE

THE NIGHT BEFORE the wedding, dinner was an intimate affair limited to Elodie's family and the royal family of Aurea. But that did not mean the meal was small. The day prior, after the seamstresses had finished with their measurements (and Floria had recovered from what she called "swooning in the face of an excess of delight"), the palace chef had called upon Elodie to provide a list of every dish she had ever wanted to eat. But while gastronomy wasn't Elodie's forte, Floria had spent her childhood poring over cookbooks from foreign lands (the only gift she ever asked for for her birthday), so Elodie had sent her sister gleefully into the kitchens with the palace chef to see what possibilities were on hand.

And the possibilities, it turned out, were beyond anything Elodie's taste buds could have imagined. Platter after platter was now marched into the throne room, beginning with golden fried dumplings filled with smoky cheese and potatoes, then a creamy soup of wild Aurean leeks. There was a salad of edible flowers, drizzled with a light citrus dressing. Individual meat pies wrapped entirely in gold leaf. Grilled mountain carp, a delicacy that could only be hooked under the light of the moon (perhaps this was why Elodie had seen those torches two nights ago). Roasted pheasant with sangberry jam, noodles made from the famous aurum wheat, and more vegetables than Elodie had seen in all the harvests of her life combined. The excess would take quite a bit of getting used to, but she was trying her best to take Henry's advice and simply enjoy it.

The king retired to his chambers after the fifth course. Elodie watched his retreat with concern. The poor man was so ashen, and he leaned heavily on the royal physician's arm. She wondered why he'd come to the dinner at all; he ought to have been in bed.

But the feast continued without him. It seemed that Queen Isabelle and Prince Henry were the ones who ran the kingdom, and they were quite accustomed to hosting without King Rodrick. Interesting.

Conversation flowed, as did the Aurean barley beer, which tasted of nutmeg and peaches and—as Henry pointed out—had the famed side effect of improving one's memory.

"So that you may remember this night, always," he told Elodie.

By the time dessert was laid out on a gold runner across the table, Elodie was stuffed beyond the limits of what she thought possible for her stomach, and she itched for an excuse to stand and stretch. She fidgeted in her seat.

"Psst," Henry whispered with a mischievous curl to his lips. "Do you want to slip outside and get some air with me?"

THERE WAS NO one out on the battlements but the sentries, keeping silent guard. Henry led Elodie hand in hand in the dark, the walls and floors of the palace a pale gold under the soft moonlight.

"All I can think of is tomorrow," Henry said as they walked.

Was he nervous, as Elodie was? You only married once, if the heavens graced you with a long and healthy life. But how do you marry a complete stranger, how do you commit to spending that entire long and healthy rest of your life with someone you've only just met? Elodie's father had been lucky with her mother, but then Lady Bayford . . . She was so tightly laced it was impossible for anything but annoyance to come out of her mouth because nothing was ever good enough. Honestly, Elodie didn't know how her father, who was relaxed and merry, could be a match for Lucinda Bayford.

But Henry and Elodie were much better suited. It was obvious even from the short time they'd known each other. He was attentive and gentle. He admired Elodie's mind. And he liked that she could mount a horse without waiting for assistance. Not to mention he was lovely to look at.

She walked over to the edge of the battlements and gazed at the mountain that towered over the Isle of Aurea. "Have you ever been up there?"

"Once or twice."

"I've never been on a mountain," Elodie said. "The closest I've come are the plateaus in the Inophean desert, but those are really just hills with their heads shorn off. Will you take me up to Mount Khaevis, perhaps after our wedding?"

Henry hesitated before answering.

"Oh!" Elodie said. "I didn't mean *immediately* after the wedding. I am sure you have plans already for, um—" She stopped herself before she began detailing what happens on a wedding night. Not that she was embarrassed. She was actually pleased she could arrive at her wedding bed armed with knowledge of how to make her husband beg for mercy, and how to teach him to do the same to her.

Still, it was a bit premature to discuss those details now.

"What I meant," Elodie said, "is that I should like to go up Mount Khaevis with you in the future, whenever the occasion may arise. I'm curious, is all. I saw torches up there two nights ago, and—"

Henry inhaled sharply. "You saw that?"

She nodded. "I couldn't sleep, and they were hard to miss. What was it? Mountain carp fishing?"

He looked away from her and stared out at the jagged horizon that Mount Khaevis cut into the purple-gray sky. "No. It was a ceremony. Every September, we begin the harvest with a week of gratitude for all that we have. During that week, we offer three prayers: The first represents our appreciation of the past, of our history. The second ceremony is for our ongoing commitment to Aurea now. And the third prayer is for the renewal of the land, for the future. During this week, we give thanks for the blessed life here." Henry shrugged and turned back to Elodie. "It's old tradition. Superstition, really."

"I don't believe in superstition."

"Well, good. Better to be grounded in reality, right?" He gave her one of his smiles, the kind that could melt solid gold to molten liquid. It warmed Elodie through her core.

"Gracious, Elodie, you are so beautiful beneath the moonlight, you almost made me forget." In a single swift movement, Henry dropped to one knee.

"What—?" she started to say.

But she lost her words when he reached into his jacket pocket and pulled out a flat velvet box. Inside on a bed of silk lay a gold necklace with a pendant of the Aurean coat of arms: a dragon clutching a sheaf of wheat in one claw and sangberries in the other. The berries were made of rubies.

"Elodie," Henry said. "I know our match was arranged, but even so, I want to ask you . . . Will you marry me?"

She gasped. Any nerves she'd felt when they stepped out onto this battlement now disappeared. And whatever questions she had going into this—about V or about what the peasant girl had said—could be dealt with later. Because *this* was how you married someone. This was how you fell in love. There would always be uncertainties, but you would face them together, two stronger than one. She didn't have to do anything alone anymore.

Elodie had been using her head too much and ignoring her heart. Perhaps it was time for her to learn to let go of control, just a little.

On impulse, she flew into Henry's arms, nearly knocking the necklace away, and kissed him.

He lost his balance, and they toppled onto the floor. She kissed him again.

And then she added, "I should clarify. My answer is yes."

ISABELLE

A FTER THE DINNER and proposal, Queen Isabelle found her
son in his chambers. Instead of rejoicing, though, he stood
gazing pensively out the window toward Mount Khaevis.

"You could choose her, you know," the queen said.

Henry startled from his thoughts. "Choose her?"

"Elodie," the queen said. "I saw how you read and reread all
her letters. You are intrigued by her intelligence, her cleverness
and wit. She could be the one you keep."

"Mother—"

She shushed him by placing her hand on his. She was surprised to find it rather steady, when she'd thought him distraught.
"Henry, you are a dutiful prince. When Jacob ran away from
Aurea, you took on the role of heir to the throne without hesitation, and you have carried the burdens of prince of Aurea without complaint for so many years. But you deserve to be happy, as
well."

"That, I disagree with," Henry said. "A future king does not
think of his own happiness. The kingdom's well-being must always take precedence."

Queen Isabelle looked down at the golden tiles. If she could have, she would have borne more sons to share Henry's burden. The king had had five younger brothers with whom to divide the heaviest of duties, and still, Rodrick had crumbled under the weight of obligation.

But unfortunately, Isabelle had been unable to give Jacob and Henry more brothers. The king rarely visited her bed. Not because Rodrick had mistresses—he didn't—but because he spent most of his time in solitude. Days were easier for Rodrick in the warmth of his solarium or in the company of his dogs that demanded nothing of him, unlike people.

Still, such demands would be made upon Henry, for although Isabelle ostensibly ran the kingdom, she and Rodrick would abdicate in Henry's favor, once Henry decided to marry for good.

"If I cannot convince you to seize your own happiness," she said, "then I can at least remind you that it is also your duty to produce heirs. That is how we ensure a lineage that will honor the traditions of Aurea. Elodie would not be a bad choice."

Henry closed his eyes, and now there was a trace of the conflict the queen thought she'd spied in him when she first walked into his chambers.

"If you had talked to me yesterday," Henry said, "I'd have agreed that Elodie could be the one. But today in the fields, she kept asking question after question. And she intervened on behalf of a peasant girl . . . No. Elodie has too many ideas of her own. She would fight too hard against customs that cannot be changed. That is why she cannot be the one I choose."

The queen bit her lip. The yoke of Aurea's traditions required a strong woman as queen once Isabelle grew too old to reign. She had thought Elodie a good candidate. But Henry's logic also made sense, so she just kissed her son gently on the cheek.

"Then I shall see you tomorrow at the wedding, as planned?" she asked Henry.

He nodded. "As planned."

The queen took her leave, but glanced over her shoulder one more time at Henry. He was again peering out at Mount Khaevis, but there was no hint of wariness now, only upright, military posture.

As she closed the door behind her, Queen Isabelle wondered when he'd changed so, when he'd hardened into a version of herself—charisma on the outside, but cold granite within.

And she lamented how she hadn't noticed when Aurea stole the last scraps of her once-innocent son's soul. She would have liked to kiss him goodbye.

ELODIE

ELODIE COULDN'T STOP smiling as she and Floria sat at the vanity in the tower top room. Elodie had returned from her walk on the battlements glowing, and not only because her new necklace shined like a beacon of its own.

Flor ran a gold comb through Elodie's silken hair. "I am so, so happy for you!"

"I can hardly believe it," Elodie said.

"Believe it. You are good and kind, smarter than anyone I know, and you've always taken care of me. I look up to you in more ways than you know, El. And if anyone deserves this kind of happily ever after, it's you."

Elodie looked down, almost shy for a moment. "Thank you, Flor. That means a lot to me . . . I'm going to miss you so much when you're gone."

"Let's not think about our imminent parting," Floria said. "I don't want to be sad. Let's think about tomorrow night's wedding instead."

Elodie swallowed the lump in her throat and nodded as her sister ran the comb through her hair one last time. Then Floria picked up the necklace from the vanity and held it up in front of Elodie. The Aurean coat of arms caught the candlelight, the dragon glimmering as if it was alive.

Flor sighed dreamily. "Henry showers you in such riches."

Lady Bayford suddenly stormed into the room, her reflection appearing in the mirror. "You would look better in emeralds," she snapped at Elodie.

Floria startled at their stepmother's sudden presence, and she dropped the necklace onto the vanity before scooping it up again and sending a daggered glare at Lady Bayford. "What has gotten into you, Stepmother?"

"I came to tell you—" Lady Bayford stopped short as she looked at Floria. "I—I must speak to Elodie alone."

Elodie frowned. Lady Bayford looked . . . odd. She was usually well put together. Now, however, her normally tidy bun drooped, locks of dark hair frizzing out every which way. The top button of her high-necked gown was undone, as if she'd torn at it in frustration. And she kept clenching and unclenching her fists, grabbing handfuls of her skirts each time.

"I have no secrets from Floria," Elodie said. "Anything you wish to say to me, you can also say to her."

Lady Bayford looked out the tower window, toward the mountain, as if she could somehow find an answer to her predicament out there. When she turned back to Elodie and Floria, she spoke with her hands pressed firmly to her sides. "This place. It isn't . . ."

Her gaze flitted back to the window. "This match will not last. Save yourself—no, save your *father* the dishonor. Say you will not go through with the wedding."

Elodie, who was rarely without words, could only stare with jaw hanging open at Lady Bayford.

But Floria had plenty of words for their stepmother. "Why

are you saying this? Why are you trying to take this away from Elodie?"

Lady Bayford ignored her and grabbed Elodie's hands. "You're not listening. I'm trying to tell you—"

"My girls!" Father boomed, strolling into the room as if this were a joyous family reunion rather than an incomprehensible scene of a stepmother trying to stop the most fortuitous marriage ever made. "Is everyone ready for the big day?"

Lady Bayford shot him an icy scowl before whirling on her heel and marching out of the room.

Father laughed oddly. "Don't mind her. The royal physician gave her something for the lingering seasickness, and it's making her . . . irrationally anxious. Anything she said, disregard. All is well!"

Then, without another word to Floria and Elodie, he hurried after her.

Floria gawked after them. "What just happened?"

Elodie shook her head sadly. "This wasn't Stepmother's idea, so she doesn't like it. She always needs to be in control of what you and I do. But I'm a grown woman, and she doesn't get to make my choices anymore. I get to choose, and I am going to marry Henry, if it's the last thing I do."

ELODIE

SOMEHOW, THE GOLD castle of Aurea shone even brighter on Elodie's wedding night. It was as if the servants had spent the entire day polishing every wall, every floor, even every roof tile, to make it gleam beneath the moonlight as it did. Outside, the indigo sky was cloudless, and an orchestra practiced in the royal gardens. The anticipation made it impossible for Elodie to eat. Only when she almost fainted putting on her wedding gown did she finally accept a few bites of the roll Floria shoved in her face.

But oh, the wedding dress! It was a marvel of elegance, just as her sister had imagined, and Elodie was glad to have caved to Floria's exhortations. Heavy cream-colored silk fell like a waterfall from Elodie's shoulders all the way down to her legs. Crimson and gold embroidery—the colors of Aurea—trimmed the edges of the fabric, following her neckline, down the folds of silk across her torso, and along the hem of the long train that trailed behind her. She wore Henry's gifts—the pair of gold combs in her hair and the ruby-and-gold necklace with the coat of arms resting at the base of her throat—and Elodie knew without a doubt that she'd made the right choice in accepting a proposal that would not only bind her to Aurea, but would also provide for Inophe from now on.

All evening, wedding guests had arrived like waves washing ashore, coming as early as was polite to maximize their time with the king, queen, and Henry. Now, however, they were all seated on the palace's rooftop terrace, the platinum light of the moon casting everything in a magical, celestial glow.

Trumpets sounded, and the orchestra began a lilting bridal procession. In Inophe, brides walked themselves to the altar, but in Aurea, the tradition was that the father led the bride there.

Elodie's father came up beside her, regal in his best jerkin, tears already filling his eyes. Tonight he was not the duke of Inophe; he was simply a man looking at his daughter and seeing all the years of her childhood flash before him, knowing that this was the moment he would have to let her go.

"I love you, Elodie. Always remember that."

"I love you, too, Father. But don't cry. It's not as if we'll never see each other again. I shall visit, I promise."

He squeezed his eyes tight, the tears spilling over. But then he pulled a handkerchief from his pocket and swiped them away. He offered Elodie his arm. "Ready?"

"I am always ready." She kissed him on the cheek, then slipped her arm through his.

The music of violins and cellos soared as they took their first steps down the aisle. All around them, the guests turned to watch her approach, and they bowed their heads in respect as she walked past. The only ones who didn't dip their heads were Floria and Lady Bayford, sitting in the front row. Floria was bouncing in her seat, grinning and mouthing *You look beautiful* to Elodie. Lady Bayford sat rigid with pursed lips, hands balled into fists in her lap, shaking her head as Elodie took her last steps to the altar.

Henry stood waiting for her under a golden pavilion. The king and queen sat in thrones behind him. Queen Isabelle looked resplendent in a gown of gold velvet and matching cape. King Rodrick seemed . . . well, he looked the part of the king, dressed in gold brocade and fur-lined robes, but he stared off into the distance as if his mind were elsewhere.

Nevertheless, Elodie's father bowed deeply to King Rodrick and Queen Isabelle, while Elodie curtsied with her arm still linked in his.

"Your Majesties," they said in unison.

When Elodie rose, Henry's radiant smile greeted her. She smiled back at him, holding her breath for what was about to come.

"Your Highness," her father said. "It is the greatest honor of my life to present you with my daughter, Elodie Bayford of Inophe. May she bring many blessings upon the royal family and all of Aurea."

He unhooked Elodie's arm from his and placed her hand on Henry's, before bowing again and taking his leave to join Floria and Lady Bayford in their seats.

"You look ravishing," Henry said to Elodie.

"You don't look too awful yourself."

He laughed and twined his fingers through hers.

A priestess in crimson velvet robes stepped forward. Tattoos of dragons covered every visible part of her skin, from her cheeks to her throat to her knuckles and fingertips. Her curly gray hair tumbled down far past her waist, where the ends were woven with rubies and gold. A heavy medallion bearing the Aurean crest hung in the middle of her chest, and it swung like a pendulum as she approached Elodie and Henry.

"Tonight we celebrate the union of two luminous souls," she began, her sonorous voice carrying across the terrace. "This wedding joins not only our beloved prince with his bride, but also marks the beginning of a new season for Aurea and Inophe. Our kingdoms are grateful for their commitments and gifts to each other. They are . . ."

Elodie found it difficult to listen. Instead, she lost herself in Henry's handsome face. She pictured what their lives would be like—diplomatic trips abroad, horseback rides up the mountain switchbacks at home, and sultry nights wherever they were in the world, tangled together beneath silk sheets. There would be trade talks together, discussions on how best to rule, alliances built with Inophe and more. And later, they would have children—sons, Elodie supposed, because that is what the Aurean royal family had always borne. Or perhaps she would be the first to break the mold and give the kingdom its first daughters. Elodie smiled at the thought.

"Do you, Elodie of Inophe, swear an oath to give yourself, body and soul, to Aurea and all that it requires of you?" the priestess asked.

Elodie brought her focus back to the ceremony before her. "I swear it," she said, standing tall and proud.

The priestess touched her tattooed hand to her medallion, as if committing the promise to the Aurean crest. Then she turned to Henry.

"Henry of Aurea, will you take this woman as your wife for as long as she shall live?" the priestess asked.

"I do," Henry said.

"And Elodie, will you take this man as your husband for as long as you shall live?"

"I do," Elodie said, before realizing that the vows were slightly different for her and Henry. They were both contingent on *her* lifespan, not his.

Maybe it was because women often died in childbirth, so it

was presumed that the husband would outlive her? But what about men dying in wars . . . ? Then again, given Aurea's geographic isolation and diplomatic aloofness, the kingdom was never drawn into wars. Aurea had been at peace for eight centuries.

But Elodie had already said yes. And no matter what, she would not renege, not when all of Inophe's future was at stake. Henry squeezed her hand.

Queen Isabelle rose from her throne. She placed her hand gently on King Rodrick's arm and whispered something to him, which seemed to rouse him from wherever his thoughts had taken him, and he stood, as well. Together, they approached Elodie and Henry.

The queen passed a golden ceremonial cloth to the king, revealing a jeweled dagger in her hands, its hilt the same gold mosaic pattern found elsewhere in the palace.

She took Elodie's hand roughly and slashed through her palm.

"What—!" Elodie cried out in both surprise and pain.

Henry held his hand out to his mother, evidently expecting the same treatment. He didn't even wince at the cut. Queen Isabelle pressed his palm to Elodie's, mingling their blood.

Suddenly—

A flash of two golden-haired boys—one merely a toddler, the other, on the brink of adolescence.

The younger one following the older everywhere he went.

Then, a few years later, Henry discovering a cold, empty bed, and the sharp blow of knowing that his brother was gone and Henry was suddenly all alone.

Elodie gasped and looked at him. But Henry just smiled reassuringly and tightened his hand around hers. He showed no sign of knowing she'd just seen into his past, and there was no indication he'd experienced anything of hers.

Queen Isabelle, however, was watching Elodie, and their eyes met. But then the queen looked away so quickly Elodie wasn't sure if she'd imagined the moment.

"Rodrick?" Queen Isabelle asked. "Are you ready?"

The king lifted the gold matrimonial cloth. His own hands shook violently as he wrapped the silk around Henry and Elodie's hands. When he was finished, he didn't let go of them. "I— I remember when gold silk was wrapped around my—"

"Hush, Rodrick, dear," Queen Isabelle said kindly, drawing him away from the matrimonial cloth. "There will be plenty of time to recount memories of our wedding later, but right now, this is Elodie and Henry's time."

The king startled and looked at Elodie as if shocked to see her there. "You're new."

The royal physician rushed out from where he'd apparently been waiting behind the pavilion, the summons for his assistance inevitable at some point during the ceremony, and he led King Rodrick back to his throne.

"Should we postpone the wedding?" Elodie whispered to Henry. "The king seems unwell."

"It shall be all right," Henry said. "We're nearly finished with the ceremony."

All of the guests smiled at them, as if the king had not just forgotten he was attending his son's wedding. Only Elodie's father, Floria, and Lady Bayford seemed concerned about what had just happened. Was Aurea so accustomed to King Rodrick's illness that they were used to carrying on without him? Elodie couldn't imagine ever doing that if it were her own father who wasn't feeling well.

Nevertheless, an attendant brought the queen a gold tiara, a circlet with a familiar mosaic pattern on it, and Queen Isabelle smiled at Elodie and Henry. She placed the tiara on Elodie's head.

"I hereby present my son and new daughter, Elodie, princess of Aurea!"

The wedding guests erupted in cheers. The proclamation quickly erased any thoughts of the king, and Floria leapt to her feet, clapping and shouting. Father looked at Elodie wistfully, crying while trying to maintain his dignity at the same time. Even Lady Bayford's eyes glistened with tears.

Elodie turned to take it all in.

I am a princess, she thought. Just like in a storybook, except for the blood oath part. Still . . .

I am a princess, and this is all real.

THE WEDDING BANQUET was held in the royal gardens, and it was even grander than the feast from the night before. The dishes were larger and more elaborate, from seafood platters served in abalone shells as large as shields to a six-foot-tall pastry shaped like a dragon and filled with beef and roasted vegetables. There was roasted wild boar served with fried saffron rice cakes, whole lambs over a crackling firepit, and sangberry jam–glazed Cornish hens nestled in aurum wheat noodles. For dessert, there was silver pear ice cream, dark chocolate tarts, and rose petal pie. And of course, Aurean barley beer with its aroma of peaches, nutmeg, and crisp memories.

During the serving of the wedding cake, which was modeled after Elodie's dress, the aristocracy of Aurea lined up to pay their respects to the new couple. The orchestra played music that sounded familiar as the guests began to dance. Was it the same song Elodie had heard from the tower when she'd first arrived? A popular Aurean song, then. But she couldn't really listen to it, as she had to pay attention to those bowing and bearing wedding gifts for her and Prince Henry.

After the twentieth nobleman—or was it the twenty-second?—Elodie leaned over to Henry and whispered, "How long must we stay? It's late . . . it must be well after midnight now." She was quite tipsy, in part from the euphoria of the night, and in part because she had drunk too much of the delicious Aurean beer. Whereas a sober Elodie might have been able to sit patiently through her new duties as a princess, an intoxicated Elodie was more than eager to begin her first night with her husband in their wedding bed.

Henry laughed as he moved her hands, which she'd placed suggestively on his thigh, back onto the gold table. "Try to enjoy yourself. This banquet is all in your honor. It ought to be the greatest night of your life. At least, I'd like to think it so."

Elodie could think of other ways to make the night even greater, but she kept the innuendo to herself for now. There would be plenty of time for that later anyway.

The music shifted to something more playful in tone, and a troupe of acrobats tumbled and cartwheeled into the gardens. Meanwhile, another nobleman stepped up to Elodie and Henry's table and bowed.

The nobleman opened his mouth to begin the requisite speech about the graciousness of His Highnesses, but he was interrupted by shouts and a commotion at the other end of the lawn.

"Halt!" a knight yelled. "Hold her!"

Elodie rose to see what was happening.

The guards held a frantic girl, punching and kicking like a fox trapped in a snare. She flung her thin limbs fiercely, and one of her kicks smashed forcefully against the side of the guard's knee, bending it in a way it was not supposed to bend. He crumpled in pain and the girl broke free, tearing through the dancers. She leapt through a hedge of roses and ran toward Elodie, her arms bleeding where the thorns had scraped.

It was the girl who'd been shoved by the bullies in the wheat field. She sprinted straight for Elodie's table. "It must stop!" she shouted.

Several knights threw themselves in front of Elodie and Henry. Swords were drawn.

Elodie jumped to her feet. "She's just a child!"

The girl shouted, "Princess, you must not—"

One of the guards hit her in the back of the head with the hilt of a sword.

The girl fell limp and unconscious to the ground.

"What have you done?" Elodie cried.

No one answered her. In a scrum of shining armor, the knights removed the girl from the wedding.

Henry brushed himself off, smoothing out the wrinkles on his tunic. He clucked his tongue. "Antimonarchists."

"But she's just a child," Elodie repeated, staring wide-eyed at where the girl had stood.

Everyone else around her seemed unfazed, though. Conversations picked up where they'd been interrupted, the lute and the dancers began again, and servants descended immediately upon Elodie and Henry, as if they'd simply been waiting in the wings and now was their moment to shine. And shine they did. They polished all the goblets and glasses, the forks, knives, and spoons. They replaced used porcelain with clean ones, even though the cake had already been served and there was, as far as Elodie knew, no more food forthcoming. They even wiped off a tiny splatter of wedding cake on Elodie's velvet slipper, which she hadn't noticed and probably wouldn't have, had they not so diligently tidied *her.*

Then everyone and everything about the wedding night continued as if the peasant girl had never been there.

How could that be?

Henry noticed Elodie sitting frozen. He gave her a full stein of Aurean beer and placed a comforting hand on her cheek. "Nothing to fear, my princess. The knights shall see the girl home safely with a firm reprimand to her parents. All is well."

"But . . . she seemed so upset. What was she shouting about?"

"The vast majority of Aurea respects the royal family, but there are always one or two bad apples. The antimonarchists are simple folk; they cannot understand how much we do for the kingdom, and how much more we are willing to give than they would, were they in our place. But let's not allow a single dissident voice to ruin your night. In fact, drink your beer, and then let us dance. We shall waltz our worries away."

Still stunned, Elodie followed his directions, draining the stein while reviewing everything that had just happened. The beer did, indeed, endow the drinker with crystal clear memory. Elodie could remember every detail of the girl's embroidered tunic, every bit of wheat chaff that flecked the fabric, as well as the distress and urgency in her eyes.

There was something bizarre in Aurea's ability to look the other way when something inconvenient happened. A king forgetting he was at his son's wedding. A girl bursting into a royal reception and being erased a moment later. Even without the beer, Elodie wouldn't be able to forget this night.

When Elodie set down the empty stein, though, Henry rose and bowed before her, offering his hand. "Will you honor me with a dance, my princess?"

Unease stuck in Elodie's throat like a wedged fishbone. But at the same time, she was very aware of the fact that although she was a princess now, Inophe's future still balanced on the Aurean family's goodwill, and that meant the will of Henry and the queen.

Elodie also admitted to herself that she was uneducated in the ruling of a kingdom. Helping her father manage a small, impoverished duchy was complicated enough. And there was so much Elodie didn't know yet about Aurea.

Perhaps I should not jump to conclusions without understanding more, she told herself. Her instinct was to side with the girl, because Elodie had a soft spot in her heart for the less powerful. Being Inophean, she'd known firsthand what that was like all her life.

And yet, here was Henry standing before her. A kind and generous ruler, beloved by all those around him. As a practical woman, Elodie was not one to discard evidence simply for gut emotion.

She rose and accepted Henry's hand and followed him to the lawn where the wedding guests were dancing. Perhaps, with time, she would understand Aurea and its people, and everything would make sense.

Wouldn't it?

ELODIE

DANCING HAD THE ability to make Elodie feel more graceful than she usually was. After Henry, Father had asked for a turn with Elodie. Swirling around the gardens, they floated to the music like dragonflies on the wind. Two admittedly tipsy dragonflies, but Elodie was quite sure that they were, regardless, the paragon of elegance.

As the song came to a soft close, Father pulled her into a tight embrace. "You know I love you, don't you, Elly? To the moon and back again, and then to the sun and beyond," He pulled back and shook her. "You know I love you, no matter what?"

Elodie gently pried loose his grip. "Yes, Father, I know. What's gotten into you, other than the beer?"

"No, not the beer. I could not bear the beer tonight and all the memories it would bring. I partook of wine, glorious wine, which blurs one's past until one no longer has to face it. I—"

"Father, you're rambling. Perhaps you ought to sit down?" Elodie said, guiding him to a stone bench under a trellis of golden roses. She sat beside him and held his trembling hand.

Floria, who had just finished dancing nearby with a nobleman's son, spotted Elodie and their father. She skipped over, cheeks rosy from the exhilaration of the last waltz. "Everything all right?" she asked.

"My other precious daughter," Lord Bayford said, drawing Floria into a maudlin hug.

Floria tilted her head in question toward Elodie while making a drinking gesture with her hand.

Elodie nodded. Father did not get drunk very often, but when he did, he was prone to outpourings of affection. There were worse qualities in a man, though, than to heap love on the women of his family when he'd had one too many glasses of wine. Lady Bayford usually whisked him off to his bedroom around now.

"Where is Stepmother?" Elodie asked.

"She . . . felt unwell," Floria said.

The sisters sighed in unison. How typical of Lady Bayford to come up with an excuse to skip out on Elodie's wedding reception because she didn't approve.

Henry poked his head around the bend of the garden path and caught sight of them under the trellis. "There you are, my love. I thought my new bride had run off."

Queen Isabelle trailed in behind him. "Princess Elodie. I trust you are enjoying your celebration?"

"Indeed I am, Your Majesty."

"Wonderful. If I may, then, I would like to introduce you to another Aurean wedding tradition. It will, unfortunately, take you away from these festivities, but if you are willing, it will be the highest honor of your life."

"It would be my privilege," Elodie said.

"Wait!" Father cried. He hurled himself at Elodie and planted a sloppy kiss on her cheek.

Floria giggled. But then she took her turn kissing Elodie on the cheek, too. "I hope I'm half as beautiful someday as you are today."

"You'll be twice as beautiful," Elodie said with a final kiss on the top of her little sister's head.

WHEREAS ELODIE'S EXPERIENCE with the palace thus far had involved climbing *up* staircases, the queen now led her down, deep into the heart of the castle. Or, more accurately, the bowels, for they were far underground, below even the kitchens and the laundry in the basements. The walls here were not gold, but granite, and the only light was the flicker of torches set into sconces in the cold rock.

Henry had not come with them; he'd said this part of the night was dedicated to women only.

Elodie tried to puzzle out what was to come but had no inkling. Was there a special vault down here with the crown jewels or archives that the queen wanted to show her? But that wouldn't require excluding the men. Perhaps it was a ritual to prepare Elodie for her wedding bed, a private prayer ceremony to bless them with children?

She cringed and hoped that wasn't the reason.

They turned a corner and stopped in front of a heavy oak door. Purple mist seeped out from the crack beneath it and around its edges, and chanting emanated from behind it.

"You are about to take part in a sacred ritual," the queen said. "Will you do the great honor of opening the door, Elodie?"

A sacred ritual. The gravitas settled into Elodie's chest, and she nodded, half proud to be a part of this, half disbelieving that she was truly a princess who *got* to be a part of this.

She heaved the door open, and the purple mist rushed out to engulf Elodie in tendrils of herbed smoke. A round chamber revealed itself, the walls lined with elderly women in crimson robes, all holding fat candles and chanting softly. In the center of the room, the heavily tattooed priestess who had conducted Elodie and Henry's wedding ceremony burned branches of sage and dried lavender.

"You were not raised in Aurea," Queen Isabelle said, "so you are unfamiliar with our customs. This may all seem . . . unnatural to you."

Elodie smiled politely. "Our people have their customs, as well. I am sure they would seem just as unfamiliar. But I am a princess of Aurea now, and I am eager to uphold any traditions this kingdom may have."

Queen Isabelle looked her up and down, and for a second, Elodie thought she caught a glint of sadness in the queen's eyes. But it must've been just a trick of the candles, because a moment later, the queen nodded and said, "Very well then. Let the priestesses of Aurea prepare you."

The women along the walls bowed deeply to the queen, who then took a seat in the corner in what appeared to be a smaller version of her throne. The head priestess shut the heavy oak door. Then the others set their candles into iron sconces in the granite walls and approached Elodie.

The first priestess removed Elodie's necklace. Then the next took out the gold combs from her hair.

"Wait," Elodie said. "Henry wanted me to wear those."

"We shall put them in the imperial vault for safekeeping, Your Highness," the priestess said. At the same time, another woman unfastened Elodie's earrings and whisked them away before Elodie could protest further.

"Tonight, you honor our Aurean ancestors," the head priestess said. "Generations before us have practiced this sacred ceremony on the evening of every royal wedding. You are special,

Princess Elodie, and yet you are but one in a long line of those who have sworn a solemn oath to Aurea, to give yourself body and soul to its needs, to honor it with all that you are."

Elodie dipped her head in acquiescence.

Suddenly, the head priestess by the fire let out a feral shriek that seemed to go on and on.

Elodie jumped. The women around her grabbed her, keeping her in place, as if afraid she was going to bolt.

"I'm not going anywhere," Elodie said, confused by their overreaction. "I was simply caught off guard by the, er, screaming."

They released their hold on her but still kept close watch as they began another low, rumbling chant in a language she'd never heard before. It sounded ancient, full of hard consonants and whispers.

Rykarraia khono renekri.
Kuarraia kir ni mivden.
Vis kir vis,
Sanae kir res.

"What does that mean?" Elodie asked.

The priestess closest to her smiled kindly but shrugged. "The meaning has been lost over the centuries, but the instructions to recite it are clear. So we honor the ritual with the chant, knowing that the symbolism remains intact."

Elodie quirked her mouth. *What if you were unknowingly summoning a demon?* she thought wryly. But she kept the comment to herself, not wanting to seem disrespectful or take away from the solemnity of the priestesses' ritual. Lady Bayford would have been proud of Elodie's restraint.

The priestesses removed Elodie's gown, her whalebone corset, and chemise, leaving her with only her tiara on her head. She wasn't cold—the fire kept the underground chamber warm— but she *was* unnerved being in such a state of undress in front of so many.

Be openminded, she chastised herself. *This ritual is important to Aurea, and therefore it is important to me.*

Elodie stole a glance at the queen, but Her Majesty's eyes were closed. Not dozing, because she sat upright with arms perfectly ninety degrees on the armrests. It was as if she were meditating, her chest rising and falling with slow, deep breaths.

So Elodie followed suit, filling her lungs with the scents of lavender and sage, and a fog of calm slipped over her. Perhaps it was the flowers and herbs in the air. Perhaps it was acceptance of her new place in this new land. Regardless, she committed to finishing the ceremony with poise and grace.

Seeming to sense this, the priestesses stopped watching her as intensely. They gathered long stalks of rosemary from baskets along the edges of the chamber, and began to anoint Elodie's entire body. In rhythm with their chants, they used the rosemary to brush on a golden oil that smelled of sunflowers and sunlight, summer days and abundant fall harvests.

Rykarraia khono renekri.
Kuarraia kir ni mivden.
Vis kir vis,
Sanae kir res.

When the golden oil had soaked into Elodie's skin and the excess had been wiped away, the priestesses began to paint her arms, her legs, her neck, chest, belly, and back. Their movements were efficient, like a corps of dancers who had practiced together for years. One woman moved in with a blue-daubed stalk of rosemary. Another flitted out of the way at the exact second to make space. Then another swooped in with pink while the priestess who'd just brushed orange on Elodie's thigh darted away.

The reverent touch of the rosemary brushes lulled Elodie into a sense of peace. She was part of something bigger than herself now, not just a royal wedding, but a grand history. How long had this wedding night tradition been going on? Henry had mentioned that his family had been the guardians of Aurea for eight hundred years.

It was entirely possible that Elodie was participating in a ceremony that was almost a millennium old. The sanctity of it took her breath away.

Soon she was covered from the tips of her ears to the soles of her feet in artistic daubs of paint. The lavender and sage mist swirled around her, infusing its scent with the paints and the oils and the trace of rosemary left behind by the brushes. Elodie felt transformed into a living work of art.

They plaited her hair in intricate braids and weaved it in and out of her tiara, as if ensuring that even if she jumped off the peak of Mount Khaevis, her tiara would still remain fastened on her head.

She was dressed again in her chemise and whalebone corset. And then, finally, they brought out a new gown. Unlike the weighty silk of Elodie's wedding dress, this one was spun of a pale purple fabric so light it was ethereal. The gown was many layered, with a different gemstone stitched into each hem. One layer was edged in rubies, another in tigerlike topaz. A third was edged in yellow diamonds, then emeralds, then blue sapphires, and last, amethysts. And shimmering thread had been woven throughout the impossibly delicate fabric, giving it an iridescent glow when the candlelight hit it just so.

This moment seemed to encapsulate all that Aurea had

been for Elodie in the last three days—too much, and yet, a saving grace. As she stepped into the dress, Elodie looked down at the opulence covering every inch of her skin and didn't quite know how to feel about it. And yet she did what she did best— swallowed her personal feelings and stepped up to duty.

It was the one thing she could guarantee about her future in the Isle of Aurea.

ISABELLE

THE HEAD PRIESTESS approached the queen and bowed deeply. "She is prepared, Your Majesty."

Queen Isabelle did not want to open her eyes. Not yet.

But this was part of the tradition. And the queen forced herself to sit through this ceremony every time, to bear witness. To sit in the awful magnitude of this ritual and accept responsibility. It was the least she could do to honor the life she was about to sacrifice. And it was a way to remind herself that she, too, had once been a princess, but she had been spared and allowed to become queen.

Forgive me, Elodie.

Isabelle took one last, deep inhale, and then she opened her eyes.

"You look like an angel," she said to Elodie.

"Thank you, Your Majesty. Now what comes next?"

You do not want to know.

CORA

WHEN THE DOOR of the cottage opened, the knight tossed the girl onto the stone floor without ceremony.

"Cora!" her father cried, rushing to scoop her into his arms. "Where have you been? I searched the wheat fields all night for you!"

"She breached the palace and threatened the princess during the royal wedding," the knight said.

Her father paled. "Why would you do such a thing?"

"I didn't threaten the princess," Cora said, rubbing the back of her head, which ached dully where the hilt of the sword had hit her. "I tried to tell her the truth."

The knight took off his riding gloves and crossed his arms. "This is why custom dictates that children do not learn about Aurea's traditions until they are ten years old. How old is she, Mr. Ravella? Seven?"

"I'm nine," Cora spat.

He shook his head knowingly. "Too young. They cannot understand the fragile balance of our lives here."

"We tried to shield her," her father said. "But the children talk in the fields, and—"

The knight waved his hand, not unkindly but dismissing the excuse nonetheless. "You must explain to her why our ways exist. You understand why it is worth it. She cannot storm through the castle gates again. Next time . . ."

"No, please."

"I have a family of my own," the knight said, "and I would do anything it took to keep us together. It would break my wife's heart if one of our children were . . . Well, let us not dwell on such things. Speak with your daughter, make her understand. And keep a close eye on her."

"I will, thank you. Thank you for bringing her home."

The knight grunted, put his gloves back on, and left.

Cora's father burst into tears and wrapped her in his arms again. "You silly, silly girl. How could you? What were you thinking?"

"It's not right, Papa! What the princess—"

"Shh." He squeezed Cora tighter. "Sometimes it's better not to think too hard. You will understand when you are older. Life in Aurea is like a pond at sunrise, serene and reflecting golden light. You'll break it if you throw rocks in the water."

"But what if I like throwing rocks?"

"You don't, my love, trust me. Aureans don't even play at skipping stones."

ELODIE

THE CORRIDOR ELODIE and the queen took didn't ascend back up into the castle, but rather continued within the depths of the granite. If possible, it grew even dimmer in the gray passageways; the flickering sconces were spaced farther apart than before, casting long shadows as they walked. Elodie clenched and unclenched her fists at her sides, attempting to ignore her fear of tight spaces, which seemed to close in on her as the rock walls angled into the corridor. Memories of being trapped in the crevice of the Inophean plateau—sun burning, sweat robbing her of precious water, hours alone with buzzards circling— echoed through her head.

Stop it, she thought furiously. *If this is to be my home, I must become inured to these underground paths.* However, Elodie also hoped there would be no need for her to visit the priestesses beneath the castle again. At least not for a very long time, until the day Elodie was queen and presiding over her own child's post-wedding ceremony.

After what was likely only a few minutes yet seemed an eternity, Elodie and Queen Isabelle reached an iron door with a knight in full regalia standing beside it. Elodie barely stifled an undignified sigh of relief that they were at the end of the narrow stone corridors.

"Your Majesty, Your Highness," he said, bowing. He opened the door as if it weighed nothing, letting in a puff of chilly night air. "Your carriage awaits."

"Carriage?" Elodie asked, but she needn't have, for as soon as she stepped outside, the golden coach stood before her. It was more luxurious than the one that had whisked her and her family from the harbor when she arrived. Not satisfied to be made merely of gold, this one was shaped like a dragon's head, with the shield-shaped mosaic pattern covering the entire carriage.

Oh, dragon scales! Is that what all the tiles and the ceiling pattern were supposed to represent?

For a peaceful farming kingdom, Aureans sure like their dragons, Elodie thought. Perhaps the dragon—a powerful creature of legend—was their way of psychologically compensating for their quiet way of life? Maybe knights without wars to fight needed *something* to make them feel like warriors.

Speaking of which, a good two dozen knights sat on horseback behind the carriage. Every soldier and steed boasted the full crimson and gold regalia of Aurea, although that was not out of place, as they had just come from a royal wedding.

However, it *was* a bit odd that they were here in the back of the palace, not in the main courtyard.

"You are a vision," Henry said, emerging from the coach. "The paint and the purple gown suit you."

Her husband's smile melted away Elodie's nerves.

"I'm curious where this is all leading," she said. "A solemn underground ceremony, yet another new gown, and now a golden carriage escorted by knights? Is this how our honeymoon begins?"

"Your curiosity will soon be sated," Queen Isabelle said. "Henry, I shall see you both there."

What does the queen have to do with our honeymoon? Elodie wondered as she curtsied deeply to her departing mother-in-law.

Henry took Elodie's hand and helped her inside the carriage. The plush seats were made of crimson velvet, the walls paneled in gold silk embroidered with the royal coat of arms.

"Oh, my combs and necklace!" Elodie's hands touched her throat.

"Do not worry," Henry said. "They will be safe in the imperial vault."

The coach began to move. Elodie pressed her face to the windows.

Suddenly, the cold darkness of the night swallowed them, and Elodie realized they were climbing up the switchbacks into Mount Khaevis.

ELODIE

THEIR CARRIAGE STOPPED halfway up Mount Khaevis. The coachman opened the door and helped Elodie out onto a rocky path. A frigid wind whipped through the jagged face of the mountain, immediately cutting through the gossamer layers of her gown and chilling her to the bone.

"Where are we?" she asked.

"Go on," Henry said. "I'm right behind you."

"But where am I going?"

"Straight ahead. There's a trail. Didn't you say you wanted to come up to Mount Khaevis with me?"

There was something mocking in his tone, though, something very different from the Henry who had courted her over the past eight months. Elodie shivered, and not only because of the cold.

Still, it was possible she was wrong about his tone and wrong about the slippery sense of foreboding that slithered through her. Besides, Elodie was a blade forged from the harsh heat of Inophe, who had been willing to give everything for her people.

What were a few steps in the dark when she'd already spent two decades fending off starvation and thirst? If Henry wanted her to follow a trail, she would. He was not only her husband, but also the partner she'd wished for her entire life. No longer would she have to bear the weight of Inophe's future alone. They would provide for Inophe and lead Aurea, together.

With that assurance in mind, Elodie started down the rocky path, taking careful steps so as not to slide in the gravel. It was difficult to see in the moonlight, for clouds had moved in since the wedding ceremony, but she navigated the best she could. She was still freezing, though.

The narrow path rose upward from where the carriage had deposited them. But it was only a handful of minutes later when Elodie crested the ridge.

Below, a deep, narrow gorge opened up; it must be the valley she'd seen from the palace, the one that cut through the side of Mount Khaevis. Fog rose from it as if from a cauldron, its depths obscured from view.

But that wasn't what Elodie was looking at anyway. For the other side of the gorge was lined with cloaked figures, each wearing a golden mask and holding a long, spearlike torch, the flames flickering wickedly in the wind.

She gasped and turned back to Henry.

The torches reflected in his eyes.

For a moment, she couldn't speak, because she'd seen this before, in her dream. It had chilled her then, and it chilled her now, like frost crystallizing up her spine.

But then Elodie gathered her wits, remembering that premonitions did not exist, that dreams could not tell the future.

"What is this?" she asked.

Henry put his hands around her waist roughly, possessive

and controlling in a way he hadn't demonstrated before. "You are the princess of Aurea. This is your responsibility now, too."

"I didn't say it wasn't." She peeled his hands off her and tossed them away, insulted that he'd think her oath to the kingdom so flimsy that she'd betray it on her first night as princess.

More cloaked figures came up behind Henry, their faces eerily anonymous behind their gold masks. The knights who had accompanied the carriage stood in a line behind them, penning everyone in.

Elodie swallowed hard.

"Walk forward," Henry said.

"But it's a gorge . . ."

"Th-there's a bridge," one of the cloaked figures said.

Elodie turned to him. She knew that voice. "Father?"

The man looked away, pulling his hood farther down his already masked face.

Now the torchlight made it possible to see a little bit into the bottomless bowl of fog that was the chasm before her. Winged, reptilian statues carved of purple-gray granite rose from below. They were identical to the dragons in the sea on the approach to Aurea.

From the other side of the narrow gorge, another familiar voice rang out.

"A land can only thrive if we offer it our blessings," Queen Isabelle proclaimed. She wore a gold mask with sharp, twisting horns. "We have been chosen for this sacred duty. For generations, it has been our task—our burden—to protect our people. To keep fertile our isle. To meet the price."

Beside Elodie, Henry shouted, "Khaevis desires and we must sacrifice."

"Life for life!" the cloaked figures yelled. "Blood for fire!"

The circle of torches closed in behind Elodie, the knights following two steps after. They funneled her to the edge of the
ridge, toward the pale stone bridge that traversed the gorge
through the fog.

Panic raced through Elodie's veins.

"Let her walk the path of communion," the queen said, her
voice echoing against the mountainside.

Oh. A wave of relief washed over Elodie. They only wanted
her to cross the bridge. Another unfamiliar Aurean tradition, but
one she could manage.

"May I have a torch?" she asked Henry.

"It is not the way of the ceremony," one of the cloaked figures said gruffly.

She frowned. "But it will be nearly impossible to see in the
middle section where the bridge dips below the fog. What if I fall?"

Henry reached over and squeezed her hand, his hold lingering for a few seconds. "My angel, your feet will never touch the
ground."

The wind whipped through her flimsy dress again.

"At least give me your cloak."

"Don't question the requirements, Princess. Do your duty,
and it will all be over soon."

She bit back an insult she'd learned from the sailors. This was
not the time. Besides, Henry had a point. Elodie was a princess
now, and she would do what they asked—not because they told
her to, but because she understood duty and what it required of
those who chose to lead. And she had chosen.

She took a tentative step off the ridge and down onto the
bridge. The stone was slender and covered in frost, but she
would proceed carefully.

"Left foot first, right foot after," she began to whisper to her-

self. It was a poem her mother used to recite whenever Elodie
was on the brink of trying something new.

> *Nothing to fear, no disaster.*
> *Right foot, left foot,*
> *Cross the ground,*
> *And ere long*
> *You're safe and sound.*

The stone bridge sloped downward into the gorge, traveling
some distance in the thick fog before ascending to the ridge on
the other side where the queen and her half of the masked,
cloaked men stood with their long torches.

The lack of visibility in the center of the bridge was not as
bad as Elodie had feared. Once she descended into the fog, the
flickering torchlight cut through parts of it, and she was able to
see not only the towering dragon statues, but also other elaborate etchings on the sides of the gorge.

They were carvings of women in flowing gowns, much like
what Elodie wore. Some had long waves of hair, others, braids
and buns, but every woman wore a circlet tiara on her head. *I
wonder if this pays homage to ceremonies past?* Perhaps these represented the generations of princesses who had crossed the bridge
before on their wedding nights.

Elodie skidded on a patch of ice. "Oh god!" She fell onto
hands and knees, sliding toward the edge of the bridge, toward
the open maws of a stone dragon.

Momentum! she thought as logic overrode fear, and Elodie
threw what she could of her weight in the opposite direction of
her slide.

She stopped just short of falling over.

Elodie sprawled on the frosty rock for a moment, panting. She had a view straight down into the gorge.

As soon as her heartbeat had slowed to merely racing, she clambered to her feet. She took each step even more carefully now, looking only at where her foot moved and not at the dragon statues rising up through the fog or the murals of women carved into the rock walls.

Slowly but thankfully, Elodie reached the portion of the bridge that began to climb upward again. When she emerged from the fog, she let out a long exhale. *Thank the skies.*

Queen Isabelle stepped forward. There was no sign of King Rodrick; he must have remained at the palace, for the cold and the pomp and circumstance of this ceremony probably wouldn't do him any good.

"You have walked the path well," the queen said.

"Thank you. But I don't understand the meaning of what I've done."

"During the marriage ceremony, you mingled your blood with Henry's," Queen Isabelle said, answering Elodie but not meeting her eyes. "You are part of the royal family now. And with our shared bloodline comes our history."

She presented a ceremonial gold coin on a pillow of crimson velvet. The coin was almost the size of Elodie's palm.

Unsure what to do, Elodie curtsied as solemnly as possible given her shivering from the wind. She accepted the coin with both hands.

On one side was the image of three women wearing tiaras. On the other, a scaly, spiked tail.

A cloaked figure handed the queen a folded length of fabric. She unfurled it, holding it high in the torchlight for all to see.

It was the matrimonial cloth stained by Elodie's and Henry's blood.

The queen tossed it into the chasm, and Elodie watched as it fell—not slowly like a feather, but plummeting into the dark. Another chill shivered up Elodie's spine.

"When our ancestors arrived on the shores of Aurea," Queen Isabelle intoned, speaking to all gathered around the gorge, "they were tired and hungry, seeking refuge and a new land on which to build a new future. The isle greeted them with fertile plains full of golden wheat and forests bursting with healing fruit. It was the salvation they had sought, the reward for bravery after their long voyage across the sea.

"But our courageous people were not the only ones on the island. There was a monster here, too. It had no use for the land's bounty, and yet it would not surrender it. And so the king and queen sent their knights to dispatch the beast, so that the rest of their people could settle Aurea in peace."

The cloaked figures around the gorge murmured in appreciation at the difficult situation their predecessors had faced. At the same time, a lone figure on the other side of the ridge mounted a horse and began riding around to the side where Elodie and Queen Isabelle stood.

"The hubris of the humans angered the monster," the queen said, continuing the story, her voice hypnotic as it carried on the cold wind. "And so it left its lair to destroy the king and queen, and their three innocent daughters."

Elodie looked down at the gold coin in her hand. Three women wearing tiaras on one side. A monster on the other.

Queen Isabelle glanced at Elodie, and for a moment, Elodie thought she saw the queen's hard exterior falter. But then the queen clenched her fists and finished the rest of the tale.

"The king was desperate to save his people, to give them this newfound paradise as their home. He threw himself before the dragon and begged for mercy."

The monster was a dragon.

Elodie's stomach rolled over itself. The kingdom's obsession with dragons made sense now. All of it—the mosaic of scales, the coat of arms, the spiked tail on this coin—was homage to their history.

"The royal family made a pledge to give the beast anything it wanted if it would leave their people alone." Queen Isabelle turned now and met Elodie's gaze. "What dragons love more than anything, you see, is treasure. And what is more valuable to a king than his own children?"

The lone rider from the other side of the ridge arrived. He slid off his saddle and strode to the queen's side.

Henry.

He did not say a word to Elodie.

"The pact was made," Queen Isabelle said. "The king sacrificed his daughters to the dragon, and in return, the dragon left the kingdom at peace. And every year during the season of harvest, Aurea must renew its pledge to the monster, three gifts of royal blood."

"Life for life," the cloaked figures around the gorge chanted. "Blood for fire."

Three prayers, Henry had said when Elodie asked about the torches she'd seen on the ridge on the night she arrived. And she was one of the "prayers."

"No." Elodie shook her head in disbelief. "You *bought* me to feed to the dragon?"

The queen's expression was hard and unforgiving, but her eyes told a different story, one of centuries of sadness and regret. She would not apologize for what the royal families had had to do in order to protect the rest of the kingdom, but she carried the weight of the guilt with her.

"Consider it an honor," Queen Isabelle said. "You are giving

yourself to protect an entire country. Weren't you already willing to do that to save Inophe, when you agreed to this marriage?
This is but one step more."

"Father!" Elodie shouted across the chasm to the hooded figure whom she knew despite the gold mask. "Did you know
about this?"

He only bowed his head lower in shame.

This couldn't be happening. Not after the luxury of the palace, the gifts in her tower room, the bliss of the wedding.

Or maybe that was precisely why it was happening. Everything leading up to this moment was only to fatten up the goose
for slaughter. And Elodie was the goose.

"I was willing to do almost anything to save Inophe!" she
yelled at her father and at everyone around the gorge. "But I
would never have taken the lives of our own people."

She turned to Queen Isabelle, "I will *not* succumb to my
death so docilely."

"It would have been easier if you had," the queen said, her
voice suddenly soft. She gave Henry a look, then she walked
away.

"I'm sorry," Henry said, giving Elodie a rough kiss on the lips.

Distracted and confused by his mouth, she couldn't defend
herself when he hoisted her up over his shoulder and took off
running down the bridge.

"Henry, what are you—?"

She didn't have time to finish the question. Because one moment she was in his arms, and the next, he had hurled her into
the dark and her heart was in her throat, and like the matrimonial cloth thrown before her, she was plummeting

Down

Down

Down . . .

ELODIE

ELODIE'S BODY HIT the bottom of the gorge and bounced once, twice, three times, body limp and bruised from the rocks and roots that had scraped her on the way down, arms and legs flying like the limbs of a discarded doll. She skidded across the ground, and Elodie wasn't sure how she was still alive, but she could still hear the ghost of her own screams echoing against Mount Khaevis's walls. She curled herself into a ball as if that could somehow make the sound—and the all-too-clear memory of Aurea's betrayal—disappear.

"How could you do this?" she moaned. It was a question for the royal family. For her father. And even for herself, for thinking she could simply marry a stranger and everything would work out not only fine, but happily ever after.

Instead, she'd been thrown over a bridge to her death.

Wait a minute. Elodie slowly uncurled and sat up. She *wasn't* dead. How had she survived a fall like that? She could barely even see the bridge and the fog from down here.

Down here was a spongy layer of moss so thick that when Elodie plunged her arm into it, she couldn't find the bottom. The moss had a springy quality to it, so much so that it must have cushioned her landing.

Thank the skies!

No. That was Henry's saying. An Aurean one. Elodie refused to use it.

She got up on her hands and knees on the moss. Actually, did the queen and Henry know this was down here? And her father? Perhaps they hadn't meant for her to die after all.

Oh, for goodness sake. Elodie sighed as she realized the truth. Of *course* they hadn't meant for her to die. There was no dragon—how absurd to think even for a second that a monster from myths and legends was real. Elodie had let the macabre ambience of the hooded, masked ceremony get under her skin, and in that moment of weakness, she'd believed.

"Queen Isabelle *did* warn me that their traditions would seem bizarre," Elodie said to herself, brushing off moss from her arms.

But why go through the whole mountainside ritual then?

Perhaps it was a rite of passage. A test. Like the game she and Floria used to play when they were children, where one had to fall backward into the other's arms.

A test of trust.

Elodie grimaced. Perhaps she'd already failed her first ceremony as princess by not trusting the queen. But what was Elodie supposed to do? Just say, *Yes, Your Majesty, I absolutely want to toss myself into the deep unknown and possibly into the maws of a hungry beast, just to prove my loyalty?*

She sighed as she rose to her feet.

But her knees gave out on her, and she tumbled back down onto the moss. Every part of her body shook. Either it hadn't caught up with her brain yet, or it didn't buy the logic her brain was peddling. Regardless, it took a few more minutes for her to be steady enough to try standing again.

This time, she crawled over to one of the rock walls and used it as support.

"Hello? Anyone up there? I'm ready to come out now!"

No response.

"Father? Henry? Anyone?"

Nothing.

Elodie's pulse began to race again.

It's all right, she tried to tell herself. *This was just a test. Someone will come. Father will come. They wouldn't actually leave me in here.*

There were no sounds from above. No clatter of knights on the bridge preparing to retrieve her. No unspooling of ropes. Not even eerie chanting.

But then, she heard something. The whinny of horses. And then hoofbeats.

Galloping away.

What? No!

"Come back!" Elodie screamed, all dignity lost. "You can't leave me here! Help me, somebody help me!"

She tried scrambling up the wall, but the rigid boning of her corset was designed for looking pretty and maybe a gentle waltz, but not for climbing sheer rock faces.

"Argh!" In frustration, she tore at her dress, loosening the bodice and digging beneath the ephemeral, jeweled layers to get at the whalebone prison underneath. "Get off, get off!" She yanked at the laces on her back, jerking herself this way and that to free herself from the cage.

Finally, she undid the laces enough to wriggle out of the corset, and she hastily tightened the bodice of the dress again, woefully exposed beneath the thin layers of lavender. But Elodie didn't care about scandal at the moment. She cared only about being able to breathe and move. Besides, there was no one here to be scandalized by her appearance anyway.

The fog above her shifted, and for a second, moonlight hazed through, illuminating a part of the rock wall a few yards away. There was an ornate V carved into the stone, and Elodie gasped. It looked just like the V of the hourglass—a curved lip dipping down into a deep, slender arrow point, then rising to another curved lip, like the profile of a blooming lily. "What is that doing here?"

But then the fog shifted and obscured that part of the wall. Only moments later, a different, warmer light flickered on the opposite side of the gorge, revealing a tunnel of some sort.

Elodie was understandably hesitant to follow what looked like more torchlight.

But then again, it could be Henry and the knights coming to retrieve her. That made sense. It would be much more difficult to extract her from the bridge above; they didn't know she could easily climb up a rope, because it wasn't exactly a skill most la- dies had. So they would come through a different passage in the mountain, one on the level she was at.

Buoyed by the thought, Elodie ducked into the tunnel. She would follow the light and meet the rescue party on its way, and this entire ordeal could be over a lot sooner.

The light was faint, and the tunnel wide but crooked. Elodie kept one hand on the rocks at all times, advancing slowly and feeling her way forward. Out of habit, she mentally recorded each turn she made, as if designing one of her mazes for Floria to solve.

"Ouch!" Elodie snatched her fingers back from the tunnel wall. A burst of hot steam had burned her. "What in the name of . . . ?" She leaned closer to the spot again, taking care not to get *too* close.

A hiss of hot, moist air puffed out of a crack in the wall.

Dragon? She jumped.

But it was just a thermal vent, and she felt ridiculous for succumbing to the superstitious harvest ceremony tale.

Besides, it made sense that there was natural heat down here. Mount Khaevis was a volcano ages ago. This was just what remained.

The light source glowed a bit stronger now. Elodie picked up her pace.

A few minutes later, the tunnel widened, then ended abruptly in an open space. She took a very tentative step forward.

The sound of something moving—*slithering*—echoed through the mountain.

Elodie froze.

"Hello?" she whispered, unsure whether she wanted to draw the attention of the source of the noise. It certainly was not the sound of armor-clad knights.

It couldn't possibly be . . .

"Vo drae oniserru rokzif. Mirvu rokzif." The voice was low and raspy, like charcoal smoke when a fire burned too hot.

Eyes wide, Elodie retreated a few steps back into the tunnel and pressed herself against the rock, moving as slowly and quietly as terror would allow her. Because that was talking. Definitely talking. But in a language she didn't know.

Dragons are not *real,* she told herself.

She remained very, very still.

Then there was nothing, and Elodie began to wonder whether she was losing her mind. Perhaps fatigue had conjured voices in her head. Nevertheless, she stayed in the tunnel for several more silent minutes.

The light ahead flared brighter, orange now, rather than yellow. Elodie forced herself to the end of the tunnel and peeked out.

A burning ball of fire was bobbing up and down above, illuminating a large, dank cave. Stalactites hung from the ceiling like sharp gray teeth, and stalagmites rose from the ground like the other half of a massive jaw.

Then the fireball crashed to the ground and emitted a mournful chirp.

It's a bird! Elodie rushed toward the poor, injured thing.

Flames danced on the cave swallow's wings. Elodie looked around frantically for something to put it out before realizing she was already wearing the answer. She threw herself onto the ground next to the bird and enveloped it in her skirt.

Deprived of oxygen, the fire snuffed out in seconds. Elodie unwrapped the little swallow. But it was too late. Its body lay limp in her lap.

"What happened to you?"

Another fiery swallow flapped into the cave. Elodie gasped. She set the first dead bird on the ground, her hands sticky with a dark brownish substance that had coated its wings, and she wiped her hands on her dress as she stood to look at the new swallow engulfed in flames.

"How is this happening? What's going on?"

The bird shrieked in pain as it careened around the cave, and other cries replied. It was only now, by its fiery light, that Elodie saw the cave walls were lined with swallows' nests, not the kind made of sticks, but the sort constructed of bird saliva and mud. Each nest cradled tiny babies, which now screeched in fear.

A large shadow darkened the tunnel from which the second fiery swallow had come. A thunderous, rhythmical sound reverberated through the cave.

What was that? There was something vaguely familiar, and yet altogether not. Elodie could feel the vibrations. Whatever was making the noise was large enough to displace a great deal of air, hence her ability to feel the movement. Her heartbeat pounded to its frantic beat.

It sounded like . . .

Like what?

"Wings!" Elodie shouted as an entire flock of burning swallows exploded into the cave. They shot past Elodie, around her, up and down, crashing into stalactites and into the ground like a desperate storm of shooting stars singing a hideous chorus of pain and terror. One bird managed to reach its nest, but in its dying throes, it miscalculated and hit its wailing babies, and the nest shattered like a firecracker of feathers and ash.

Elodie stood rooted to the spot, gaping in horror at the flaming massacre around her.

And then . . . that slithering sound again. Louder, closer than the first time she heard it. Leather sliding against granite.

What birds remained living shrieked and dove out of the cave, into the narrow tunnel Elodie had come from. Darkness fell on the cavernous chamber, only faint light coming from the dying flames of swallows' corpses among the stalagmites.

Elodie could feel *it*. Any hopes that it was a corps of Aurean knights coming to find her had now been eviscerated by the burning birds, and she knew for certain that whatever was making that noise was an *it*.

The slithering noise grew even nearer, and the cave began to warm, as if all the thermal vents had opened at once to release their steam. Elodie shivered nonetheless, and she crouched behind a stalagmite, hoping that whatever it was would pass her by.

And hoping that it wasn't as colossal as it sounded.

Perhaps it was just the echo of the caves . . .

Scales on stone.

Elodie heard it to her left. And also her right.

Oh god, is it circling me?

She huddled against the rock, but in the fading light of the dead swallows, she saw a stalagmite nearby that hadn't been there before.

It moved.

A tail!

Elodie clambered up her own stalagmite, thankful for all her years climbing trees and boulders in Inophe. She didn't know where she was going, just that she had to get off the ground, away from that *thing.*

"Please, don't hurt me," she whispered, clinging to the top of her rock. The tip of the tail alone was bigger than she was. It was covered in armored scales, and short, sharp fins protruded from it like a mace.

An enormous violet eye opened to stare at her. Its center was a gold slit, predatory and reptilian.

"Dev errai?" it asked, its voice rough and ashy.

"Wh-what?" Elodie cried.

The eye closed, and she was plunged into darkness again. Then it opened, but it was in a different place in the cave. And all the while, the constant scrape of leather and scales against rock.

"Ni fama. Dikorr ni fama."

"I don't know what you're saying! What do you want?"

"What do you want?" it mimicked, almost mocking in tone.

"You can understand me," Elodie gasped, forgetting for a moment to be scared.

"Ed, zedrae."

"What are you?"

"Khaevis."

Elodie tried to process the sounds that it had made. They didn't connect to any word she knew.

Impatient at her lack of response, it spoke again. Its enormous violet eye was once more in a different place. Closer.

"I am *KHAEVIS* . . . DRAGON."

ELODIE

"**D**RAGON," ELODIE BREATHED. It was real. It wasn't just a story. The Aurean royal family truly had meant to feed Elodie to the beast. *Oh god oh god oh god.*

She could smell its smoky breath, the bitterness filling the air and stinging the back of her throat. It had burned all those swallows. It had circled her in this cave.

"What do you want?" she asked, even though she knew full well what it wanted. To have her in its belly.

"*Dek vorrai.*"

"What do you want?" Elodie shouted, feigning bravery she didn't feel.

"That is what I said, *zedrae. Dek vorrai.* What do you want?"

She furrowed her brows. *What?* Why was it repeating what she said? Was that the way dragons spoke?

Or perhaps the dragon was repeating her words because . . . because it wasn't used to speaking to humans and needed to go through the process of translating itself?

That would make sense. The dragon probably didn't get much company in the mountain.

Oh. Mount *Khaevis*. It meant Dragon Mountain.

The little that Elodie had eaten at her wedding threatened to come back up.

"*Vorra kho tke raz. Vorra kho tke trivi. Kho rykae,*" the dragon said. "*Vis kir vis. Sanae kir res.*"

She had no clue what it was saying. But she couldn't wait around and have a one-sided conversation with it. As it spoke, she slid down the stalagmite.

Hoping it was distracted by its little speech, Elodie began tiptoeing toward the tunnel.

"I can see you in the dark," the dragon said, one violet and gold eye flicking open just to the right of her.

Elodie screamed and fled up a different stalagmite, despite what little good it would do when the dragon decided to pounce.

The dragon inhaled deeply. "Your blood smells delicious. Princess blood. *Strong* blood."

Its breath was too near now. Too hot, the sulfur in it too sharp.

Both of its eyes opened wide, violently purple, staring straight into Elodie's face.

"Oh god!"

This close, she could see the mosaic of its scales, exactly like everywhere in the Aurean palace, except the dragon's were dark gray, not gold. Each of its teeth was the length of her arm and sharp as a blade. Its triple-forked tongue flicked in and out, as if sampling the air around her, a preview of how she would taste in its mouth.

"I want my part of the bargain," it rasped. "*Vis kir vis. Sanae kir res.* Life for life. Blood for fire."

"I thought dragons were just supposed to be stories," Elodie whispered.

"*Erra terin u farris.* I am the *end* of stories."

"Please . . ."

"But strong *zedrae* blood is the most powerful blood . . . So show me if you are strong, *zedrae* . . . Run."

It opened its jaws and pointed upward, unleashing flames and lighting the cave like the gates of hell. The dragon was even larger than she'd thought, its wings like bladed sails, its powerful jaw full of teeth the size of swords. Elodie screamed and bolted for the tunnel.

As she ran, feathers and bones crunched and squelched underfoot, the remains of the burning swallows that hadn't made it far from the cave. In her haste, she kept slamming into rock every time the tunnel turned.

The dragon laughed. "This is my favorite part."

It blew a long flame into the tunnel that licked the heel of Elodie's shoe. She screamed and ran faster, arms smacking into rock, knees scraping against jagged stone, but never paused.

The leathery sound of slithering began to follow her. The dragon could have snapped her up in an instant, but it was taking its time, enjoying her terror, feeding off the smell of adrenaline wafting off her skin.

Elodie burst out of the tunnel into the moss-covered landing where she'd been thrown in, at the bottom of the gorge. It suddenly felt like an arena, the type where prisoners of war were sent to fight lions and tigers, only to be mauled to death while their audience of captors watched and applauded. This space was too open, too easy for the dragon to lunge and swallow her whole.

The fog overhead had broken since her fall, though, and moonlight illuminated the chasm. On the other side of the gorge, beneath the bridge, she thought she saw another cave opening.

"*Zedrae* . . . Princess . . ." The dragon's voice echoed through the tunnel and reached her like tendrils of smoke wrapping around her.

Elodie ran for the other cave opening.

But the moss was thick, and the sponginess that had saved her from breaking her neck earlier now slowed her speed, her feet sinking as if in green quicksand. She fell, scrambled up, fell again, lost a shoe in the depths of the moss. It was faster to crawl, and more terrifying, because the dragon's next taunt was right on the edge of the tunnel from which she'd come.

"*Fy kosirrai.* Now you understand."

"I understand nothing!" she shouted as she continued, determined, to scrabble forward on all fours. She was only ten yards away from the edge of the moss. Almost back on solid rock.

"*Errai khosif, dekris ae. Nydrae kuirrukud kir ni, dekris ae. Errai kholas.*" Then, as if remembering she couldn't understand it, the dragon said, "You are alone down here. No one will come for you. *You are mine.*"

"Not if I can help it." Elodie reached the end of the moss and jumped, landing on her shoed foot and sprinting for the cave entrance.

The dragon sprang after her, its massive wings catching the wind and whooshing as it lunged. One of its talons struck the back of her right calf.

Elodie shrieked. But the cave opening was right there, only a yard away. It was small, exactly the kind of place Floria would have loved for hide-and-seek when they were children, and exactly the kind of tight fit Elodie hated.

Her stomach somersaulted. *Please no, anything but a tiny space . . .*

But that also meant it was too small for the dragon.

She dove for the opening.

The ceiling here was low and she had to hunch as she ran, but she sprinted as fast as she could on a bleeding leg, not caring where the shaft led as long as it was away from the monster who wanted her as supper.

The dragon roared. It could not pursue, but its flames faced no such limitation. Fire shot into the passage behind Elodie and caught on her hem. She beat at it, trying to put it out, but then it touched the sticky residue left on her skirt by the dying swallow. The gooey substance was like oil to the flame, and the fire exploded.

Elodie screamed and fell to the ground, rolling against the rocks to try to smother the flames. It burned her legs and her arms, the sharp stones cutting into her flesh, the gravel grinding into her wounds.

I'm on fire, maldí-seù, *I'm on fire and there's nowhere to go and the walls are so close and I'm going to burn and suffocate, and I can't breathe, I can't breathe, I can't—*

Her rolling snuffed out the fire, and the tunnel filled with smoke. She choked, both ash and claustrophobia lodged in her throat.

You have to get ahold of yourself, she thought, tears and snot trickling down her face. *Don't think about the space. Pretend you're outside, that the dark is just the sky on a cloudy night.*

But it's not!

She gagged as fear gripped her stomach and squeezed.

No, damn you! There's a dragon chasing you, and you are not *going to die from claustrophobia you pathetic little—* Elodie slapped herself in the face.

She forced herself to her feet and started running again. The dragon had gotten quiet, but that didn't mean it wasn't a threat. It could unleash another column of fire any second.

Elodie sprinted hard, trying to commit every turn in the narrow passage to memory. Her brain was clouded by fear, though, and she couldn't hold on to more than four turns before she forgot the previous ones.

I won't even live to use the knowledge, the grim voice in her head said.

But the will to survive was an irrational one, and it was what kept her moving. Finally, the rock shaft widened and opened into another cave. It was a six-foot drop but she jumped down into the cave, barely registering when her ankle twisted, just grateful to be able to stand to full height, grateful to not be enclosed anymore in so small a—

"*Resorrad kho adroka a ni sanae.*"

Elodie barely suppressed a scream as the violet eyes opened a few yards away from her.

The dragon had not seen her yet, but it had been waiting, had known this was where she would emerge.

An image of the innocent, fluffy lambs she'd seen on her first carriage ride in Aurea flickered in her mind. *I've been herded like sheep.* There were only two ways in and out of this cave: the passage she'd come through—the one that was six feet off the ground—and the one the dragon was blocking.

The terrain in this cave was similar to the other one, though. Lots of stalagmites and stalactites, and a few long cracks in the walls. Which meant the possibility of hiding and buying at least a little time.

But then Elodie's gaze landed on several broken skulls—one missing half its jaw, another with only one eye socket, the third with the entire top part of its head smashed in. Scattered around the cave were charred bones, and the walls bore the smoke-damaged marks of fire and ash.

Perhaps worst of all, Elodie saw a tiara just like her own, not too far from where the dragon was. There were still wisps of platinum, blue-ribboned hair attached to it.

Oh god oh god oh god, the woman from the other tower?

The dragon was sniffing the remnants of a lavender dress horrifyingly similar to Elodie's, as if luxuriating in the smell.

Did the bloodstains still hold the scent of its dead owner? Could the dragon smell the woman's terror, even in dried blood?

Elodie ripped off a piece of her skirt that was already hanging by mere threads. If the monster liked the scent of princess blood so much, she could use that as a distraction.

She wiped the strip of cloth against the talon wound in her calf, wincing as she squeezed it to make it bleed more. She wanted the fabric soaked with her blood.

Elodie eyed the most promising of the crevices in the wall, just wide enough to slide into sideways. If this worked, she'd need a place to run to. Perhaps the dragon would just roast her right away. But it seemed to enjoy the hunt, and Elodie hoped it wanted fresh blood more than it wanted her dead. For now.

As quietly as she could, she wrapped the blood-soaked fabric around a palm-sized rock. Then she hurled it into a cluster of stalagmites to her right.

The dragon lunged at the sound. Elodie ran to her left toward the crevice. She was even slower now, because her ankle must have sprained when she dropped down from the passageway. Elodie reached the crevice and crammed herself inside, just as the dragon reached the stalagmites and discovered her trick.

It whipped around to find Elodie gone.

"*Syrrif drae.* A clever one." The dragon breathed deeply from the bloody fabric, as if her scent were a fine wine. "*Syne nysavarrud ni.* Pity it won't save you."

Elodie remained as still as possible, even though she was stuck inside the smallest space she'd ever been in in her life. Her heart rose up into her throat.

She hoped her blood near the dragon's nostrils was enough to distract it from the smell of where she actually was.

It opened its mouth and released a jet of fire that curved along the arc of the cave wall, heating it red hot. Elodie shrieked as the rock burned her skin like a branding iron, and she squeezed herself deeper into the fissure to try to get away from the heat. The promise of cooler rock propelled her farther and farther in.

"*Kuirr, zedrae . . .*"

Elodie held her breath and her tears.

"Come out, princess."

She would not.

Instead, Elodie stood like a statue—a badly burned one—and listened for every movement the dragon made in the cave. Every slither, every sigh, every flick of its triple-pronged tongue. Magnified by the claustrophobic terror of being wedged in what could be her final resting place.

It waited for several hours, hoping she would think it gone. Hoping she would slide out from her hiding place and into its open jaws.

She would not give it the satisfaction.

Finally, when Elodie felt she was already half dead from her wounds and from being crammed into the crevice, the dragon laughed, filling the cave with its smoky breath. "Congratulations on surviving, *zedrae*. For now."

It exited the cave, its leathery scales scraping against rock as it left.

Elodie exhaled.

The dragon was gone. *For now.* She squeezed her eyes closed and clenched her fists, wishing that none of this was real, that it was only a nightmare from which she'd soon wake, and that instead, Floria would be there, bouncing on her bed, and they'd be back in Inophe, where they had never heard of Aurea and Prince Henry.

But when Elodie opened her eyes, she was still stuck in the impossibly narrow crevice.

And she began to sob.

FLORIA

FLORIA DANCED AROUND her room in the tower. The wedding reception was over, but the lutes and trumpets still played in her ears, her mouth still remembered every sweet and savory flavor that had delighted her tongue, and she could still recall with crystal clarity how beautiful and happy her sister had looked with the prince of her dreams beside her.

Well, admittedly, Henry was more like the prince of *Floria's* dreams—handsome and rich and charming. If Elodie could have chosen for herself, she would likely have picked a scholar prince, someone who wrote her brainteasers instead of love letters, and who'd want to travel and visit every library in the world with her, rather than stay on a reclusive island kingdom for the rest of their lives.

But Elodie would be happy, Floria knew. Because her sister had always been the adaptable one, stepping up to do the market shopping and cooking and running of the household when their mother died, tucking Flor in every night and reciting epic poems to her as bedtime stories. Elodie mourned the loss of their mother quietly, but she always took care of what needed to be done, and the effort never showed. Elodie was the kind of woman who could balance the tenant accounts while teaching Floria algebra while reading the philosophy of the ancients, allowing Father to dismiss the governess.

Well, actually, the governess ended up marrying Father. That was how Miss Lucinda Hall became Lady Bayford.

But Floria shoved thoughts of their stepmother out of her mind, because she wanted to think about *this* wedding. Yes, Elodie would be happy. *Very* happy. Who wouldn't be, in a place like this? And Henry had showered her with compliments and flowers and beautiful dresses. Floria flopped onto her bed and sighed.

I wonder how El's first night as princess is going.

The queen had taken Elodie away for "some Aurean traditions." Perhaps a ceremony to give her more jewels to match her tiara—a royal ring? Or maybe a scepter?

Or perhaps there were words of wisdom a queen needed to impart to a princess. Like how Elodie had taken over running Father's accounts after Mother died, now she'd have to learn how to rule a kingdom.

Whatever the Aurean traditions were, Elodie hadn't returned to the reception afterward. And Henry had disappeared, too.

Suddenly, Floria blushed. She might have only been thirteen, but once Father had announced Elodie's engagement, Flor had heard some of the older girls in Inophe giggling about what went on between a man and woman on their wedding night . . .

"Ew." Floria made a face and shook her head back and forth, as if to jostle out thoughts of her sister and Henry doing *that*. To further cleanse the palate of her mind, Flor hopped off the bed and stood in front of her mirror, admiring her dress again. The seamstresses had let her design it—although they made sure it would not upstage Elodie's wedding gown—and Floria grinned at the delicate posies and buttercups and butterflies that dotted the skirt, as if she were a meadow come to life.

"When it's my turn to get married, I shall have a gown of pale silver, like moonlight on the clearest night."

And so Floria eventually fell asleep, still in her butterfly dress, dreaming of her own future, and a wedding and husband as perfect as Elodie's.

CORA

S OMEONE KNOCKED ON Cora's bedroom door.

"Sweetheart, it's Mama. Are you still awake?"

Cora curled up a little tighter on her bed. She wasn't looking forward to more disappointment from her parents, but she had to say yes. Her mother was a sailor who would head out to sea once the harvest was ready, to bring Aurea's grain and fruit to the rest of the world. Cora had learned from a young age to spend whatever time she could with Mama, who was away from home more often than not.

"I'm still up," she said. "You can come in."

The door opened, and Mama came over and sat next to Cora on the bed. "I heard you broke into the palace."

"I might have done so . . ." She braced herself for another reprimand.

But instead, Mama ruffled Cora's hair. "How did you manage to get past the guards?"

Cora blinked in surprise. "You're not mad?"

"Oh yes, I am plenty mad. But also impressed."

The pleasure of making her mother proud tingled in Cora's

toes. "I walked in with a troupe of acrobats who were going to perform at the reception." Cora was lithe and strong from her work in the fields, so it hadn't been a stretch for an outsider to believe she was part of their group.

"Brilliant." Mama laughed. But her amusement quickly faded. She lowered her voice and said, "Papa told me why you went."

Cora looked down at the bed and picked at the comforter. Unlike peasants in other countries, the farmers of Aurea slept on down mattresses and blankets woven from cloud-soft aurum wool. They owned their own land, which thrived under always perfect weather, and everyone had plenty to eat. But Cora hadn't known it was any different elsewhere until Papa explained tonight that it was the presence of the dragon that made Aurea so.

"I don't need another lecture," Cora said. "I know I was wrong."

"Were you?" Mama asked.

The genuineness of her tone made Cora look up. She was a kind mother, but she was a parent nonetheless, which meant she did not often ask for children's opinions. Now, though, Mama tilted her head and waited patiently for her answer.

"Papa said that life is harder outside of Aurea," Cora said. "That there are kingdoms where every single person suffers, in one way or another."

"And?"

"And we are blessed to have this paradise. Living dragons emanate magic from the strength of the blood that courses through them, so we must keep the dragon happy, in order that Aurea may remain as good as it is. Life is never fair, Papa said, and everyone has to make compromises."

"He shares the view of most Aureans. But sometimes I wonder, what compromises are worth making?"

Cora furrowed her brow. "What do you mean?"

Mama rose and began pacing. "Peasants usually do not live like this." She gestured to Cora's room. It was small but tidy, with tiles hand painted with flowers, a pretty mural of the aurum wheat fields on the wall, and satin drapes around the picture window. "I've sailed to many a country and seen what their working men and women are like. Skin baked and cracked from the sun, unpredictable snowstorms in winter and tornados in summer that destroy their crops, coffers empty from too much taxation."

"That sounds awful," Cora said, shaking her head.

"It is. Believe me, most would do anything to be able to live in prosperous peace like we do."

She nodded.

"But not everybody. What if"—Mama looked straight at her—"you were born in one of those kingdoms? And what if Queen Isabelle came to you and said, 'Cora, I invite you to my perfect island where you shall never want for anything. The price is only a small one—you must choose three girls to die.'"

Cora's eyes widened.

Mama continued. "If you make that choice, then you and thousands of others can enjoy a rich life of all you can eat, all you can buy, and all you can love. Just three lives a year, in exchange for the happiness of an entire kingdom. Could you do it?"

"D-do I have to know the girls personally?"

"Does it make the decision any less morally fraught if you don't?"

Cora hugged her stuffed sheep toy to her chest. She was too old for it, but she needed something to hold on to. She understood that Mama was asking if everything she'd ever known was a crime.

"If I said no to the queen," Cora said slowly, "then I would have to live an ordinary life, in an ordinary country, and suffer?"

"Perhaps you suffer, perhaps you don't. There would still be plenty of moments of joy and love. Families and friends still exist out there. But there's no guarantee of bounteous harvests or fair weather or money for pretty dresses. No promises of down comforters and songs in the wheat fields with a benevolent sun shining over our heads."

"But if I say yes, I condemn someone to death. *Three* someones, every year."

Mama closed her eyes for a moment and said nothing. Then she nodded. "Yes, and those three souls are on your conscience forever, whether you choose to think of them or not."

Cora curled up around her toy sheep. "Am I a bad person if I want to be happy?"

Her mother sat back down on the bed and stroked Cora's hair. "No. You're only human. We do what we must to survive. Life is not as simple as good and evil. It is mostly lived in the pages in between."

They were quiet for a while, both lost in their own thoughts. Cora thought about how beautiful Princess Elodie had been. How compassionate in leaping to her aid when the boys shoved Cora in the ditch. And how by doing nothing, the people of Aurea had sentenced a good person to her death. At the jaws of a dragon.

"But what can we do?" Cora asked, breaking the silence.

"I don't know," Mama said. "The antimonarchists want to revolt against the royal family. But that is too simplistic. The king, queen, and prince are all that stand between us and the dragon. Without them—without the horrible peace their ancestors negotiated—the dragon would destroy us all. We are, as ever, mere guests on this isle. To live on Aurea is to accept this price."

"We could slay the dragon," Cora said, eyes darting to a play sword in the corner. There was a matching shield, too, bearing the coat of arms of Aurea—ironically, with a prominent dragon.

"First of all, if we did that, we would lose the magic that grows the aurum wheat and silver pears and sangberries and more."

"Oh. That's bad."

"Yes, it is. But even if that were not so, it's a fantasy to think we *could* slay the dragon," Mama said, her shoulders drooping. "That's where the founding royal family made their first mistake—their hubristic belief that they could beat such a legendary beast. No, the more realistic outcome of picking a fight with a dragon is that we start a war we can't win. And then many, many more innocent lives are lost than only three." The bags beneath Mama's eyes seemed heavier than when she'd walked into the room. She had clearly lost plenty of nights of sleep thinking over this dilemma.

"And if life isn't just good and evil," Cora said, "maybe the dragon is not solely a villain. Perhaps we ought not kill it, even if we could. Who are we to say which life is worth more than another?"

Mama gave her a sad smile. "You are very wise for such a small person."

Cora shook her head. "But it leaves us with the same problem as before. It's wrong to sit back and let Aurea's tradition continue. It's also wrong to try to save the princesses or slay the dragon. We're stuck."

"There *is* one other possible solution," her mother said, although she didn't seem very happy about it.

"What is it?"

Mama leaned over and whispered in her ear.

Cora furrowed her small brow as understanding sank in. Then she grabbed her stuffed sheep and hugged it tighter, biting her lip to try to keep in her tears.

ALEXANDRA

A LEXANDRA RAVELLA SHUT her daughter's door gently after she'd soothed Cora to sleep. In the hallway outside her room, though, Lieutenant Ravella leaned against the cool wall and squeezed shut her eyes.

She had almost told Cora her secret. But at the last second, Alexandra had pulled back, because she'd already burdened Cora too much tonight. Cora was only nine; she didn't deserve to shoulder all the guilt her mother carried.

But knowing that Cora had broken into the wedding that *she*, a mere child, had more gumption and conscience than she, a woman in her fifties . . .

Alexandra sank down onto the tiles. She couldn't do it anymore. To her family and everyone else in the village, she was a mere sailor on a merchant ship that sold the fruits of Aurea's harvest. No one knew she was a scout, tasked with finding women from other shores who would sate the dragon's hunger. After all, Aurea did not want to give up its own daughters to marry Prince Henry, only to be tossed into the chasm of Mount Khaevis.

Hence, the scouting ships sailed to new lands in remote parts of the world. Alexandra's job was to search for families who were willing to betroth their daughters in exchange for gold or grain or other resources they lacked. She never lied about what would come after the wedding, and still, there were men who fell at her feet for the contract.

Bloodhound. That was Alexandra's nickname. She'd started as a ship girl when she was fourteen, carrying messages among the crew and taking care of small tasks like mending sails and helping on the night watch. But soon word of her keen insight into the personalities and motivations of the other sailors made its way to the scout on board, and Alexandra was brought under his training as an apprentice. In the decades since, Alexandra had helped recruit dozens of potential candidates for princess. While some scouts specialized in identifying greedy fathers, Alexandra's specialty was recognizing the despairing, dutiful ones who felt honor bound to help their people, no matter the personal cost. Including giving up one's daughter to a dragon.

Lord Bayford of Inophe was this type of man, who could be convinced that he was making a noble decision by giving away one daughter for the lives of many. Alexandra had told Lord Bayford of how lavishly Elodie would be treated in her final days. How this young woman who had grown up in a parched land would be showered with gifts and gowns and food and drink, how she would be spoiled beyond her wildest dreams, and how this would honor her for what she was about to do.

Alexandra had built a bond with Lord Bayford, explaining how she, too, understood the difficult decisions a person must make when charged with the well-being of many. Aurea may have been wealthy, but it was much like Inophe in that something had to be given in order for the rest to survive, to thrive.

It had been Alexandra who arranged for Elodie to begin a

correspondence with Prince Henry. Alexandra's fault that Elodie fell for the prince's practiced charisma. Alexandra's doing that Elodie agreed to the betrothal and set sail here, to her doom.

And yet, even though Alexandra was sick for days after every arranged marriage, she had always kept her head down, blinders on as much as possible, just like her husband and everyone else in Aurea had. She had accepted the devilish bargain and her role in it.

Until Cora dared to try to put a stop to it.

So now it had come to this, the only solution Alexandra could think of. She wished there were another answer, but she had spent many years vomiting her guilt on her voyages, and she could think of nothing but this single way out.

Alexandra opened her eyes and forced herself to stand from the hallway floor. Her small daughter had shown her what bravery looked like. Now it was her responsibility to show Cora what to do with it.

ELODIE

ELODIE WIPED THE tears from her puffy eyes and the snot dripping from her nose. Her skin felt like it was still on fire, her ankle throbbed, and who knew what shape her calf was in, other than the unexpected blessing that the dragon's fire seemed to have cauterized the claw wound.

I'm glad Flor isn't here to see me like this, she thought. For the obvious reason that she would never want Floria to have to face a dragon, but also, Elodie was supposed to be the courageous older sister, the one who didn't cry and who could take on anything.

She hadn't known that "anything" included a traitorous husband and in-laws who would hurl you into a gorge for a bloodthirsty dragon. And what was Father's role in all this?

Pain washed over her like lightning strikes alternating with typhoon waves of nausea. Elodie turned her head sideways and threw up.

But she hadn't been able to get clear of herself because she was still wedged inside a crack in a cave wall, and now she was covered in her own vomit in addition to the priestesses' ceremonial paint. And she was burned. And probably on the brink of infection in her leg.

The walls of the crevice seemed to close in on her, and Elodie began to hyperventilate.

"I c-can't do this," she whispered through a fresh onslaught of tears.

She was going to suffocate here, her skeleton trapped between slabs of sharp rock, her burned skin stretched taut like a charred mummy's. She would never see the sun again, never smile at the lightness of Floria's laugh, never see the beautiful sandy landscape of her homeland again.

And how would Floria feel when she went home to Inophe and wrote letters to Elodie but never received a reply? She would think Elodie had abandoned her, that Elodie thought it beneath a princess to write to a poor daughter of an unimportant lord in an insignificant land.

Would Flor really think that of her?

Elodie's heart ached at the possibility.

And what about when Flor grew older and found her own match? Who would comb her ebony hair for her on her wedding day? Who would help her into the gorgeous gown she designed? Who would offer the first toast at her reception?

"It's supposed to be me," Elodie said.

And suddenly, a rush of anger flooded through her veins, because *how dare* Henry and Queen Isabelle take those milestones away from Elodie? How dare they leave Floria alone in the world, without her sister and best friend by her side?

I won't let that happen, Elodie thought, teeth gritted.

She swiped the tears from her eyes, and this time, they did not return. Because she was going to make the people who put

her here pay. She didn't know how, but it was a promise to herself and to Floria.

But first, Elodie had to find a way to stay alive.

AN HOUR LATER, she had managed to squeeze herself about fifty
yards deeper into the crevice. It was slow going, because Elodie
had to keep pushing down the claustrophobia that threatened to
subsume her. But it was necessary, for she'd decided that going
back out into that cave—with the big tunnel that might be hiding
the dragon just out of view—was not a risk she was willing to
take.

The crack in the rock wasn't level, either. At some parts, it
ascended and widened; at others, it went down and narrowed.
Now, Elodie navigated a section that had twisted sideways, and
she had to inch along practically horizontal, with who knew how
many tons of granite above her, only inches from her face, possibly about to cave in and crush her and—

Stop it. Elodie bit her lip and forced herself to take a long,
slow breath while she stopped her spiraling thoughts. She needed
to take this one step at a time. Or one wiggle at a time, as it were.

The mental image of herself wiggling made Elodie laugh a
little. And then a lot.

She couldn't stop giggling, caught halfway between hysteria
and soul-crushing fatigue. She laughed and laughed, thinking
about how ridiculous it was that she was a princess in a torn-up
ceremonial gown, wriggling around like a rainbow-painted cat-
erpillar trapped inside a . . . inside a what? Elodie was too worn
out to come up with a suitable analogy, and for some reason,
that made her laugh even harder.

I am losing my mind.

Elodie snorted.

A good ten minutes later, the giggling died down, and bone weariness settled in. Her eyes drooped, and for a second, Elodie fell asleep.

Merdú! She jolted awake. She would *not* sleep yet. If she did, she might as well die here as infection took hold of her leg, and then dehydration and starvation finished her off. Perhaps the other way around. But in any case, she would *not* die in the middle of a crack in a rock.

"I am not going to die at all," she growled to herself, and pushed onward.

Soon, the crack twisted forty-five degrees, so at least Elodie was upright (mostly) again.

"*Sakru, kho aikoro. Sakru errad retaza etia.*"

Elodie froze.

The dragon's voice was faint, but menacing. Was it near her? Or was the wind carrying the threats through the caves?

"*Kho nekri . . . sakru nitrerraid feka e reka. Nyerraiad khosif. Errud khaevis. Myve khaevis.*"

She shuddered. But the dragon couldn't reach her inside this small space, right? If it hadn't already roasted her, it probably wouldn't do it now. She hoped.

Strong blood is the most powerful blood, Elodie remembered it saying. It wants a chase, an opponent. Not just an easy kill, she reasoned. In the other chamber, the dragon had tried to heat the rocks with its flames to force her out. The temperature was enough to scald her skin but not to kill her. It could have sent fire into the crevice, but it didn't, because then it would lose both its challenge *and* its dinner.

Please let that assumption be a sound one.

Regardless, Elodie couldn't stay here, so she pressed on, even as her calf went stiff and her ankle swelled, even as the granite walls scraped off raw patches of her burned skin.

Thirty yards later, she came face to face with what looked like a bright blue slug. It was glowing.

Elodie blinked, sure she was seeing things.

But no, it was really there, about two inches long and half an inch wide and giving off a pale blue luminescence.

If there's life here, then perhaps it means I'm close to another cave? She hadn't seen anything else living inside the barren crevice, but if there was a glowworm here, then it must have come from somewhere nearby that *did* have a food source. Maybe not food for Elodie, but at least food for sluggy things. She hoped she was right, and she hoped where the glowworm lived was big enough for her to stand and stretch out in.

She squeezed by the worm, doing her best to avoid touching it with her face as she passed. Close up, she could see that it secreted a viscous blue goo from its pores, which is where the light came from. She suppressed her gag reflex as it waggled its feelers at her. Thank goodness she didn't have anything else left in her stomach to vomit up.

Not far past the first glowworm, she encountered two more. Then a half dozen. The crevice widened a little, too, enough that she could actually walk forward rather than scooting sideways like a crab.

Suddenly, she stepped in something that squelched.

"Oh, yuck . . ." Elodie lifted the foot that was shoed. The sole was covered in blue worm corpse. The glow from its goo lit up the narrow passage a little, though.

"At least your death wasn't in vain," she said. She took off her shoe and held it like a makeshift candle, and despite the disgusting origin, she was thankful for the light.

Elodie continued, although the glow from her shoe soon faded. The potency of worm goo could only last for so long after the worm itself died, she guessed. But more blue slugs began dotting the crevice, so she kept going, and then she was really, really *going*, because the crevice angled sharply downward and the rock grew slippery with algae. Elodie had no traction on her bare feet and she fell on her backside and slid with increasing velocity down slick granite, glowworms and algae smashed by her careening body, until suddenly the bottom disappeared from underneath her and she screamed as the crevice turned into a vertical chute. She shot through its slime-covered walls and then popped out of the end of it, landing with a hard, wet splat.

Flat on her back in a pile of decaying algae and smashed slugs, she groaned. *"Caráhu . . ."* The sailors' curse for whenever they slipped or dropped something seemed immensely apt.

But when Elodie opened her eyes, soft blue light greeted her from above. She was in another cave, just as she had hoped. And the glowworms indeed lived here. Their colony, far from repulsive, looked like a shimmering sea on the ceiling of the granite chamber. When they moved, it looked like tiny waves of the incoming tide.

Beautiful. Peaceful. The claustrophobic tension in Elodie's chest eased now that she was in a space that was big enough to stretch out in, and she let her limbs sink against the bed of cool algae. It soothed the burns on her skin and took all the weight off her injured legs.

The glowworms moved slowly, in complete silence, shifting in hypnotic, bioluminescent patterns. It was like watching the ocean, its gentle waves washing in and off the shore. Elodie knew she ought to rise and get the lay of the land. She ought to figure out whether it was safe to stay here. But she was just so, so relieved to be off her feet and out of that crevice, and her eyelids were heavy, and perhaps she would just close her eyes for a moment, because she deserved a small respite, and then she would get up, and . . .

She was snoring within five seconds.

ELODIE

THE DREAM WAS of princesses falling from the sky, like a royal hailstorm of gowns and tiaras and confused faces. Some were pale and others were brown; some were flaxen haired and others had tight, black curls. The platinum-haired woman from the other tower fell from a storm cloud, her blue ribbons like a torrent of rain. A brunette princess tumbled heels over head and bounced as she hit the moss. Another one, strong-boned, landed on top of her, and then another and another, until the bottom of the gorge was a pile of royalty.

Then there was a crash of thunder, the roar of wings. More princesses kept falling from the sky, but the bottom of the gorge tilted, and the spongy moss poured the pile of sacrificed wives into a narrow passage, and from there, they sobbed and crawled, arms and legs sliced up by jagged rocks.

Elodie tried to shout at them in her sleep. "No! Don't go that way! You're being herded like sheep!"

But they couldn't hear her, and so they pressed on, a line of discarded women on hands and knees. Soon the tunnel ended in a steep precipice, and a curly-haired princess flung herself over the edge. Her legs gave out and broke as she landed with a crunch six feet below. She cried out as dark violet eyes flickered before her, their gold pupils dilating at the scent of her blood. She tried to rise but couldn't. The beast snatched her with a single swipe of its claw. Her tiara, a few curls of hair, and a scrap of lavender cloth fell behind a stalagmite, the only evidence the woman had ever been there.

The princesses kept coming. And they kept falling. Some would look before they jumped and land without breaking bones. Others, overcome by fear, leapt straight into the dragon's open maw.

And then the dream began again, with fog and lightning and princesses raining out of the sky.

This time, though, one in particular was lit up as she fell. Her dark red hair was like the Aurean flag fluttering through the air, and she seemed to fall slower than the others.

Are you V? Elodie thought in her dream.

The woman's piercing green eyes met Elodie's.

Elodie gasped, both from recognition—the vision from the hourglass!—and because no other princess in the dream had been able to see or hear her.

The redheaded princess stopped falling, and she floated while she held her arm outstretched, as if she could reach Elodie.

"Me?" Elodie asked.

The woman nodded and held out her hand again.

Elodie extended her own, but she was too far away, for the princess was in the sky, and Elodie was somewhere else, watching from both inside and outside the dream. The distance between them was miles yet also infinite.

"I can't!" Elodie shouted.

You can, the woman mouthed. And then she drew a V in the storm cloud and smiled, just as the dragon roared into the gorge with eyes blazing—

Elodie jerked awake, hand still reaching for the redheaded princess, mouth formed in a scream of *Watch out!*

She sat up, dazed, sweat dripping down her forehead, heart pounding like a mallet inside her rib cage.

"Just a nightmare," she said to herself.

It had felt so real. But perhaps that was because Elodie had just lived through all the same terror. Perhaps the dream was her brain's way of processing what had happened, an attempt to make some sense out of the madness. As for the V, maybe it was because Elodie had seen a similar V carved into the rock at the bottom of the pit where she'd been thrown in. And of course, the hourglass.

Still, there was something about this cave that felt . . . off. A warm fug hung in the air, but more than just the heat from the thermal vents. Rather, it was as if an invisible mantle of *something* permeated the chamber—no, permeated every part of the tunnels and caves that Elodie had been in so far, even the tight, endless crevice in the rock. An unseen mist that smelled faintly of blood and ancient forests, of old cathedrals and amber and musk.

A couple of minutes passed before Elodie could shake off the grogginess and distinguish between what was reality and what was not.

That's when she noticed the creepy, crawly tingling all over her body.

"Ack!" Glowworms had clamped themselves on to her, smearing their blue mucus all over her skin. She could feel their little feet and their gooey torsos, their slippery feelers and their nibbling little mouths. Elodie jumped up and started swiping at them. "Get off, get off! I'm not your dinner! I'm *no one's* dinner!"

The slugs toppled off in heaps onto the slimy bed of algae. Only then did she see that she'd slept not only on the algae, but also partially on a slab of rock stained a deep brown rust.

The color of . . . blood. Very old blood, lots of it, layered over time until it seeped deep into the veins of the stone so that some parts stood out darker than others, like a sanguinary map of the past.

Oh god! Elodie leapt onto the dry rock floor nearby. She was covered head to toe in gray-green decaying plant matter and glowworm excretions and had slept on centuries of suffering. Would the nightmare never end?

Her calf tingled.

Please, no . . .

Elodie didn't want to look, but she had to . . .

Glowworms were all over the back of her calf where the dragon had slashed her open with its talon. And now the voracious maggots were having a party in her flesh, moving faster than she'd thought them capable when she'd fallen asleep to their slow-shifting patterns on the ceiling, drooling inside her wound and feasting as if this was the best day of their lives.

Elodie leaned over and dry heaved over the pile of algae. Some bile came up, leaving bitterness on her tongue.

She had to get the glowworms out. She tried to think of anything besides their viscous mucus or whatever that was, anything besides their bloated, wriggling bodies like gorged larvae ready to burst—

Elodie's stomach revolted and tried to vomit again.

Light-headed and mouth coated in bile, she cringed and began scooping up the glowworms as fast as she could. They were slick in her hands, coating her fingers and palms in blue ooze. "I hate you I hate you I hate you!"

She flung the last of the foul slugs into the algae.

Then she looked down at her calf to assess the damage they'd done, and . . . there was nothing. No torn open flesh. No red swell of infection. Only a faint hint of pink scar tissue on the new skin that had grown over what had been a gaping gash.

"H-how?"

Elodie checked her arms and the rest of her exposed skin, which had been burned by the fire the dragon unleashed against the rocks. But like the talon wound, no evidence of the attack remained save a slight tenderness to her skin and the pale shine of fading scar tissue.

She stared at the mass of glowworms on the algae.

"Did you heal me?" she asked.

They didn't pay her any more attention, though, since their work was finished. Instead, the worms were already industriously making their way back up the cave wall, slowly but steadily inching home to their ceiling colony.

How had they healed her so quickly? Had they been working on her for hours while she slept, or had they just begun more recently?

Elodie supposed it didn't matter. They'd made her better, and it was more than she could have hoped for.

"I'm sorry I said I hated you. I . . ."

She sighed at herself for judging them so harshly. Then Elodie rose and gave the glowworms a long curtsy. It was silly, but it was also the most respectful thing she could think to do. Curtsies were reserved for those who ranked above oneself, those who deserved one's greatest admiration. "Thank you," she said solemnly. "Thank you, thank you, thank you."

Only her sprained ankle hadn't healed, which made sense, because all the work the glowworms had done on her had been where their powerful excretions could touch. Elodie sat on a boulder, tore off a length of her gown—the hem with the jewels had long torn off, so she was left with plain lavender cloth, albeit many layers of it—and used the fabric as a bandage to stabilize her ankle.

She stood and tested it out. Not bad. She would have to move gingerly with that foot, which might be easier said than done, but at least the glowworms had helped with the worst of her injuries, the ones that could have festered and killed her.

Elodie could finally take in her surroundings. It was what she should have done before falling asleep, but now she was glad that wasn't the order of how things had transpired, for she would have fled this place before it could help her.

The glowworms' chamber was dank and small, many of the rock faces covered in slick algae. There was the hole in the rock to the right of their colony, which was the end of the chute Elodie had careened out of. But the rest of the cave was unremarkable; there was a scattering of boulders, but not much else.

Elodie's eyes almost skipped past another unassuming rock, but a slight change in color caught her attention and she looked again.

She gasped. Above the boulder was a faint V etched into the cave wall. It was partially covered by algae, but it was carved with the same swoopiness that the redheaded princess in the dream had drawn in the clouds, the same ornate style of the V in the hourglass.

Elodie ran over and wiped the algae away. She traced the carving, her fingers following the groove of the V in the cool granite.

Is this what you were trying to tell me in the dream?

She stretched out her arm, as if trying to reach the redheaded princess again.

No words of wisdom came to her. But as she let her arm drop back down to her side, Elodie spotted another V carved farther along the wall. And then another.

A trail!

She still didn't know who V was, but Elodie plastered herself to the granite and kissed that letter, because at this moment, that imaginary princess was her best friend in the entire world.

VICTORIA

N EARLY TWO WEEKS had passed since Victoria had entered the gorge. Her red hair lay greasy and limp and tangled with small branches. She was thin—*too* thin—and the former rosy glow of her cheeks had turned pale from malnourishment and lack of sunlight. Her lips cracked like old parchment, the result of living on the brink of dehydration, and her embroidered tunic dress was closer to brown than white. Her gold coat was in no better shape, and she'd lost two of the brooches that fastened it closed.

Well, she hadn't "lost" the brooches; she had sacrificed them because she'd needed the pins to carve her initial into the granite.

But now, Victoria knelt next to a pile of broken volcanic glass. She picked up one of the shards, feeling its weight in her hands, catching her bedraggled reflection in the smooth black surface. She looked like the dragon had already chewed on her, then spit her back out.

Victoria's grip on the black rock tightened.

She still hoped for escape. Yet she knew the odds were against her, and thus she would do what she could to help the next princess sacrificed to the dragon. And the next, and the next. If Victoria did not succeed in saving her own life, she would endeavor to save the lives of those who came after her. She would leave her marks on the walls, share what she had learned of these dismal, twisting tunnels and caves, show them how, perhaps, they could survive.

Victoria glanced up at the blue glowworms on the ceiling. Then she turned back to the granite and pressed the volcanic glass hard against it.

V—she carved in the same way she used to always begin signatures of her name. A flourish of a curve. A dip into a narrow, swooping point. Then up for a final flourish.

She walked farther down the cave and scratched another V into the rock. And another. And another.

Follow me . . .

ELODIE

LODIE WOULD NOT have found the tunnel entrance on her own. It was only two feet tall and obscured by a disk-shaped stone with a V carved into it. She'd rolled the rock aside and crawled in, having no better option than to trust this clue.

The tunnel was small, but nothing compared to the crevice Elodie had traversed earlier. The ground was smooth, too, not made of sharp, uneven granite but more like polished marble. *Too smooth to be natural,* she thought. Had so many princesses before her crawled through this passageway that all the roughness had been rubbed away? Elodie's chest tightened at the possibility. Because it would mean that an endless parade of other women had suffered before her. But it would also mean Elodie wasn't alone in her experience. She felt a little guilty for being glad of their company.

But although the rock was smooth, it was hot. Nothing like dragon flame, but hot enough that her hands and knees would burn if she didn't move quickly. Aurea was a volcanic island, and that meant there was still lava deep inside the ground, fueling the thermal vents of these caves.

Oh god, please say I don't have to worry about dragons and *a volcanic eruption?* Elodie crawled as fast as she could.

No stone blocked the exit on the other side, and she soon emerged and stood up in a chamber about the size of her tower room in the Aurean palace. The distance from the glowworm cave to this one was actually quite short. The wall between the chambers was riddled with small holes, like bubbles in ancient magma had left pinpricks in the lava rock when it solidified. The glowworms' light shined through each opening and illuminated this chamber with a soft luminescence and a constellation of tiny blue stars.

Puffs of steam rose from the floor. More thermal vents. The hot, moist air plumed around her, and she hovered over it as if it could steam her fears away. At the very least, it loosened her muscles a little and kept her warm in an otherwise too-thin dress.

She continued surveying the cave. There was one other opening in the opposite wall, a little taller than Elodie. Her pulse quickened. Could the dragon slither through? It seemed too tight, but then again, she knew from the deserts of her homeland that snakes and lizards could be found in the most impossibly narrow of spaces. They could unhinge their jaws and squeeze their bodies as if their bones were made of jelly.

Elodie backed up to the passage leading back to the glowworm cave, ready to retreat. But as she crouched down, the light coming through that low tunnel shone on a message carved in Ingleterr into the chamber wall:

SAFE HERE.

IT CANNOT REACH.

~V

Oh god. Tears of relief streamed down Elodie's cheeks, and she collapsed on the ground, able to truly relax for the first time since she'd arrived on Mount Khaevis.

"Thank you, thank you," she cried, letting herself sob again, but this time, she didn't feel so alone. She crawled over and pressed her palm against the words, as if absorbing the comfort they gave. *Safe here.*

Next to V's message, a cluster of names was etched into the rock, most names accompanied by a bloody thumbprint, as if providing further proof each woman had been here:

And on and on, close to a hundred names of women who had traveled from all over the world to this isolated kingdom, promised a royal life of serenity and prosperity, only to be tossed off a mountainside to appease a voracious monster.

Elodie read each name aloud, shaking, knowing that every name represented a real person who had suffered through the confusion and terror that she herself had just lived through. So many beautiful, bright sparks of life, snuffed out because the royal family made a deal with a demon.

Perhaps that was why they could only give birth to sons, Elodie thought. Perhaps it was the universe's way of punishing the Aurean family for mistreating the original three princesses—they fed their own daughters to a monster, and therefore they forfeited their right to ever have daughters again.

But that didn't do any good for the other princesses who

came after. It was *their* blood that had stained the floor of the glowworm chamber, *their* blood that had soaked into the rock and left behind a legacy of pain and despair. Elodie let the tears continue to fall as she said a quiet prayer for each woman represented by a name on the cave wall.

There weren't enough names, though. Henry had said his family had ruled Aurea for eight centuries. Three princesses a year for eight hundred years meant there ought to be close to twenty-four hundred names here.

"Oh," Elodie breathed, as understanding settled like a lead weight in her belly. She remembered the remnants of the blond tower princess that the dragon had sniffed greedily, and the other skulls and charred bones. The names listed on this wall here were only the princesses who survived long enough to discover the Safe Cave. Less than 5 percent of those sacrificed.

The ones who died faster were erased from history.

"Fy thoserrai kesarre." The dragon's voice echoed through the cave walls, amplified through the tunnels and sending a tremor through the rock. "You may hide now. Others thought the same. *Kev det ni antrov erru ta nyrenif?* Why is your cave so empty, *zedrae?* Have you thought of that?"

Elodie felt all the blood drain from her face and rush back to her heart, which pounded frantically at the sound of the dragon's threats.

"Where are you?" she whispered.

But the dragon didn't answer. Perhaps it was far off and merely its voice was carrying.

Or perhaps it was right outside the nearest tunnel, waiting.

She pressed herself against V's message. *Safe here. Safe here. I'm safe here,* she reminded herself.

The dragon could taunt her, but it couldn't reach her.

But she couldn't ignore its question. Why was the cave so empty?

Because even the princesses who carved their names in the rock eventually died.

Elodie noticed now that the walls were damp, especially near the thermal vents. The warmth had been welcoming to ease her tired muscles when she first arrived, but now she recalled the scalding heat of the short tunnel between this cave and the glow-worms'. This chamber might be safe from the dragon, but Elodie could already tell it would be too hot to stay in all the time, like trying to live inside a sauna. And although the walls were damp, there wasn't enough moisture to make water she could drink. There was also no food.

The Safe Cave was only a resting point, not a permanent shelter. She'd have to venture out again if she wanted water and food to survive. If there even was any water or food down here.

The only thing Elodie knew for sure that was out there was the dragon. She squeezed her eyes shut, as if that would change reality.

"Akrerra audirrai kho, zcdrac." The dragon's voice was like the tip of a cold sword blade dragged down along her spine.

Elodie whimpered.

She hated that she didn't know how close or far the dragon was. And she hated that she didn't know what it was saying.

But I've heard something like the language before . . .

The chant of the priestesses! When they were anointing Elodie with oils and preparing her for the ceremony, they'd sung lyrics with ancient words, sounds with the same hard consonants and sinister r's. That must be all that was left of human knowledge of the dragon's language.

But that meant it was possible to learn it. That at some

point in the past, people *did* know how to speak the dragon's tongue.

"Kuirr, zedrae."

There. That word, *zedrae.* The dragon kept using it. Elodie straightened as she tried to recall the context of the other times the dragon had spoken it.

Nearly all of it came back as clear as glass. She never thought she'd be thankful for getting drunk, but right now, Elodie thanked the heavens for the copious amounts of Aurean barley beer she'd consumed at her wedding reception. It had still been in her blood when she was thrown into the gorge. Which meant her memory of every detail during that time was preserved to near perfection, whether she liked it or not.

She grabbed a chunk of volcanic glass that lay under the cluster of princess names, found an empty stretch of rock, and began scratching what she remembered of the dragon's language into the wall. It could keep taunting her if it wanted to, but V said this cave was safe, so Elodie was going to use that to her advantage for as long as she could stand to be in the heat.

Zedrae, she quickly figured out, meant "princess." She had refused to give the dragon her name, and so it used *zedrae* to jeer at her.

I am KHAEVIS, it had said.

KHAEVIS = DRAGON, Elodie carved.

Some of what she could recall was only in the dragon's own language. It apparently didn't think it necessary for Elodie to understand it completely; perhaps it knew how threatening its voice alone could be.

But there had been other sentences the dragon had translated, to ensure she understood.

Vis kir vis. Sanae kir res. Life for life. Blood for fire.

Errai khosif, dekris ae. Nyfe kuirrukud kir ni, dekris ae. Errai kho-

las. You are alone, down here. No one is coming for you, down here. You are mine.

Elodie shivered at the memory of the dragon's cold-blooded promise.

Still, she wrote it down. It might help her to know what her hunter was saying, if she could decipher enough of the language to learn it. And if not, then she would at least leave the information behind to help the next princess who made it to this cave . . . A small gift to the sad sisterhood, just like V had left behind with her initials.

"I will have you sooner or later," the dragon said, its voice rattling Elodie from her work. "*Sy, zedrae* . . . Until then, princessssss."

Quiet descended on the caves. Elodie waited to see if it would say anything else. She hoped for more because it gave her something to hold on to—words—but she also hoped that the dragon would just leave her alone.

After a long stretch of silence, she let the shard of volcanic glass fall with a clatter from her hands. The dragon was done with her, for now. Or perhaps it was biding its time outside this cave and would give chase as soon as she emerged.

Too tired to care, Elodie slid to the ground, leaning her head against the wall.

Only then did she notice the crude map drawn on the opposite side of the cave. It looked like one of the mazes she used to draw for Floria, although an unfinished one with big gaps remaining to be filled in.

Still, Elodie smiled weakly. Because the dragon's language might be a yet-to-be-solved mystery, but maps and navigation, Elodie understood.

LUCINDA

LUCINDA TORE THROUGH the harbor like a hyena who'd discovered that the carcass it meant to have for breakfast had already been picked over.

"What do you mean we cannot set sail immediately?" she shouted at Captain Croat. "The wedding is over. I don't want to spend another minute with these . . . these scoundrels who live in gold castles and throw jewels as if they were confetti. We need to leave today!"

"I offer my sincerest apologies, my lady," the poor captain said. He'd been napping on deck—a rare luxury, as life at sea was usually packed to the brim with responsibilities and emergencies—and had been startled awake by the first mate, who'd informed him that Lady Bayford was down on the pier, demanding that she speak to him at once. His first mate had attempted to make excuses for him, but Lady Bayford was not one who relented quite so easily. Or ever.

"My lady," Captain Croat said as politely as possible, while looking balefully back up at the ship where his comfortable, sunny napping spot was now covered by a fat cloud. "We are set to sail tomorrow. It will take all day to load the grain and other bounty that are Lady Elodie's bride price."

Her bride price. A weak wail escaped Lucinda's lips, and she grabbed hold of a post on the docks for support. Elodie was truly gone.

"Lady Bayford! Are you all right?" Captain Croat rushed to take her arm. "I truly am sorry that we cannot depart immediately. Can I fetch you something? Water? A chair? Perhaps a sugar cube would help restore your strength . . ."

The man babbled on about understanding that marrying off a daughter was a big life milestone, but assured Lucinda that she would still see Elodie, just not as often. Then he began shouting for his first mate to find a chair and blankets and coffee with sugar to relieve Lucinda's sudden bout of weakness.

But she knew none of it would help. What ailed her was deep inside, eating away at her bit by bit. She had been Elodie and Floria's governess, had taught them arithmetic and science, and had watched them grow from small children to poised young ladies. When their mother died, Lucinda's heart had broken for them. And when Lord Bayford found consolation in her conversations and, later, in her bed, she had thought marriage would make their family whole again.

But Elodie, oh, fierce-willed, clever Elodie . . . She missed her mother so, and did not want another. Floria was only three when their mother died, but Elodie had been ten. She had a decade of memories to hold on to. A decade of ideals with which to compare Lucinda and find her lacking.

Because I never could compare to Madeleine, Lucinda thought, recalling the intelligence, beauty, and grace of the first Lady Bayford. And perhaps Lucinda's own self-doubt was partially to blame, but she could not get close to the girls. She had once been the taskmaster who forced them to recite their Latin roots and castigated them if they forgot their sums. But when she tried to take on the role of their mother, she couldn't shake the governess habit of scrutinizing everything Elodie and Floria did in meticulous detail. Lucinda felt like a usurper who didn't deserve to take Madeleine Bayford's place.

And now Lucinda had committed the ultimate failure—she had let Elodie become a sacrifice for a dragon. She had watched while one of the girls she loved as her own was taken away to slaughter.

Lucinda was no better than the Aurean royal family she despised.

"Lady Bayford," Captain Croat was saying. "If you won't sit down here on the dock, may I see you safely to your carriage and back to the palace?"

She looked out at the sea, at the dragon statues in the distance that marked the boundary of Aurea. How she wished they could be on the open ocean already. How she hoped they would be caught in a violent storm. How she wanted to pitch herself into the dark waters and be swallowed whole, before the guilt gnawing inside her devoured her, bite by bite, from within.

"No, Captain, thank you," she said. "I have no desire to return to that accursed palace quite yet."

Lucinda turned and staggered away on unsteady legs, sailors scattering to avoid her unpredictable path. As she left the docks, though, a woman and a girl stepped out of the shadow of the harbormaster's building.

"Lady Bayford?" the woman asked. She looked vaguely familiar, but Lucinda couldn't quite place her, as her face was obscured by a straw hat.

"Yes, I am Lady Bayford. How did you know?"

"I sailed here with you—"

"Oh!" Lucinda's hand fluttered to her chest. "Lieutenant Ravella! I didn't recognize you outside your uniform!"

"Please, call me Alexandra." The lieutenant bowed as gracefully as ever, even though she wore a peasant's tunic and breeches rather than the elegant gold and crimson of a royal envoy. When Alexandra rose, she said, "This is my daughter, Cora. You might recognize her from your own daughter's wedding reception at the palace."

Lucinda suddenly felt light-headed and needed to sit down. She did remember the girl; she was the one who'd caused the commotion and been dragged off by the knights. It had been unclear what she'd been yelling about, but nevertheless, it had plucked the guilty string in Lucinda's chest. She'd retired from the wedding reception soon after, claiming a migraine.

"Wh-why have you come here?" Lucinda sank down onto a golden bench, a particularly Aurean luxury for a place as prosaic as a harbor. She hoped Alexandra and Cora had not come to thank her for the gift of her stepdaughter. Lucinda couldn't bear it if they had.

"Is that your ship, my lady?" Cora asked. "The *Deomelas*?"

Lucinda nodded.

"In that case," Alexandra said, "we were wondering if we might speak to you about a few things."

ELODIE

THE MAP SCRATCHED into the wall had contributions from many different hands. The caves were labyrinthine and messy, with tunnels that led to dead ends or that, even worse, were exposed and vulnerable to the dragon. That was what Elodie had to be most careful about, because the portions of the map that were unfinished most likely meant one of two things: They hadn't been explored yet, or they had, and the princesses who went there didn't make it back alive.

Nevertheless, the map gave Elodie a basic understanding of her prison. The Safe Cave was home base, although it was too hot and muggy to stay in for long. The gorge into which she'd been tossed was to the northeast, and the first cave—the one with the swallows on fire—had been even farther east. The passageways she had traveled were documented, as well, including that horrible crevice she'd spent so long inching through.

There were also symbols, and that's what Elodie was most interested in right now. There was a large chamber marked with a flower and music note, another with a cross, and a few with wavy lines that she really hoped meant Water.

She hadn't had anything to drink since the wedding reception, which was who knew how long ago. Time was impossible to keep track of down here because there was no rising and setting of the sun. Elodie's only light was from the glowworms next door.

"So thirsty." She could get by with less water than most people, having grown up in and adapted to the harsh clime of Inophe. But there were still limits to the human body.

Elodie studied the map for a minute more. Under normal circumstances, memorizing the path she wanted to take would have been simple, but Elodie was functioning on only a nightmare-ridden nap and frayed nerves. So she triple- and quadruple-checked.

"All right, I can do this." She touched the wavy symbol. "Please don't lie to me."

ELODIE TIPTOED OUT of the Safe Cave, taking tiny, slow steps so she could listen for the dragon and barely sticking her nose out whenever she had to take a corner. Every little skitter of gravel falling from the ceilings made her jump, and she nearly passed out from holding her breath so tightly.

She also quickly discovered that the map was not entirely accurate. Not five turns out of the Safe Cave, Elodie ran into a landslide where there ought to have been a tunnel. At first she'd thought it was her mistake, but she backtracked to the Safe Cave and no, she'd been right. Perhaps there *had* been a tunnel there in the past, but no longer. Elodie grabbed a piece of volcanic glass and updated the map.

Given the potential inaccuracies, she also needed light if she wanted to navigate the tunnels without getting lost. Would that signal too loudly to the dragon that she had left the cave?

But the dragon could see her in the dark *or* the light . . .

"I have to take the risk," Elodie said. If she didn't have light, she'd never be able to find her way through the tunnels. And she'd never see the dragon coming at her.

Although not knowing might be preferable to watching death approach.

Focus on what you can *control,* she said to herself. That was how she was going to get through the next hour or however long it took to find water. One task at a time. Everything thought through thoroughly, and everything undertaken very, very carefully.

Now, for the light. The best would be a torch; the sticky residue on her dress—left behind by the dying swallow—could be used as fuel for a flame. But she didn't have any fire, and certainly didn't want any from the only source down here that could provide it.

Which left the glowworms. Their light would be dim, but still better than nothing. If Elodie could collect some and bring them with her . . .

The dress! Its diaphanous fabric would be perfect for wrapping around the glowworms. The cloth was thin and translucent enough that their light would shine through.

She crawled back through the short passage into the glowworms' chamber.

"You've already helped me a great deal," she said to the blue lagoon of worms on the ceiling. "But could I trouble you for a little more? Who wants to come with me on an adventure?"

She tore off a wide swatch of her skirt, thankful for its many layers. Elodie held it up to the worms above her, as if presenting them with a grand palanquin on which to travel.

But of course, they had no idea she was talking to them, let alone what she wanted. And they were too high up for Elodie to reach.

Hmm.

She had to think of a way to get them to come down of their own accord. Unfortunately, she didn't know how or why they moved, because she'd been asleep last time. She'd only woken up to them on top of her, trying to eat her. Well, *heal* her (she knew that now), but at the time, it had been alarming to find them on her wound and—

"That's it! If I'm injured, you'll come, won't you?"

Elodie found a sharp rock and braced herself. She sliced into her forearm, wincing but making sure it was deep enough to draw blood. *I am either brilliant or I have completely lost my mind.*

She was about to find out.

Elodie walked under the glowworm colony and waved her arm in the air. They probably couldn't see well—in fact, she hadn't noticed any eyes on them, and Elodie had been in pretty close quarters with the glowworms, so if they had eyes, she thought she would have noticed. After all, she'd noticed everything else, their creepy little feelers, the blobs of luminescent mucus that they excreted from their pores, the plumpness of their slimy bodies . . . *Ugh.*

Be nice, Elodie, she chastised herself. *They can't help the way they look. Besides, what kind of lady insults the very creatures she's entreating for help?*

Elodie snorted. Okay, she really was losing her mind.

But then a glowworm plopped down from the ceiling. And another. And another. It was working, it was working! She waved her bleeding arm around again, and a dozen more fell down at the smell of the blood.

"I have never seen more beautiful sluggy things in my life

than you," she cooed as she scooped them onto her wound and let them heal her.

When they finished, she gathered them into a bundle of fabric and tied a loop over her wrist. The worm lantern cast a soft blue light. Elodie grinned, pleased with herself. Then she set off again.

This time, Elodie turned to the northwest instead of pursuing the faulty fifth turn that had led to the dead end. She moved slowly and as quietly as possible, hampered by her sprained ankle and always aware that there was a hungry dragon with her in the caverns. Every so often, the blue light would illuminate a mark on a tunnel wall—sometimes a V, sometimes another symbol like a sun or an arrow or strange hashmarks she didn't know the meaning of.

For now, though, all Elodie cared about was finding the cave with the wavy lines.

As she wound through the narrow tunnels, the terrain grew rougher and steeper, and the air colder. The temperature in these caverns varied wildly based on proximity to thermal vents, she figured. Elodie shivered, wishing she could huddle into Father's big, warm arms like when she was young. Wishing Father were *here* to hold her.

Except then she remembered him at the masked ceremony. And his inability to meet her eyes.

Were you aware of what they were going to do to me, Father?

But the truth was, she didn't want to know. Not right now. She needed to stay sanguine and focused. So even though Elodie shivered again, she shoved the memory of Father's hunched, masked figure into the darkest recesses of her mind.

Instead, she pressed onward. Left turn. Go straight and pivot right at the next bend. Pass an X symbol, which she took to mean Do Not Enter, and then at the next fork in the tunnels, take the second branch, which ought to bear true west. Her ankle was beginning to throb again.

And always, in the forefront of her mind was the question *Where are you, dragon?* She did not like how quiet it was. Elodie slowed down to listen even more carefully.

Most of the passageways were as marked on the map, but some, as she'd discovered earlier, had since been blocked off by rockslides, often scattered with old bones and the occasional torn-up glove or melted tiara. The tunnels and caves were one big cemetery of sacrificed princesses, and Elodie shuddered every time she came across more evidence of those who had unfortunately come before her. She had to force herself not to look too hard, to back away and refocus on recalling the layout of the map, to retrace her steps and try alternate routes.

Finally, she and the glowworms reached a dank, frigid cave. Three wavy lines were carved into the rock at the entrance.

"Oh, thank heavens." Elodie's mouth was as parched as an Inophean summer, and against all caution, she picked up her pace, practically running into the cave.

Straight into a calf-deep puddle of mud.

"Ugh!" Her bare feet made loud sucking noises as she extracted herself from the cold muck. Strands of rotting plant matter clung to her skin, and the air stank of decay.

Elodie shined the glowworm lantern on the mud. "Please tell me this isn't what's left of the water."

The cave was long but not wide. She paced its entire length and found a couple of clusters of mushrooms and more puddles of mud, half frozen in the chilly chamber, but nothing else. Elodie was so thirsty she knelt down and considered eating ice chips off the surface of the sludge.

She had set down the bundle of glowworms and was on her knees, reaching for a piece of muddy ice, when a droplet of water hit her hand. Elodie startled and drew back, away from the puddle.

But then another droplet fell, hitting the spot where her hand had just been.

Her eyes traveled upward, following the path of the drop's fall.

An icicle. Not just one, but clusters of them, right over each of the mud puddles.

"I'm such an idiot," Elodie said, although she was smiling in relief. Gravity had collected the water into puddles, but the water had to have come from somewhere before that.

The icicles were too high for her to reach, though. What she needed was a cup, but those were in rather short supply down here.

The mushrooms. Elodie hurried back to the parts of the cave where she'd seen them sprouting. There were two groups of them: large, red-capped ones and then, on the opposite side of the cavern, tiny, delicate pink ones.

Above the red mushrooms was carved: EAT.

Above the pretty pink ones: NO!!!

"I'm trusting you," Elodie said as she picked the biggest of the red mushrooms, its cap the size of a chalice.

She returned to the frozen puddle and set the mushroom on top, flipping the cap so its underside could catch water.

Drip

Drip

Drip

This was going to take a while.

Elodie's stomach growled. "I suppose I might as well eat while I wait," she said as she returned to the red-capped mushrooms. "And I really hope that the princess who marked these was a botanist and got the labels right."

VICTORIA

EIGHT CENTURIES AGO

VICTORIA AND HER younger sisters, Anna and Lizaveta, huddled together in the icicle cave. They looked as bedraggled as they had when they'd been refugees on the sea, except now they were prisoners in a dragon's lair. Dark, puffy circles smudged below twelve-year-old Anna's eyes, and fourteen-year-old Lizaveta's skin had taken on a wan, almost translucent quality, closer to the color of the icicles than it ought to be. They smelled of sweat and tears and old blood soaked into their gowns.

They were thankful for the source of water, but it was cold while they waited for the icicles to drip, so they shared their body heat to keep warm.

"These mushrooms taste like sawdust," Lizaveta said, taking a bite out of a red cap.

"It didn't stop you from eating the five previous ones," Victoria said with a smirk, albeit a fond one.

"That's because I'm starving."

Anna sighed. "I miss Chef's cooking. What I wouldn't give for a proper mushroom and thyme pie right now," she said, making a face at the red cap in her small hand. Unlike Lizaveta, Anna had only nibbled at hers.

"Just pretend that's what you're eating," Victoria said, trying to encourage her youngest sister. They had been in the caves for five days now, and Anna was growing weaker and weaker. It was a miracle they had survived to this point, and Victoria was determined to keep them alive and help them escape.

Anna dropped her mushroom onto the muddy ground and got up to check on the icicles. Lizaveta picked up the abandoned red cap and ate it. Victoria closed her eyes and chewed on her own red cap. It was, indeed, difficult to imagine it was anything other than sawdust-flavored fungus.

She must have dozed off, the cold and the lack of food affecting her, for she woke with a start to Anna chirping, "Sisters, look at what I found! They look like tiny fairies, and they're delicious!" She held out a handful of lacy pink mushrooms that indeed resembled small pixies in gauzy dresses.

"Ooh, can I try them?" Lizaveta asked, leaning in to pluck a few from Anna's palm.

"No!" Victoria leapt to her feet and swatted the fairy mushrooms from her sisters. "Those are Fae's Bait! They're highly poisonous . . . Oh god, Anna, how much did you eat?"

Her face went ghostly pale. "Not much . . ."

"How much is not much?" Victoria grabbed her already-frail sister by the shoulders and shook her. "How much is not much!" she shouted.

"I don't know!" Anna said, beginning to cry. "I was so hungry, and they tasted like candy, and I—I . . ."

"You what?"

"I . . . I can't . . ."

"You can't what?" Lizaveta yelled, stomping the Fae's Bait

into the ground, as if no longer seeing them could make the ones in their little sister's belly disappear.

"I can't . . . breathe." Anna clawed at her throat. Her face began to turn purple.

Victoria spun around, looking for anything that could help the girl she'd known since the moment she was born. The girl who danced before she could walk. The girl who, when she played dress-up, had always wanted to pretend she was Victoria.

A harsh, gurgling sound came from Anna's mouth. Tears streamed down her purple face as she fell to her knees.

"Help her!" Lizaveta cried.

But there was nothing here in the caves to save Anna. Even out there, in the world that still existed beyond this dragon's hell, there was no antidote for Fae's Bait.

All Victoria could do was gather her baby sister in her arms and hold her while she died.

"I'm sorry," Victoria said, choking on her fear, her anger, her guilt. "This is my fault. I shouldn't have brought you here, I should have come alone . . ."

Anna's eyes bulged. She clutched Victoria's hand tight.

"Don't go!" Lizaveta sobbed.

"I love you," Victoria whispered. "I will never forget you."

"No!" Lizaveta screamed.

Anna convulsed and closed her eyes.

Her body stilled.

And then there was no sound in the cave except the icicles' steady

Drip

Drip

Drip.

ELODIE

DRIP DRIP DRIP drip drip drip drip
    DRIP drip drip DRIP drip drip DRIP drip drip
DRIP DRIP drip DRIP DRIP drip DRIP DRIP drip DRIP
DRIPDRIPDRIPDRIPDRIPDRIPDRIPDRIPDRIP
Elodie leapt to her feet at the sudden melting of the icicles.
She opened her mouth, catching the cool water, gulping it down
in glugs. Nothing had ever tasted so necessary and so delicious at
the same time. She laughed at the chilly downpour and twirled
in place and filled her mushroom chalice and drank. Even after
her belly was full, she kept drinking and drinking and drinking—

Until she realized she wasn't cold anymore.

And the cave had brightened, lit not by glowworm blue, but
something yellow. Something orange.

Something like fire.

Every muscle in Elodie's body tensed as she looked where
she didn't want to: up.

The ceiling of the cave was part rock, but part ice. Thick ice,
probably fifty feet. And yet the dragon's silhouette on the other

side was unmistakable, its serrated spine a bladelike shadow against the light of the flames it shot at the ice, the only thing separating it from Elodie.

"*Nyerru evoro, zedrae. Nyerru saro.*"

Elodie froze, chills sluicing down her spine.

The dragon hissed.

Elodie snapped out of her paralysis. Screaming and snatching her bundle of glowworms, she ran as fast as she could on her sprained ankle. She tore back through the tunnels the way she'd come, begging her brain to remember the path backward. Right, right, hairpin turn, pass that fork, don't go down the path marked X, turn left—no that's a dead end, a pile of gnawed bones, oh god!—retrace, turn right, sprint on the downhill.

"*Vis kir vis. Sanae kir res,*" the dragon's voice growled through the caves. "*Vorra kho tke raz*—I want my share of the bargain!"

"I never agreed to the bargain!" Elodie yelled, even though she actually had. She'd encouraged Father to accept Henry's offer, knowing what it would mean for the people at home. But Elodie hadn't known the full terms of the proposal.

She slammed into a rock face with a hard *oomph*, too much speed on the decline. But she was nearing the Safe Cave now. Just a few more minutes

Elodie turned a corner and shrieked. What had previously looked like a divot in the top of the tunnel was actually a hole, and right now that hole was filled with a vivid purple and gold eye.

"*Demerra vis er invika. Kir rever, annurruk vis tu kho. Voro erru raz.*"

The dragon's smoky breath seeped in through cracks in the rock. How stable was the structure? If the dragon tried, could it break the stone and claw Elodie out?

She summoned as much courage as she could muster and said, "Your taunts have no effect on me if I can't understand you. You're just noise. Insignificant noise!"

A thunderous roar shook the caves, and rocks tumbled from the ceiling. That had been stupid to ridicule it.

But if she was going to be cornered, she was going to get something out of it, too. She would make it talk, goad it into revealing information. And she would remember its words and write them down. Translate them. Help herself and help future sacrifices not be so afraid.

The dragon snarled. "I said, I allow life on the isle. In turn, life is paid to me. Such is the bargain."

"And I already told you," Elodie said, inching away. "I did not agree to the bargain."

Impossibly, the dragon laughed. Then it said, "*Esverra zi kir ni kir ta diunif aeva, zedrae.* I have waited for you for such a long time, princess."

"You just ate another princess a few days ago!" Elodie thought of the sad ribbon-haired woman from the tower.

"She was tasty, but not good enough."

"And what would have made her more delectable? Chocolate sauce? What more do you want?"

"*Nyonnedrae. Verif drae. Syrrif drae. Drae suverru.* Not anyone. The right one. The clever one. The one who survives."

Now it was Elodie's turn to laugh. "Has it occurred to you that a princess can't survive if you eat her?"

But she was done talking. She had all the language she could remember for now, and the longer she stayed here, the more likely the dragon would find a way to break through that rock and get to her. So Elodie turned on her heel and ran.

Behind her, the dragon shrieked. Then it shot a plume of fire down through the hole in the tunnel.

Elodie sprinted harder, ignoring the sharp pains screaming up her ankle. The fire licked her just as she got out of range, and it caught on the bundle of glowworms. The lantern fabric, made from the outermost layer of Elodie's skirt and therefore covered in the sticky flammable residue from the dead swallow, burst into a ball of fire.

"Oh god!" It burned her wrist, and she dropped the lantern to the tunnel floor. The glowworms writhed in pain inside, the flames turning a bright blue at the moment the fire consumed them.

"I'm so sorry," she whispered. "You were just trying to help me, and—"

"ZEDRAE!"

Elodie jumped at the anger in the dragon's voice. It was not amused by her anymore, and she had to go. Now.

"I'll come back and give you a proper burial, I promise," she said to the dead glowworms. If she could, she'd take them with her, but the fabric was ash. Everything was ash. And if she didn't run, she would be, too. But she would come back.

She ran hard, putting too much weight on her bad ankle but having no choice.

Elodie took the turns in the tunnel fast. Left, left, 180 degrees, another pivot.

The dragon roared again.

Terror lifted every hair on her arms and the back of her neck. The instinct of being prey wanted her to freeze, to make herself small and hide in plain sight and hope the dragon would not see her if she didn't move. But that instinct was wrong, because she wasn't a small mouse, she was a full-grown woman, and there was no way the dragon would miss her if she didn't run.

Keep going, she yelled at herself.

Right turn, slight incline, a zigzagging tunnel, then another right turn. She put on another burst of speed, as much as her limp would allow.

Elodie didn't let up until she crashed into the princesses' cave and the wall marked SAFE HERE.

"I'm all right," she panted, trying to catch her breath and convince herself at the same time. "I'm all right," she said again.

But as she looked at the names of all the princesses before her who hadn't made it out, Elodie suddenly felt the weight of all their deaths upon her.

No one ever made it out.

No one.

Elodie hugged the wall and wept. She wasn't all right at all.

ELODIE

Minna sang softly to the glowworms as they tended to the burns on her face and her torso. The dragon had almost succeeded in killing her this time, but she still had some fight in her yet. She smiled at the short dagger she'd fashioned from volcanic glass by chipping it against a boulder. A princess-warrior of Kuway would not go down meekly.

The vision played through Elodie's mind as lucidly as if it were her own memory. She jerked back from the cave wall. Why had that happened? How?

It was like the dream she'd had the first time she stumbled into the glowworm cave and fell asleep on the bed of algae, the dream of princesses falling through time. Before she even knew they existed.

But Elodie hadn't been sleeping on algae alone. There had also been an old, dark stain of blood left behind by princesses past.

Now she looked at the wall of princesses' names and gasped. Next to many of them was a thumbprint, inked in blood. Elodie had been too panicked the first time she arrived in the Safe Cave to think about the significance of those thumbprints, and too hungry and thirsty and scared since then to do more than glance over them.

But now she reached out and pressed her own thumb against the rusty brown smudge next to Minna's name.

Minna sang softly to the glowworms as they tended to the burns on her face and her torso. The dragon had almost succeeded in killing her this time, but she still had some fight in her yet. She smiled at the short dagger she'd fashioned from volcanic glass by chipping it against a boulder. A princess-warrior of Kuway would not go down meekly.

Elodie pulled away from the bloodstain, heart pounding. She had to work to breathe, the air seeming thicker than it had only moments before. She had gotten used to the closeness of the caves, the warm fug that filled any open space with an invisible weight. Before, she'd thought it smelled like amber, old forests, and ancient religion. Now she suspected something else.

This is the smell of magic.

Of course. The dragon had lived on Aurea for centuries; its musk and power permeated every tunnel and chamber underground. Perhaps the glowworms were already magical on their own, or perhaps it was an effect of magic on their evolution. And perhaps it was also because of the dragon that aurum wheat and sangberries and silver pears existed. The presence of its magic might affect all of Aurea, not just the caves. Elodie couldn't be sure, but it would make sense.

What she *did* know for certain, though, was that she couldn't access other people's memories in Inophe just by touching blood. If she could, she would have seen Floria's thoughts hundreds of times for every instance Elodie had to clean a scrape on her sister's knee or patch her up when she tried to feed a desert goat.

Yet not every Aurean could use blood as a window into the past. At Elodie's wedding, her wounded palm had been pressed to Henry's, and he hadn't given any indication of seeing visions. In fact, if this sort of magic were common in the kingdom, others would be using it.

But wait . . . Elodie remembered Queen Isabelle watching as Elodie touched Henry's bloody palm. The queen's eyes were the first things Elodie saw after the flashback of Henry's childhood.

Strong zedrae blood is the most powerful blood, the dragon had said.

Every princess who had made it into the Safe Cave was strong enough, Elodie realized as she looked at the names carved in the walls. The thumbprints began at the end of the second row. That must have been when Princess Minna figured out what her blood could do, that the power that coursed through her veins could leave flashes of what was happening to her. And then princesses of subsequent centuries followed her lead.

Greedily, Elodie pressed her own finger against another bloodstain.

SIX CENTURIES AGO

Ailing marked a cross on the map in the Safe Cave. The chamber she'd stumbled on today had ceilings that soared like a cathedral. She was not a member of the religions that worshipped in churches, but when she saw the skeletons of previous princesses lying down in disintegrating dresses, with arms crossed reverently across their chests, she understood.

This was where they'd come to die. Those who were not eaten right away by the dragon, or who could not escape, came here to meet death through dehydration and starvation.

It was as if there was a silent pact among the princesses—the Safe Cave was a sanctuary, a chamber of hope for the newly arrived. They would not taint that by dying there. And so this cathedral chamber was a mausoleum, their final resting place . . .

That was the entire memory. Elodie was chastened by it, yet she also tightened her fists, feeling viscerally the dark, long history she'd become a part of.

Rashmi carved hashmarks into the map. She had found a cave full of edible stalks, their stems bursting with sweet flesh. It was a far better option than the flavorless red mushrooms in the other chamber.

The visions were brief, as if the droplet of blood captured only that moment. But no matter. Elodie was certain they were real. She could feel a tangible connection to the ghosts of those who came before her, as warm and true as memories of her mother hugging her, kissing her good night, telling her how proud she was of her brave little girl.

Part of Elodie hoped she wouldn't find any more blood outside of this wall, because every drop spilled meant someone had suffered. But part of her desperately hoped there were more clues to the past.

When she finished the memories by the names, she prowled the Safe Cave, searching. She found another blood spot on the ground, an inadvertent one, shed while an injured princess was deep in thought.

Eline paced the Safe Cave, considering the new fact she'd discovered: The dragon had once had a family, too. A beastly reptilian one, but a family nonetheless.

Is that why it was so keen to devour the princesses of Aurea? A twisted form of revenge on humans, who had plenty of their species to spare, while the dragon was the only one? Eline was not sure, but she felt it must have something to do with its bargain with Aurea. If only she could figure out what.

"I wish I knew the answers, too," Elodie said. She especially didn't know what to make of the revelation that the dragon had not always been the only one of its kind here. But before she could think on it longer, she walked into another memory in the corner of the cave.

ONE CENTURY AGO

Camila plucked anthodite needles out of her arms. She'd spent the day harvesting the spiky flowers, and tomorrow she would embed them in the tunnel walls as defenses. The needles wouldn't kill the dragon, but perhaps they would at least hurt it and slow it down.

And Camila would take any advantage she could get.

"Yes," Elodie whispered, her heart beginning to race, not with fear this time, but with renewed determination. For in this cave, Elodie was not alone. There was a sisterhood here, and a belief that even though their lives spanned centuries, they were still stronger together. The past princesses' selfless contributions to everyone who came after them roused Elodie from her self-pity.

She picked up the volcanic glass she'd used earlier and began recording what she could recall from her last "conversation" with the dragon. She was beginning to piece together how the language worked and what more words meant. She didn't know if it would be helpful to anyone, but she wanted to give future princesses whatever information she could get.

It wasn't just repeated words that Elodie wrote down. Years of being around foreign merchants and sailors in Inophe's harbor had taught her there was always a syntax to a language, an order in the way the words came together. Grammatical structures, too. Some languages had adjectives after the nouns they modified; others did it vice versa. The Inophean sailors' polyglot vernacular did that, and it also followed a structure of verb-object-subject. So a sentence like *George ate the tasty cake* sounded like *Ate cake tasty George.* The order was different from what Elodie had grown up with, but the meaning was the same.

That's what she was deciphering now of the dragon's language. From the pieces that Elodie took apart and examined, it did seem to follow the traditional subject-verb-object structure to which she was accustomed. But there were no articles like "the" and "a," as far as she could tell. And adjectives so far had ended in "-if."

Syrrif drae, it had said. Clever one.

"You are damn right about that," she said as she scratched her notes into the Safe Cave wall. Having something intellectual to work on was comforting. Even though it was figuring out the language of a murderous beast intent on devouring her, the familiarity of having a puzzle to solve soothed Elodie's nerves.

When she finished, she looked at the shiny black rock in her hand. In her dream, Princess Minna of Kuway had made a dagger out of it. Elodie wanted a weapon, too. She picked a different shard of volcanic glass—a slightly bigger piece than the one she'd been carving with—stationed herself at a waist-high boulder, and got to work.

HOURS LATER, ELODIE was drenched in sweat from the heat of the Safe Cave, and she had a stiff back, bleeding hands, and a slightly less dull chunk of volcanic glass. It turned out that chipping rock into a blade was a lot harder than she'd expected. Maybe she was getting the angle wrong, or maybe every time she thought she was sharpening a point, she was actually just breaking away any point she'd previously created.

Whatever the problem was, Elodie's hands were too raw to fix it now. She left the mangled piece of black glass on the boulder and lay beneath the map, resting her tired muscles while deciding what to do next.

Perhaps the best course of action would be using my *strengths, rather than trying to emulate those of others.* She might not be a warrior-princess, but she *was* a master of mazes—both creating them and finding a way out. If anyone could solve the puzzle of this underground labyrinth, it was Elodie.

But first she needed to get out of the Safe Cave. The overwhelming moist heat from the thermal vents was making her light-headed. Elodie didn't want to go back out into the exposed parts of these caverns, but she didn't have a choice. If she stayed in the Safe Cave, she'd pass out from heat exhaustion or suffocate from the heaviness of the air.

Her light-headedness could also be from lack of food. Elodie needed sustenance. She hadn't eaten nearly enough mushrooms before she'd had to run from the dragon. She couldn't return to that cavern, though, for obvious reasons.

But according to the vision of Princess Rashmi, there was an alternative: the hashmark cave full of sweet, edible plants.

HALFWAY TO THE chamber Rashmi had marked on the map, Elodie stopped where the glowworms had died in her first lantern. Working solemnly, she wrapped their ashes in another piece of cloth torn from her dress. "I promised you a proper burial," she said, "and I mean to make good on that."

She tucked the bundle safely into her bodice and continued on her way. She no longer felt alone; she had the sisterhood of all the women who'd come before her guiding her path now.

But only a few steps later, the tunnels began to vibrate. Small rocks skittered loose.

Elodie inhaled sharply and pressed herself motionless against the wall.

"*Zedrae* . . ." A voice like kerosene. "*Ni sanae akorru santerif.* Your blood grows stronger. I can smell it even from here."

Where was "here"? The dragon's words seemed everywhere all at once as it echoed—both near and far. Elodie had been glad not so long ago that her strength had given her a connection to the princesses of the past, but now she suddenly wished she were weak so she wouldn't be as tempting to the beast.

No, don't think that, she chastised herself as she took a quiet, careful breath. The dragon would eat the sacrifices, weak or not. But only if Elodie was strong would she have a chance to survive.

She needed food. She couldn't stay holed up in the Safe Cave, waiting to die. Elodie closed her eyes for a second, listening for the dragon's scales sliding across stone. But there was nothing. Hopefully the dragon was far away and just taunting her. She ventured into the tunnel again.

"Where are you now?" the dragon asked.

Elodie froze.

It laughed. "Explore all you want, *zedrae.* But remember . . . *Errai kholas.*"

You are mine.

She held her breath even as her entire body shook. *I am* not *yours,* Elodie thought as fiercely as she could, as much to convince herself as to defy the dragon. *My destiny belongs to me, and I will decide what that is.*

Nevertheless, she sprinted back toward the Safe Cave. If the dragon was looking for her, she couldn't be wandering around, regardless of how much she needed water and food. Its laughter chased her through the labyrinth, and even though the dragon had not yet found her, she could feel the heat of its hunger at her heels, and Elodie crashed down the tunnels.

She took the turns as fast as she could, and her bad ankle twisted again and she fell onto the rocks, scraping her hands and knees, leaving more of her blood to stir the monster's appetite.

The sound of the dragon's deep inhale reverberated through the tunnels. "Ohhh." It moaned in pleasure at finding her scent, and inhaled again. It wasn't far away now.

Get up, get up! Elodie screamed to herself. Tears streamed down her face. She scrambled to her feet, hardly able to see through the veil of tears and the terror and the pain. She ran blindly down the last stretch, into a narrow corridor.

The dragon's body slammed against the entryway only moments after Elodie threw herself into it.

She shrieked and wriggled faster through the tapering passageway, the walls so close they took off a layer of her skin as she pushed through.

The dragon hissed, spitting fire now. The flames heated the rock and a spark caught on Elodie's hair, setting it ablaze.

She hurled herself through the last part of the corridor and dove into the Safe Cave. She batted at her hair and rolled at the same time, hitting boulders but not caring because she was on fire and it was burning her scalp and almost at her face and—

The flames snuffed out.

Oh god . . . Elodie sobbed.

"I enjoyed that," the dragon said, its ashy breath so close it filled the Safe Cave. "But your time is running out. They will bring me another *zedrae* in two days. I will have *you* before she arrives."

Every year, we begin the harvest with a week of gratitude for all that we have, Henry had told Elodie. *During that week, we offer three prayers . . .*

The platinum, ribbon-haired princess on Sunday. Elodie on Wednesday. And the third "prayer" on Saturday.

Elodie wrapped her arms around her knees and began to rock back and forth, her whole body shaking. Three weddings, each only days apart. As soon as one wife was dead, Henry could marry another, anointing her as a princess. Another sacrifice. Payment to the dragon for peace and prosperity on the isle.

Did you know, Father? Did you willingly sell me to a dragon?

She suddenly remembered the night before the wedding, when Lady Bayford had barged into the tower-top room and demanded that Elodie cancel the ceremony. Lady Bayford, who often said things in a way that made Elodie bristle . . . and Elodie, who was always annoyed at her without considering what she might be *trying* to say, rather than what came out of her mouth.

Had Lady Bayford found out about the bride sacrifice? Now that Elodie turned the memory over in her head, it seemed . . . possible.

And if that was so, then when Father strolled in just a few minutes later, looking specifically for Lady Bayford and telling Elodie and Floria to ignore anything their stepmother had said . . .

Maldi-seù . . .

Father knew. Elodie had not really wanted confirmation of this; she'd wanted to believe he was unwillingly dragged to the torch-filled mountain ceremony just as she was.

But in the pit of her gut, she *had* known. And now she was sure.

How could anyone raise a little girl—teaching her how to pluck needles from prickly plums, how to ride the most mischievous of horses, and telling her every day how much you adored her—only to send her to slaughter as easily as a desert goat on a feast day?

She had loved her father with her entire heart, but now Elodie didn't even know who he was anymore, and therefore she didn't know what to do with that heart.

"I should have given my love to someone more deserving," she choked out, tears beginning anew.

Hours later, shaking from hunger, exhaustion, and overheating, Elodie crawled through the small passageway into the glowworm chamber and unfurled the cloth containing the glowworm remains. She sprinkled the ashes in the algae pool beneath the colony.

"You're home," she said softly to the ashes. "Thank you for helping me."

Unlike her father, who'd left her for dead.

ELODIE

THE DRAGON LURKED outside the Safe Cave all day, or perhaps it was all night, Elodie didn't know. She'd lost track of time, her mouth tasted like it had been stuffed with wool batting, and the delirium of too long without food began to tremor through her body and mind.

After burying the glowworms, the heat of the chamber lulled her into a restless sleep. She drifted in and out of lucid dreams, or perhaps they were hallucinations fueled by trauma and hunger. Some of the dreams made no sense, like elephants with fox heads sharing a watering hole with a walking cactus. Some were memories mixed with fables, like an arithmetic lesson Lady Bayford had taught her that morphed into a house made of numbers and sugared cookies. Elodie woke to find herself chewing on her own cracked lips.

Her ankle throbbed. It was swollen and tender to the touch, and sparks of pain occasionally shot through her tendons for no reason other than to remind her that she was doomed. When she fell back asleep again, she dreamed about sawing off her foot with the volcanic glass she'd tried to hone. "I challenge thee to a duel, dragon," Dream Elodie said, tossing her amputated foot in front of it like a glove.

The beast gobbled up the appetizer of her foot. "I accept your challenge, *zedrae.*"

But when the duel was to begin, a cave swallow flew between Elodie and the dragon. "Wake up," the little bird sang. "I have something to show you."

Dream Elodie swatted the swallow away. "I'm busy, don't you see?"

"You cannot fight the monster. You will lose," the bird said.

"Then I will die with honor," Dream Elodie said. She hopped on her remaining foot toward the waiting dragon.

The swallow darted between them again and began to peck at Elodie's face. "There is another way. Wake up, wake up!"

Elodie jolted up from the hot cave floor. A cave swallow indeed flew just above her head. It was so close it was entirely feasible it had been nipping at her face.

Fatigue fogged her brain. Elodie swiped the dried drool from the corner of her mouth.

"Are you the same bird who visited me in the palace tower?"

It danced around her, chirping.

The chances were slim. But Elodie began giggling deliriously. Even the slight possibility of this being the same swallow felt a little like having a friend in this godforsaken place.

The bird flew to the map on the Safe Cave wall. It flew in a circle in front of a series of chambers that had been labeled with a music note, a flower, and a sun symbol, in that order.

"You want me to go out there?" Elodie asked.

The swallow flew another circle around that part of the map.

"How can you read a map? Are you a figment of my imagination?"

The bird tilted its head at her like it was insulted.

Elodie snorted and started giggling again. She was really losing her grip on reality. She laughed herself to the point of exhaustion, and then she slumped back into sleep again.

WHEN SHE WOKE, the bird was gone. Or perhaps it had never been there. Certainly, Elodie's foot was still attached; she hadn't actually sawed it off and thrown it as a challenge to a duel with the dragon. It was difficult to say whether anything from the last hours was real or not.

The rest had done her some good, though. Elodie was still worn down and thirsty and hungry, and much, much too hot and sweaty in this sauna of a chamber. But her arms and legs no longer felt bonelessly weak, and she could think clearly enough to notice she no longer heard the dragon's embered breath outside the Safe Cave.

It had left.

For how long? Elodie couldn't be sure. But she rose and limped to the map on the wall, because even if the bird had been a hallucination, the hope it left behind—that there might be another way out of this than death in the dragon's jaws—lingered.

The part of the map labeled with the music note, flower, and sun symbols was the most densely marked part of the map. Did that mean something? Was it heavily notated because it was important? Or was it merely a coincidence because different chambers happened to be connected?

With the dragon temporarily gone, Elodie had a decision to make. She could stay in the Safe Cave and feel sorry for herself while being steamed to death by the thermal vents. She could strike out again for Princess Rashmi's cave, the one with the edible stalks. Or Elodie could follow an imaginary bird's advice.

Obtaining sustenance was the most practical choice. But

what would that do, other than keep Elodie alive for just a little while longer? The dragon had promised it would kill her before the next princess arrived. Two days . . .

No, *less*. Because she had slept away who knew how much of that time.

And yet, the other alternative was going to a part of a map just because a hallucination told her to.

Something stirred in the upper corner of the Safe Cave. Elodie screamed.

But it was the swallow. It flew in a circle in front of the map, the part marked with the music note, flower, and sun symbols.

"You're sure?" Elodie asked.

The bird chirped.

She had no idea what that meant. She understood some of the dragon's language now, but Elodie didn't speak cave swallow.

Nevertheless, when it flew out through the narrow corridor that connected the Safe Cave with the rest of the labyrinth, Elodie followed. It was one of the less unbelievable things to happen to her since the wedding.

GRAY STONE FOLLOWED more gray stone. Some tunnels twisted upward, others branched off and descended deeper into the depths. Most of the passageways were warm, although a distinct chill fogged the tunnels closer to the mushroom and icicle cave.

Elodie wanted to move slowly, but the bird's flight ushered a sense of urgency. And perhaps it was right. Wherever the dragon had gone, it was only temporary. Elodie had to make the most of what little time she had before it came back to hunt her.

The music came to her before she saw its source. It was otherworldly, like a choir of cherub sopranos singing, their voices like piccolos on the wind.

Elodie's lips parted in wonder as she paused—just for a moment—to listen.

How can something that beautiful exist in a place this ghastly?

She picked up her pace. The melody grew louder, echoing through the tunnels.

Elodie gasped when she stepped into the cave.

She'd seen cave swallow nests before, of course, in her first horrible hours underground. But this cavern was ten times the size of that one. The soaring walls were pockmarked with holes—*a giant lava tube,* Elodie realized—and the birds flitted around everywhere, swooping among their nests, their songs resounding through the holes in the stone walls like a giant pipe organ.

Just like in the first swallow cave, baby birds twittered and bobbed their heads in each nest. But unlike the aura of panic that pervaded that experience, here, the fledglings seemed as if they were trying to sing along with the adults, and in doing so, they contributed their own higher register of the melody.

"This is where you live?" she asked her bird guide.

It just glanced at her, then continued flying.

A tunnel—an archway, really—separated the music cave from the next one. Elodie's breath caught as she walked into the chamber. It was just as tall as the music cave, but instead of swallows' nests, this lava tube was covered in the same crystal-like flowers that had been in the bouquet Elodie received when she'd first arrived at the palace. There were blooms in every hue imaginable—vivid pink and bright yellow, deep orange and sparkling ruby. Each petal resembled a long, pointed prism.

Anthodite, that's what they were called. She'd been warned that the gemlike flowers were very sharp. But it only made Elodie like them more. Beauty combined with ferocity was a formidable thing, indeed.

She inhaled deeply, the breath bringing not only the light perfume of the flowers but also a sense of calm that first filled her
lungs and then expanded further through her body, serenity traveling with the oxygen as it made its way through her veins. The
thermal vents made it cozy in this cave, as well, despite the soaring ceilings; Elodie felt as if she was on a private tour of secret
botanical gardens.

No wonder the past princesses had marked the map with
these chambers. The caves were such a welcome break from the
fear of being roasted alive and torn apart by dragon claws. Elodie
smiled as she watched the anthodite petals shimmer in the light,
as stunning as if they were real gems, and—

Wait a second. They were shimmering. In the *light.*

Elodie looked all the way up.

A beam of sunlight shone in, coming into the cave at an
angle, its golden rays filtering downward.

"The sun symbol," she whispered, hope rising tentatively in
the pit of her stomach.

She could only see a ceiling of rock from this vantage point,
but it was possible that the lava tube angled to the northwest and
then opened up to the mountaintop.

It was also possible that it was just another layer of thick ice
up there, like in the icicle chamber. But sunlight hadn't pene-
trated into the icicle chamber.

Could this be the way out? Was *this* the real reason the other
princesses came to this series of caves?

The swallow that had led Elodie here swooped in front of
her. It chirped a happy melody, circled her twice, then flew
straight up, past the jewel-toned anthodite, past what looked like
the top of the cave. It turned northwest, disappearing from view
into the angled part of the lava tube Elodie couldn't see. A few
seconds later, she heard its same happy melody, echoing back

down through the cavern from somewhere much farther away. Its song sounded as if it were bathed in sunlight.

A flock of other swallows glided in from the music cave and soared upward, following her bird friend. They, too, sang cheerily as they flew up and into the bend of the lava tube, vanishing from sight and not returning.

That's when Elodie saw the V carved about ten feet above where she stood.

"It *is* a way out." Elodie brought her hand over her mouth in near disbelief.

Now the only thing she had to figure out was how to get up there.

VICTORIA

V ICTORIA STOOD AT the bottom of the anthodite cave. The
dragon had eaten Lizaveta six days ago. There was no body
to bury. Not even a scrap of dress. Both her sisters were gone,
and there was no one to blame but herself.

She had cried her eyes sore over the past week. Observed fu-
neral rites as best she could underground. Then she began leaving clues for future sacrifices who would be thrown into this
dragon's pit, instructions to try to help them avoid Lizaveta and
Anna's fate.

Now there was nothing left for Victoria to do but finish what
she started, to follow through with her plan.

So she looked up at the sunlight filtering in through the top
of the anthodite cave. She started reciting her sisters' names,
over and over.

And then Victoria began to climb.

ELODIE

LODIE MADE SEVERAL passes around the cave, surveying each wall for the clearest path upward. She was used to climbing ropes and trees, but a rock face was different. Especially one littered with razor-sharp anthodite.

There were three possible climbing routes. The most direct one was a minefield of flowers. The second shortest way involved some twists in the lava tube that would place Elodie at a precarious angle. And the third path—V's route—was more circuitous, but would keep her at a safer incline. Plus it avoided the denser patches of anthodite.

Well, Victoria hasn't led me astray yet, Elodie thought. She found herself a couple of good stones to hold on to and hoisted herself up onto the wall.

The beginning was easy enough. There were a few big rocks jutting out, so it only took a minute for Elodie to grab them and reach the carved V. From there, though, the real climbing began. Ten feet off the ground, Elodie grit her teeth as she dug her fingers into the cave walls.

She was tired. So tired.

But this was the only way.

Use your legs, she reminded herself. That was the trick to climbing. It wasn't as much about arm strength as it was the larger muscles in one's legs, and Elodie's were strong from all the years spent hiking through Inophe and riding with Father to visit their tenants. Even being weakened from lack of food and water, she was stronger than many would have been.

The other trick to climbing was finding good handholds and footholds. The rocks looked different from the tree trunks to which she was accustomed, but Elodie was no novice, and she'd made it up this far.

She looked down. Oh. Not very far yet . . . but still.

Elodie pushed up with her legs and grabbed a stone protruding from the cave wall. It came out in her hand in a shower of dirt. "No!"

The momentum of pulling the rock loose sent Elodie backward. She hit the ground with a thump.

"Caráhu!" She sat up and rubbed her shoulder, which had taken the brunt of the fall. Thankfully it hadn't been far; Elodie had fallen out of trees much higher than the mere ten feet she'd climbed up the cave wall.

She tested her ankle. She hadn't landed on it, thank goodness, but she tore off yet another strip of cloth from her dress and wrapped the ankle tightly again to restabilize it. She'd need to put force on it to get up the wall.

A wave of exhaustion hit her. But Elodie tried to fight it back by imagining what it would be like to reunite with Floria and flee Aurea. Elodie even seized upon irrational small details, like how old Captain Croat's emergency kit would have everything she required to wrap her ankle properly. The cynical part of her didn't fall for it, but she tried anyway, because she needed every ounce of hope she could gather.

And it worked, in a way. Imagining herself and Floria at the stern of the *Deomelas* brought Elodie to her feet. She examined the rock walls again and decided to start from a different place this time. Just because the V was carved in one place didn't necessarily mean it was the best route. Many centuries of erosion and anthodite flowers had come and gone between Victoria's time and Elodie's. A clear path back then might not be a clear path now.

Elodie climbed again, resting here and there on protrusions that served as narrow ledges. She reached a good hundred feet before there were no more handholds or footholds. Only lots and lots of anthodite.

She took a deep breath, grabbed one, and yelped as its gemlike petals sliced into her palm. Losing her grip, she half slid, half tumbled, her momentum slowed only by hitting each rock ledge on her way down.

At least she didn't slam into the ground at full force. Nevertheless, the impact rattled through her body and knocked the wind out of her lungs.

The air in the cave, which had seemed cozy before, was now too hot and too humid. It weighed down on Elodie, and she labored to catch her breath. Every rise and fall of her chest took great effort to achieve.

Finally, though, she was able to breathe again. Elodie rolled over and groaned.

She was going to have to find a way to use the anthodite as holds. Even though they looked like flowers, they were firmly embedded into the rocks, like crystals growing from the cave wall. For a brief moment, Elodie marveled at the kind of root structure the anthodite must have to be able to implant itself like that—and to grow into solid rock!—but then she shook the thought away because now was *not* the time for scientific inquiry.

If only I had gloves and boots. All Elodie had was her dress, which was quickly running out of spare fabric. At this rate, she would emerge from the dragon's lair wearing nothing but dirty undergarments like a feral princess. Whatever was left on her skin of the priestesses' anointing ceremony must look like battle-worn war paint by now.

Perhaps I have become a feral princess, Elodie thought as she tore off the penultimate layer of her dress and wrapped the fabric around her feet and hands like mittens and socks.

"Here we go again."

Elodie picked the same path as the last time, because it still looked the most promising. When she got to the part of the wall without handholds and footholds, she said a quick prayer, then reached up and carefully held on to a flower.

Before using her legs to push herself all the way up, Elodie tested the thickness of her makeshift mittens. They seemed to be all right. Then she wiggled the anthodite to ensure that it really was rooted into the rock and would hold her weight.

It would.

"This better lead to a real escape, V," Elodie said as she pushed up with her legs, her left hand on the first anthodite, and her right hand grabbing another.

They both held.

Yes!

Elodie climbed at a steady pace, not needing to pause as long between moves since she didn't need to search out rocks to latch on to; there were more than enough flowers to serve as handholds and footholds. The swallows flew back in from above and swirled around her, singing their buoyant, flutelike melody as if cheering her on. As Elodie climbed higher, the light also got brighter. Perhaps it was only because the sun was rising outside. But she liked to think of it as a marker of progress, a promise that the end to this ordeal was near.

She reached a stretch where the wall shifted a little, so she was no longer climbing straight up but was actually on an incline of approximately fifteen degrees. Although mathematically small, the change was significant enough to give her aching muscles a bit of relief. She could rest more of her weight against the stone instead of holding all of herself against the greedy clutches of gravity.

The sunlight grew brighter, and then all of a sudden, Elodie was high enough that she could see where the chimney of rock began to bend, and she caught a sliver of blue and fluffy white.

"That's the sky!"

In her glee, Elodie reached for a handful of anthodite without looking, continuing instead to crane her neck for a better look at the sky. At freedom.

She missed the flowers, swiping at nothing. *Merdú!* One of her feet slipped, and she began sliding down the slope. Elodie reached for an anthodite, but this one was a cluster of baby flowers that hadn't rooted itself strongly enough into the cave yet, and it ripped off in her hands as Elodie tumbled.

"No!"

She slid to the point where the wall shifted angles, changing from a slight slope to completely vertical, and then Elodie careened down the rock face, screaming.

She snatched at anthodite and managed to grab hold of one, cutting up her hands more and jerking hard at her arm. She hung for a few precious seconds, but then the flower petals cracked, and Elodie tumbled down again, smashing and bouncing against the sharp rock ledges, and finally landing with a heavy smack on the cave floor. Searing pain flared through her arm. She cried out in agony.

And then a white-hot wave of panic washed over her. If she'd broken her arm, she wouldn't be able to climb. She'd be stuck in the dragon's labyrinth forever. Or until it heard the commotion she'd been making and came to eat her. *Oh god oh god oh god . . .* Why had she screamed when she fell? The dragon would probably be here any minute!

Elodie forced herself to sit up and examine her arm. Logic warred with hysteria in her brain, and she barely kept hold of her reason as she checked whether she'd shattered her bones.

Her right side ached. She had likely cracked a couple of ribs. By some miracle, her arm was intact, but numb. The shooting pain was only in her shoulder, and it was worse when she tried to move the joint.

It's dislocated, Elodie realized. This had happened to her before when falling out of trees. Back then, the doctor had been summoned to pop her shoulder back in. She'd had medication so she wouldn't feel it. And her mother to hold her hand.

But Elodie was on her own now. And all she wanted to do was curl into her mother's lap and cry.

Why am I even trying? She didn't know if the V meant Victoria had made it out, or only that she'd attempted it. Victoria could very well have begun the climb, then fallen to her death.

"I should just offer myself to the dragon and get it over with," Elodie whimpered, cradling her shoulder. The pain was so intense she was seeing flashes of white stars through her tears.

This is frightening, but not impossible, her mother's voice seemed to whisper in her ear. It had been part of her arsenal of encouragement, like her poem about taking one step at a time. *If you cannot do it, Elodie, no one can.*

"What am I supposed to *do*, though?" Elodie said. "Shove my shoulder back into place myself? And then what? I have nothing useful to help with the climb. I am fast running out of dress to tear up, and other than that, I only have this stupid tiara the priestesses wove into my braids, as if the most important thing when I died was to still be wearing it in my hair, and—"

Oh.

Never let it be said that women's fashion was merely shallow decoration.

Elodie could use the tiara to climb. Instead of holding on to the anthodite with her hands, she could loop the tiara over the flowers.

She looked up at the beam of sunlight coming in from the chimney above. Then she took a deep breath, counted to three, and shoved her dislocated shoulder back into its socket, trying with all her might not to scream.

AS SOON AS the immediate pain receded, Elodie recommenced her climb, aware that the dragon would probably appear soon. She had to get out, now.

Using the tiara to loop around the anthodite proved her best idea yet. Following the same path for the third time, Elodie made quick progress up the rock face.

When she reached the point where she could see the first sliver of sky, though, she refused to look at it and make the same mistake again. Instead, Elodie kept climbing, focusing on nothing but the next anthodite ahead of her. The cave wall continued its fifteen-degree incline for a while, but eventually shifted back to vertical. In fact, this part of the rock began to angle a little in the other direction, from zero to negative degrees, and Elodie had to side-shuffle to a different part of the cylindrical walls. She might have mastered the tiara-as-tool climbing method, but it couldn't adhere her to the rock like a spider. Unfortunately, Elodie was only human.

She was impossibly high up by now. A fall would be—

Don't think about that.

Lady Bayford hadn't wanted Elodie to climb up anything, but Elodie was more than glad now that she hadn't listened to her stepmother's advice. At least on that count.

Finally, she reached the part of the cave where the chimney met the main walls. The lava tube bent here, but Elodie had learned from her carelessness before, and even though she could crawl up the steep incline, she continued to hook the tiara methodically on anthodite. Slow and steady progress was better than sloppy speed. Especially at this height.

"Zedrae . . . der krerrai vo irru?"

Oh god. The dragon. It was here, below her. Elodie's heart slammed against her broken ribs.

She accidentally knocked the tiara against a sharp point of a flower, and it must have been a weak point in the gold, because the crown snapped.

She started sliding down the chimney. Desperate, Elodie tried to dig her heels into the rock, and she lunged for a passing anthodite. Her fingers curled around it, the bladelike petals slicing straight through her skin again, but despite the sharp pain, she gripped tighter.

Her momentum stopped abruptly, and her right shoulder nearly popped out of its socket again. Blood streamed down Elodie's fingers and wrist. Her hand was slippery, her hold on the anthodite weakening. She dangled on the edge of where the chimney ended and the main part of the cave walls—straight down—began, and she could see the dragon's gray armored scales below, shifting and making that soul-curdling leather-scraping noise as it circled the ground.

"*Der krerrai vo irru?*" it rasped. Smoke from its nostrils curled upward until it reached Elodie, embracing her like an unwanted lover.

But it didn't faze her, because Elodie was beginning to understand what the dragon was saying. Piecing together the grammatical rules and vocabulary she'd learned so far, *Der krerrai vo irru?* meant something like *Where ____ this go?*

Where does *this (cave/path/climb) go?* or *Where* you think *this goes?*

Not precise, but she knew the gist of it.

However, her grip began to slip again, and the feeling of being pleased with herself dissipated with the smoke.

She dug her heels further into the rock, adjusted the tattered fabric that remained around her hands, and latched on to another anthodite.

"*Nythoserrai vinirre. Visirrai se.*"

Elodie snorted. "I am very well aware that I can fall."

The dragon hissed in surprise. "How do you understand Khaevis Ventvis? My tongue?"

Khaevis meant dragon. Elodie remembered that from their first encounter, when it had shrieked *I AM KHAEVIS* at her. So Khaevis Ventvis must be the name of the dragon language.

"I am a clever one, remember? *Syrrif drae,* you said. I listened to you, and I learned."

"*Iokif.*" The dragon chuckled, its laughter like an earthquake through the caves.

That was a word she didn't know.

"*Kuirr tu kho,*" the dragon said.

"Does it look like I want to go to you?" she asked. "Why

don't you just fly up here and eat me now?" Surely the amusement of the chase must be wearing thin.

But its serrated wings remained folded along its spine. The dragon was too big, and there wasn't enough space to unfurl its wings inside this chamber. *Oh, thank heavens.* It was her only chance at getting out of here alive.

"Sodo nitrerrad ki utirre diunif ira . . ." Rocks fell around Elodie, careening past her face, and she squeezed the anthodite she was holding on to, even though they cut through the cloth on her hands.

The dragon slithered out of the cave.

Elodie shuddered. She'd caught some of what it had said, something about going another way. It might not have been able to fly up here, but it certainly wasn't just going to leave her alone.

She leaned against the chimney floor for a long moment, gathering the splinters of her courage from what the dragon's appearance had just shattered.

Only fifty yards ahead, the lava tube opened up into sunlight and blue sky.

"I can do this," she muttered. Elodie thought again of Floria, of how abandoned she would feel if Elodie weren't around to attend her wedding, to bring gifts to her children, to write letters every week back and forth. "I can do this. I *have* to."

With bleeding hands, Elodie half climbed, half crawled the steep incline of the chimney. With every new cut in her skin, she was closer to the sunshine. With every new protest in her cracked ribs and her sprained ankle, she was nearer to freedom.

Sweat and dirt blurred her vision as she approached the lip of the chimney. The sun's rays, which kissed her skin now, had never felt so nourishing. Fresh air had never tasted as sweet. The sky had never seemed so limitless. Silent tears of relief trickled down Elodie's filthy face.

Floria, Father, and Stepmother ought to be about ready to set sail soon, now that the wedding was over. All Elodie had to do was get to the harbor. According to the mental map in her head, she ought to be at the southeasternmost part of the mountain, near the base, close to the roads that led to Aurea's vast farmland. The way to the harbor would be easy compared to what Elodie had just endured.

"I'm coming," she said, as much to herself as to her family. With a surge of hope, Elodie clambered over the lip of the chimney, burst onto her feet, and ran.

But suddenly, the ground disappeared in front of her, dropping off as if the mountain had been sheared clean by a guillotine. Elodie shrieked, catching herself only steps before careening off the cliff.

Her pulse pounded in her ears. She clung to a boulder and peered over the edge.

She'd been correct that she was on the southeastern side of the map in her head, but she'd incorrectly calculated the topology. Believing that the dragon's caverns were all underground, Elodie had assumed that when she emerged, she'd be near sea level.

But instead, the caves must have subtly wound up through the belly of the mountain, because she'd been spit out at the top of a narrow peak, even higher up than when she'd been thrown into the gorge.

And there was nowhere to go.

ELODIE

IRONICALLY, THE PANORAMA of Aurea from this vantage point was stunning. The palace sparkled in the sunlight, like a precious brooch set into the mountain's bosom. Swaths of silver pear orchards, sangberry hedges, and aurum wheat covered the lowlands in a vibrant patchwork of greens and gold. Wispy clouds streaked the blue sky as if they'd been artfully daubed on by a painter's brush.

There was the harbor, the ships bobbing gently at the docks over glimmering, cerulean water. Most of the ships would be loaded with the harvest, to be sold to countries near and far; those vessels would eventually return to Aurea laden with riches. There was a small group of ships bearing yellow-and-blue-striped flags that hadn't been there when Elodie arrived. And then there was the *Deomelas*, its orange Inophean banner bright enough that she could see it even from here, whipping in the wind.

The sight of her family's ship so far away—and against the backdrop of this deceptively beautiful kingdom—made Elodie scream. "You soulless bastards! How do you sleep at night, knowing what you've done to me and to all the other women who came before?" Her voice echoed through the purple-gray peaks and valleys of Mount Khaevis. The wind carried her rage.

"You do not deserve this isle. You do not deserve the good people who toil for you." Elodie spat off the side of the cliff. "If I were a dragon, I'd burn your wretched, ill-gotten castle down."

Her chest heaved as she glared at the palace, imagining it melting into the rocks like a gold ingot in a forge. If she ever made it off this mountain, she would find a way to make the royal family pay for everything they'd done. Eight centuries of sacrifices. Eight centuries of lost lives.

But first, Elodie had to survive. She pulled herself back from the edge of the cliff and from the sword's edge of fury. She had to get down to the lowlands, to her family and then to their ship.

She couldn't go back into the caves, which left only one option: a one-and-a-half-foot-wide ledge on the otherwise sheer rock face. Elodie could not see where it went, or if it ended around the curve of the mountainside.

There was a V carved above the beginning of the ledge.

Elodie exhaled. "Thank you, Victoria." This was undoubtedly the way to go.

It hardly qualified as a ledge. More like a protrusion of rocks that hadn't realized it was supposed to fall off when the rest of the cliff side had.

Elodie crept slowly sideways, pebbles skittering off with every tentative step. Without anthodite to hold on to here, she was at the complete mercy of the mountain. All Elodie could do was press herself as close to the rock as possible and pray that the ledge did not give way beneath her.

The path began to narrow even more as it turned along the curve of Mount Khaevis. Like a fold in fabric, this part of the mountainside was blocked from the sun and instead sheltered a pocket of soupy fog. Elodie shivered at the sudden drop in temperature and the wet mist that seeped into the thin remaining layer of her dress. For a brief moment, she missed the steamy heat of the dragon's caves.

Elodie couldn't see more than an arm's length ahead, so she had to tap her toe lightly in front of her before putting her weight into each step.

Left foot first, right foot after,
Nothing to fear, no disaster.

Her voice tremored, but she carried on.

Right foot, left foot,
Cross the ground,
And ere long
You're safe and sound.

But then, when Elodie was deep in the pocket of fog, there was a loud rush of wind.

Followed by another. Rocks tumbled from above in a small landslide, and she threw herself against the cliff side to avoid tumbling down, too.

What in the hells was happening?

There was another booming whoosh. Was it just the shape of this side of the mountain—like the inside of a chalice—that made the wind reverberate so? Like how the pipe organ cave amplified the swallows' song?

The next gust came like a crack of thunder. The fog rolled in waves as the force of the air pushed it. Then another thunderous roar, and another, closer—

Elodie screamed as the dragon burst into view, its serrated

wings like colossal panels of forged longswords. It lunged for her, and she ducked, its claws striking on either side of where she'd just been.

She scrambled along the ledge, no longer able to check if the rock shelf still existed where she put down her foot. All she had now was faith that Victoria would not lead her astray.

"I will get you, princess," the dragon rasped. "Like all the ones before."

"I am not just one of the many! My name is Elodie!" she shouted. "And the other princesses had names, too. Beatrice! Amira! Charlene! Fatima! Audrey! Rashmi! Yoojin!" She yelled all the names carved in the Safe Cave wall. "You will remember them! You will respect them!"

The dragon laughed. It had drawn back into the fog, likely to regroup before attacking again. "Finally, I have your name. Elodieeeeeee. You sound delicious."

She trembled at how it savored her name, rolling it around in its mouth like an appetizer before the main meal.

It rushed through the fog again, violet eyes narrowed and nostrils flaring. Elodie braced herself as it charged at the mountainside, then violently reversed course, whipping its tail at the rocks to knock her off.

Merdú! Elodie leapt out of the way and clung to a scraggly tree growing from the granite.

The tree couldn't support her weight, though, and it began to give and tilt over the ledge.

"Please no . . ." Elodie dangled from it, face-to-face with the sheer side of the mountain. "Frightening but not impossible, frightening but not impossible," she chanted desperately, crying as she put hand over hand on the thin trunk of the precarious tree.

"Dakhi krerriv demerra se irrai?" the dragon snarled. "How far did you think I would let you go?" It surged up from the fog below. "No more playing!" It unleashed a plume of flame.

The branches caught on fire as Elodie hoisted herself up. Her dress was on fire, too, and she threw herself back onto the ledge and smothered herself against the rock to put out the flames. The little tree exploded in a final burst of fire, then relinquished its hold on the mountainside. She watched wide-eyed as it tumbled into oblivion; she would have gone with it had she been a second slower.

No, she wouldn't have. The dragon would have caught her and crushed her in its talons. Or its jaws.

The ledge along the cliff side was only inches wide now. Ten inches. No, eight . . .

But the dragon's fire had burned away the fog for a moment, and she spied a fissure in the rock face. Another tiny, hellish space. Yet her only hope.

Elodie thrust her arm into the fissure. The dragon dove for her, claws outstretched. She yanked herself into the crack, jerking herself inside just as the dragon hit the granite, clouds of rock dust exploding where its talon shredded the mountainside.

"Nyerru evoro. There is no escape, *zedrae."*

Regardless, she squirmed deeper into the crack. It began to widen, and Elodie was no longer tightly sandwiched in the rock. The fissure ran straight up to the top of the peak, from where sunlight slivered in. She squeezed in farther, and there the crevice opened up into a long and slender space, about six feet across at its widest point, and thirty or so feet deep.

"Thank heavens," Elodie breathed.

The back of the fissure was mostly cast in shadow. But the sunlight shifted slightly, and a glint of metal caught her eye.

A partially melted tiara with strands of scorched but undeniably red hair fused to it.

Above it, carved into the rock:

NOT SAFE

~V

"*Maldí-seù*," Elodie swore.

Behind her, the dragon snarled. "I heard that *that* princess led a chase, as well."

It had heard? Elodie thought. That meant *this* dragon hadn't been the one pursuing Victoria. How many other dragons had there been, and when and why did they leave or perish?

"But that *zedrae* was terrible!" it said. "*Nitrerra santaif vor kir ni.* I have higher hopes for you."

Elodie whipped around. The dragon's eye filled the entire opening of the fissure, so all she could see was malevolent violet slashed with gold.

"You heartless beast!" Elodie scooped up a handful of rocks and began hurling them at the dragon's eye. It roared as the sharp stones made contact and shook its head, rattling Elodie's prison as it held on to the mountainside.

But she kept throwing rocks, because what did she have to lose anymore? She was about to die. She knew she was just an ant to this monster, but even ants could bite, and she would go down fighting. "Why don't you just eat the princesses immediately and save them from suffering? Why must you toy with us like hapless prey?"

"Because you *are* hapless prey," the dragon snapped, its voice like sparks on wood about to burst into flame.

"I am Elodie Bayford of Inophe, and princess of godforsaken Aurea. I am—"

"You are tiresome." The dragon exhaled a stream of yellow smoke from its nostrils. It filled the fissure, and Elodie coughed on its sharpness. It stung the back of her throat and prickled her tongue with the acrid taste of rotten eggs. Her eyes watered, and she stumbled on her bad ankle as her vision began to swim.

"Kuirr. Nykuarrad etia."

"And what if I don't come out?" Elodie asked, rubbing her itchy, swelling eyes. "You'll leave me here to rot?" She pointed at Victoria's tiara. "Or will you burn me to death here in this hole like her?"

The dragon made a hissing sound, like it was sucking air in through its razored teeth. "She was not burned to death. And I would not kill you with fire unless you left me no choice. *Vis kir vis. Sanae kir res.* I thought you understood."

Life for life. Blood for fire. It kept saying that. Elodie knew the words now, but she still didn't know what the phrase signified.

But what it implied was the dragon wanted to eat her, rather than just kill her. Perhaps it *needed* her blood.

For what?

The violet eye flared again at the crevice's opening. "You can die like a coward or *kuirr* and face your fate with bravery."

Elodie scooped up another handful of rocks and hurled them.

The dragon jerked back from the fissure and bellowed. *"KUIRR. NYKUARRAD ETIA."*

"Never!" Elodie shouted. "I will never come out. I'd rather fry in here than surrender and give you my blood!"

It roared, yellow smoke pluming from its nostrils. Elodie waited for her life to flash before her eyes. The memory of her mother, singing her to sleep with a lullaby. The memory of Flor's birth. Of riding across Inophe's parched yet beautiful terrain. Of mazes and smiles, of the languages of sailors and stories that brought laughter, of nights spent with Floria making up new constellations from the stars.

But the flash of memories did not come.

Nor did dragon fire.

Instead, the monster hissed. "What is *that*?"

And then, inexplicably, the beating of wings and the dragon's retreat.

What just happened?

Perhaps it was a trick. An attempt to induce Elodie to run to the fissure's opening to see if the dragon was truly flying away. Then it would snatch her as her head emerged from the crevice.

"*Syrrif,*" Elodie said. "But not clever enough."

She stayed where she was and listened for the dragon's return.

But it was quiet out there. She waited longer, yet heard nothing. The dragon might have been stealthy inside its caves, but in the air, there was no way it could be silent. Its wings announced it with every thunderous flap.

"I'm not dead yet," Elodie said, not quite believing it.

Something had distracted the dragon. But it didn't matter to her what. All she needed to know was she had a little more time. Every moment of being alive meant another chance at surviving.

There was nothing to do in here, though. Elodie couldn't look at Victoria's tiara, couldn't look at her beacon of hope, eviscerated.

But Elodie had to stay busy. She had to keep moving so she didn't freeze. She had to do *something* so she didn't just contemplate her own grim future in Victoria's tiara.

So Elodie picked up the sharpest rock she could find and began scratching onto the walls the new words the dragon had spoken, and reasoning out possible translations. It had been surprised that she could understand some of what it was saying; she must be the first princess to ever communicate with it, the first who wasn't a mere meal.

Already, because she'd learned some of its language, she'd discovered that this dragon hadn't always been the only one on Aurea. It confirmed the other princess's memory from the Safe Cave—this dragon used to have a family. Perhaps that fact was important . . . somehow. Elodie wasn't sure *how* yet. But learning more of Khaevis Ventvis could only help her. And future princesses, as well.

She settled in to really think about the way the dragon's language sounded. Hard consonants and ominous r's—that had been her first impression. But there were a lot of r's, and Elodie realized that they were present in every verb the dragon used. *Kuirr.* "Come out." *Nykuarrad etia.* "I will not ask again," where the verb was *nykuarrad.*

"I'm right. The verbs are conjugated based on the subject," Elodie murmured to herself, recalling how the sailors' vernacular also changed the endings of verbs. In the sailor's tongue, the verb "to drink" was different in "I drink" (*bébu*) and "you drink" (*bébuz*), which was different from "we drink" (*bébinoz*) or "they drink" (*bébum*). The dragon's language seemed to follow similar rules.

Elodie dissected more phrases she could remember, both from what the dragon had just said and from their previous encounters.

After transcribing everything and breaking down the linguistics of the dragon's tongue as best she could, though, Elodie had no new ideas for how to get off the mountain. *Nyerru evoro.* Perhaps the dragon hadn't lied when it said there was no escape.

Elodie rubbed her eyes. The last effects of the stinging gas had finally worn away while she was working. She turned to Victoria's tiara.

Elodie frowned and moved closer.

There was a V smeared in blood on the ground. It led to another V and a trickle of blood, a yard to the right at the base of the wall, then the splatter became a trail of blood and V's until—

"Oh," Elodie gasped.

The corner in the farthest recess of the crevice was completely covered in old blood, a vast puddle of it. Elodie hadn't noticed before because it had been in shadow, and her vision had been blurred by the dragon's caustic smoke.

Elodie stepped into it, and instantly saw Victoria lying on the ground in a pool of blood, one of her arms torn off by the dragon.

"I love you, Lizaveta. I love you, Anna," Victoria whispered in the memory. "I will be joining you soon."

VICTORIA

DYING HURTS MORE than I imagined it would, as if my muscles are being peeled from my bones piece by piece, my soul harvested from my marrow with a spoon. My mind begins to drift, seeking distraction from the pain. As if preparing for my end, it returns to the beginning, to our hopes and dreams. To when I still had my family intact. Before it all went wrong.

I see clearly our arrival on the Isle of Aurea as if it were yesterday—my parents, King Josef and Queen Carlotta; my sisters, Lizaveta and Anna; and our baby brother, Josef II. Our original home, Talis, had been destroyed by catastrophic earthquakes and infestations, so we set out in search of a new land for our people. We sailed for four years, and we lost over half our population during our exile. Once, it was plague; another time, a hostile government. There was an island composed solely of salt mines and saltwater, and a jungle full of diseased insects that bit and stung and infected many of our strongest citizens. Sometimes our people died simply from being too exhausted to go on.

I can still feel the joy and relief that surged in our chests when our decimated fleet dropped anchor off the shores of Aurea.

Here was a plentiful land, isolated from the rest of the world and as yet uninhabited by man. The volcanic soil was fertile and bursting with silver pears, healing sangberries, and grains such as we had never tasted before—rich in flavor and nutrition, able to restore our poor health within weeks of landing. Aurea was the salvation we had been searching for.

The only problem was that Aurea was not entirely uninhabited. A territorial dragon lived in its sole mountain, and it did not like our intrusion into its paradise.

But, oh! How we wanted to stay! We had seen what the rest of the world had to offer us, and it was nothing. This was the only place our people could begin anew. The only place we had the energy to pursue. The citizens—formerly of Talis, and for four years, of no country—refused to set foot on another boat again.

Because of this, Father sent our knights to exterminate the dragon. The monster was over a millennium old. It ought not have been too difficult to slay a single enemy.

And yet it torched every soldier before their arrows were even within range. It tore them in half with its talons and flung their limp, armored bodies against walls. Some it swallowed whole. The rest, it piled in a heap of warped metal, ash, and bones at the base of the mountain for us to see.

Then it flew in fury at the temporary tents our people had constructed, intent on lighting them all aflame.

In the royal residence—a tent only slightly more stable than those of ordinary citizens—Mother huddled with Lizaveta, Anna, and our baby brother in fear. My father wept for failing his people.

But I did not believe this was our fate. Despite my parents' pleas, I burst out of the tent and screamed at the dragon, "We repent and wish to make amends!"

The monster roared at me but came to a standstill in the air, abominable wings flapping, but no longer attacking. "Amends?" it sneered. Its accent was pronounced, and it suddenly occurred to me how foolhardy I had been to run out alone and assume it could understand my language.

"Y-you know what I'm saying?"

The dragon narrowed its violet eyes. "I have consumed the blood of your soldiers, and therefore I know all that they have ever known."

I trembled at its great power and intelligence. It was no mere beast.

But I summoned what courage I had, for I was the only hope for my people. The rest of my family cowered—and rightly so—in the tent behind me.

"If you know all that our knights knew," I said, "then you understand that all we want is to live here in peace."

The dragon laughed without humor, plumes of smoke spiraling from its nostrils. "What a peculiar definition of peace you have, sending warriors to kill *me*."

I fell to my knees and lay prostrate before it. "Your Majesty, forgive us. We have been homeless at sea for four years. We are weary from much loss, and in our desperation, we erred in our judgment against you. Please, tell me how we can make amends. Anything we can offer you is yours. We only wish to coexist here without conflict."

The dragon hovered above me. "Anything?" it asked, its voice like an impending storm.

I dared not rise from my prostrate bow, for fear of offending it. "Anything in my power to give, Your Majesty."

It inhaled deeply and licked its lips, the sound of its reptilian tongue like a sword sliding over chain mail. "Royal blood," it said. "*Your* blood."

I jerked upright. "You mean . . . y-you wish to drink it?" My heartbeat crashed through my veins, the very veins that carried what this monster desired.

The dragon flew lower. It inhaled again, as if smelling me. It was so close, I, too, could smell *it*—sharp sulfur and bitter smoke, leather and the iron tang of death.

"I do not want a drink, *zedrae*. I want to eat you. The men you sent to my lair were palatable. But you—your blood sings sweetly of grace *and* power."

"No!" Anna, my twelve-year-old sister, screamed. She ran out from the protection of our shelter, and Lizaveta, only two years older than her, followed close on her heels. They threw their arms protectively around me.

"Ah, I knew I smelled more." The dragon landed, rattling the ground beneath us in terrifying semblance to the earthquakes we'd suffered on Talis. I hugged my sisters tighter.

"I shall have all three of you," the dragon said with what could only be described as a reptilian smile—teeth bared, the pleasure of a trick and a bargain in the upturn of the corners of its mouth. "And every year thereafter, I shall have three more of royal blood."

Anna buried her face in my side. But Lizaveta glared at the dragon and said, "If you eat the three of us, how are we to produce three more next year? Royalty doesn't grow on trees."

"You will find them if you wish to *live here in peace*," it snarled, throwing my own words back at me like a threat. "That is the bargain. You may stay here on the island and have your harvest. But I shall have mine, as well. *Vis kir vis.*"

"Is there no other way?" I asked, my voice smaller than it had ever been before.

"You claimed to offer *anything*," the dragon snapped, flame flaring from its nostrils. "You have three moonrises to make your decision. On the third night, if three princesses are not delivered to my lair, I shall consider the bargain null, and I shall destroy all of you."

It flapped its bladelike wings and rose into the air. Then, with a final roar that blew all the tents from their posts, it swooped away, faster than any of our ships had ever traveled on the sea.

"I DON'T WANT to die," Lizaveta cried as we ran back to our half-demolished home. Anna had collapsed under the dragon's final warning, and I was carrying her in my arms.

"You will not die," the king declared as we crossed the threshold inside. "We shall depart from this cursed isle immediately—"

"Father, no," I said. "We cannot exile our people again. They have hardly any spirit left. If we leave, they will perish. It will be the end of our history."

"I will not feed my daughters to a beast!"

"Nor would I feed my sisters to one," I said as calmly as I could. Every part of my body shook, but I knew it was up to me to find a way out. The king was frayed as threadbare cloth from years of fighting for a dying people, of leading them when there was nowhere to go. The queen was sweet and gentle, but too timid to help against what we faced.

But I had been forged from misfortune. My adolescence was one of angry seas and unfriendly lands, of starvation and disease. I became a woman while living on the brink of despair, yet I learned that leadership meant holding on to the flickering lantern of hope even as the oil ran low and the wick too short. Such responsibility and duty I held solemnly. If anyone could save the remnants of our kingdom now, it would have to be me.

"Our knights failed because they could not get close enough to the dragon," I said. "But if we are to be delivered to its lair, then we shall have the chance to accomplish what they could not achieve."

Anna whimpered. "I do not know how to wield a sword."

"Our weapon will be smaller and cleverer," I said, stroking her hair. "Just like you."

"A dagger?"

"Poison," I said.

"You think I'm poisonous?" Anna began crying again.

Despite my fear—or perhaps because of it—I laughed. "No, peach, you could never be poisonous. Forgive my poor analogy. I only meant that we shall strike in a way the dragon does not expect. Instead of providing our blood, we shall fill its watering hole with the most potent, deadliest draft our apothecary can concoct. And then our people will be free to grow roots here on this isle, for many, many peaceful and prosperous centuries to come."

As THE MOON climbed into the gloomy sky on the third night, the queen and our baby brother stayed at home, but the king and his knights accompanied Lizaveta, Anna, and me to the mouth of the dragon's lair. We had packed lightly—only what water and small provisions we could hide in the folds of our gowns and the pockets of our cloaks—for we had to appear as docile sacrifices to the dragon. I wore the poison in a crystal vial around my neck, disguised as a jewel pendant. A single drop of the draft had been able to kill a dozen rats on our ships; what I carried with me ought to be enough to slay a dozen dragons within an hour of drinking the poison.

"You do not have to do this," the king said as he held the three of us in his embrace. "We could still flee."

"No, we cannot," Lizaveta said. "Victoria is right. This is the only way for our people to have a future."

"She will keep us safe," Anna squeaked, her small head nuzzled against our father's beard.

"Yes, I will," I said, hoping it wasn't a lie. I touched the vial at my throat. "We will survive."

The king kissed us each and refused to say goodbye, as did I, for I intended to return to him with my sisters by the next night.

We entered the caves on foot, via a path our scouts had discovered, a route the knights had intended to use to breach the dragon's lair, although they never had the chance. Lizaveta, Anna, and I each carried a lantern, but still we navigated the rough tunnels carefully. One false step and we'd alert the dragon too soon of our arrival. I wanted to find a safe place to make camp where Lizaveta and Anna could stay while I poisoned the dragon.

"*Kosor, zedrae. Oniserrai dymerrif ferkorrikh.*" The dragon's voice echoed through the caves.

Lizaveta and Anna shrieked.

"Show yourself," I said while pushing my sisters behind me. How naïve of me to think we could hide in its own dominion.

It laughed. "I shall reveal myself when I choose. For now, I think I shall give you time to explore my domain."

"Why would you do that?" Anna asked.

"I like the taste of blood laced with fear," it said.

Lizaveta huffed. "So you're just a giant cat, playing with its food."

"*Ed, zedrae . . .*"

A terrifying silence followed. And then, suddenly, a loud, hissing whoosh as clouds of stinging yellow gas rushed from the tunnel to our left, burning our eyes and lungs. We ran screaming deeper into the caves, tripping over ourselves and gashing open our hands and knees, smashing our lanterns and flailing blindly into the underground depths.

Miserable days followed. I cannot bear to recount them. All I will say is my decisions led to my sisters' deaths; I carry their souls in my heavy heart and feel their terror and pain with every beat.

After that, I hated myself for still being alive. And yet, I knew that if I could not slay the dragon and survive, then I would have doomed not only Anna and Lizaveta, but many more princesses to come.

So I recommitted to poisoning the dragon, while leaving as many clues for the future as I could, in case I failed but could help others find a way out.

However, my original plan to poison the dragon's source of water proved impossible. I could find no wells underground, and if there were any other subterranean fountains or rivers, they were hidden and protected, and I knew not where they lay.

Hence, I did the only other thing I could think of. I have drunk the poison myself, and my coveted blood will be the dragon's undoing.

The monster has already taken my arm. I retreated here because, for a moment, my courage failed me and I fled deep into this crack. But I am losing precious blood and time, and I know what I must do. Soon I will step back outside and offer myself— and the rest of my tainted blood—to the angry beast.

I take full responsibility for my actions. In my hubris, I made a bargain that would require the sacrifice of many more lives in the future. In order to provide the dragon with more royal sacrifices every year, the king and queen will have to marry the baby prince thrice each harvest, then cast his wives to the wicked monster.

But if I had to do it again, I would still make the bargain with the dragon. Because the monarchy's duty is to put the needs of the whole above the needs of the few. And that is what I did.

I hope my plan works. I hope the dragon will consume my flesh and blood. If so, in only an hour's time, my people will be saved.

If I fail, however . . . I am sorry that future generations will have to suffer, and that they will have to die to protect Aurea. But even so, they ought to be proud that they are part of a noble tradition, and their lives will not be given in vain. My sisters' lives, and *my* life, were not given in vain.

Vis kir vis.

I am proud of our sacrifice.

ELODIE

ELODIE FLUNG A rock at Victoria's bloodstains. "That's supposed to make me feel better? I'm a noble sacrifice? You selfish, arrogant ronyon!" Elodie grabbed more rocks and threw them at V's bloody confession. "You festering plague sore! You supercilious, self-righteous scullion! You . . . You evil bitch!"

She spun on her heel and hurled a larger stone at Victoria's bloodstain. Then another and another, until her rage fizzled out into disillusionment.

Elodie sank to the ground and curled around her knees.

"You were my hero," she said. "You were that lantern of hope I held on to . . . But now it turns out that you were actually a villain, as well. How am I supposed to feel about that?"

Then she slumped further. Because part of her understood what Victoria meant. After all, Elodie had agreed to give herself to ensure the well-being of her people. She hadn't outright agreed to be sacrificed to a dragon, but then again, Victoria hadn't expected to condemn eight hundred years of future princesses, either.

In fact, according to Victoria's memory, the original bargain had been for *any* imperial blood, not only that of princesses. Which meant that it was the Aurean royal family that had made the decision to sacrifice women. Since they'd only ever borne sons after the deaths of Victoria and her sisters, a harvest ceremony of three *princesses* was a convenient "tradition" to avoid ever having to condemn their own children to death again.

Elodie's stomach rose, and she had to turn away, not able to bear looking at Victoria's blood and tiara.

Instead, Elodie rose and began pacing the length of the fissure. She tried coming up with plans for escape, but it was futile. The ridge along the cliff side ended here. There was no going forward, only back. And she had no intention of returning to the dragon's lair.

As she paced, Elodie kept an ear on the outside, listening for the beast's wings or its smoky breathing. But it was as quiet as if she were on Mount Khaevis all alone, far from civilization.

"This kingdom certainly *is* far from civilized," Elodie muttered. Only anger and the task of problem solving kept the panic and despair down in the pit of her belly. If she let go of her outrage or logic, she'd vomit pure fear, in which case she'd be useless and might as well just surrender to the dragon.

Elodie kicked at a pile of rocks, sending them skittering out of the mouth of the crevice. They flew out into nothingness, plummeting straight down until, eventually, they hit something much farther down the mountainside. The noise of the impact— of shattering rock—was faint and far away.

That's how far Elodie would fall before her body smashed to pieces.

She closed her eyes for a moment. *Perhaps that is the best way to end this. I refuse to give the dragon what it wants. But if my death is a foregone conclusion, perhaps I should be the one to choose how that conclusion comes.*

It would be a long fall, plenty of time for terror to fill her to the brim. Preferable, Elodie thought, to waiting in this cave for the dragon to tire of her intractability and decide to roast her as punishment.

She tiptoed to the entrance of the fissure. If the dragon were close, it would have reacted to the rocks she'd kicked outside. Pausing at the mouth of the crevice and hearing nothing, Elodie dared to stick her head out.

There truly was nothing out there. For whatever reason, the dragon had abandoned her.

But why would it do that? It had Elodie cornered. The chase was up.

It wouldn't leave unless something more immediate had distracted it.

Then she heard it. Voices, not in the dragon's tongue, but in her own language.

The wind shifted, temporarily parting the fog. In the distance, Elodie spied a handful of torches in a shadowed part of the mountain with which she was unfamiliar. They were sheltered by a series of broken ridges, almost as if the area used to be horizontal lava tubes, but bits and pieces of the ceilings and sides had fallen off over time. In this way, they were protected from a dragon's assault from above, but would still have been visible to the dragon from its vantage point outside Elodie's fissure.

A different route to the caves? She now remembered that part of V's confession, how Victoria and her sisters had entered the dragon's lair. They hadn't been thrown in like Elodie had, which made sense since the original princesses volunteered for the mission. Rather, they'd been equipped with food, water, and poison, and had entered the caves on foot.

Below, a flag fluttered in the breeze. It was not crimson and gold, but rather, orange, the color of Inophe.

"Father?" Elodie whispered.

Her heart clenched as she remembered how he had betrayed her trust. But at the same time, her pulse raced at the sight of him. He was coming to rescue her, along with six of the sailors who had accompanied them on the journey to Aurea. She was a mass of conflicted emotions, but one dominated them all: hope.

"Hello? Can you hear me?" she yelled. "I'm up here!"

They didn't respond; the fog swallowed her shouts whole.

"*Bocê pudum me ovir?*" she shouted, trying the sailors' polyglot vernacular. "*Púr favour me ajjúdum!*"

But they couldn't hear her, no matter what language she yelled.

She had to go back down.

Elodie hesitated. There was a part of her that didn't want to ever see her father again. Why had he agreed to such a marriage? And even afterward, why hadn't he objected to the ignominy of throwing her into the gorge?

But she shook the questions vigorously from her head. They could be dealt with later, when she was safe. Right now, though, the most important thing was that Father was coming to help her, and she needed to be there when he arrived.

Especially if the dragon had already seen them. It would intercept them in the labyrinth . . . Lord Bayford and his men had no idea what they were up against. Elodie scrambled out of the fissure.

It was nearly impossible to go back the way she'd come, but she had to.

She left Victoria's crevice and began to scoot along the narrow ledge. Elodie needed to hurry to meet the Inophean rescue party, but she also had to slow down so she didn't plummet off the side of the mountain.

With every step, the fragile ledge threatened to crumble beneath her feet. Rocks cascaded down the cliff. Where the tree had come out of the rock face, she had to hop sideways along the skinny, broken ledge to reach the other side.

Elodie held her breath as she put one foot in front of the other, scooting like an injured crab, just inches at a time.

Every so often, she checked over her shoulder on the progress of her father's men. They were still under the shelter of the ridge overhead, shielded from aerial attack. For now.

Elodie kept going, picking her way slowly back toward the dragon's caves. Fog shrouded her view. Gravel and dust from missed handholds battered her face and stung her eyes. She tried not to think too hard about what was at stake, about reuniting with Father. Or what would happen if the dragon intercepted them first.

She was a short distance away from the lip of the chimney in the anthodite cave when she noticed the rescue team down below, unspooling ropes. They'd reached a point where the old lava tube they were following had collapsed, but there appeared to be an opening below, leading into the caves.

Elodie did a quick check of the labyrinth map in her head. The rescue party would be entering the dragon's maze on the southwestern side, a part of the map that wasn't well documented. The lava tube might be the path Victoria and her sisters had taken to enter the caves, but since it wasn't drawn on the maps as a way out, it must have collapsed soon after Victoria's time, like some of the other tunnels Elodie had tried. There was probably nothing of use there in terms of survival, other than steep walls that required ropes to scale.

The Inophean sailors *had* ropes. But as soon as they entered the caves, they would be in the dragon's territory, vulnerable to attack.

She would be, too. But at least she knew the terrain underground. And since the dragon thought she was still stuck in that fissure in the cliff side, it wouldn't be looking for her here. All its attention would be on Father and his men.

I'll be there soon, Father, Elodie thought as she gave them one last look. Then she hurried as fast as she could and descended back into the anthodite cave.

ALEXANDRA

ALEXANDRA LED THE Inopheans down the tunnel, their ropes the only way they could avoid sliding down the slippery chute onto the rocks below. She was a scout and sailor now, but she'd grown up in a family that loved foraging for mushrooms, and the damp, shadowy slopes of Mount Khaevis were the best places to pick. The dragon never threatened the people of Aurea, and in fact, the citizenry never saw the beast. For after the dragon received its annual tributes of princess blood, it retired into the bowels of the mountain for the rest of the year. No one knew what it did down there, but as long as the Aureans didn't bother it, it also left the Aureans alone.

But now, Alexandra breached that long unspoken tradition. Her daughter's fearlessness had been driven by naïveté, but Cora's heart was in the right place. Which, in turn, had led Alexandra to question her own heart—how could she let the princess who'd shown kindness to Cora be fed to a monster? Every year, innocent young women were murdered for the beast. Women like Alexandra could grow older, but the princesses never would.

And so, unbeknownst to her family, Alexandra had offered to

be Lord Bayford's guide in the mountains, should he believe there was a chance Elodie was still alive and wished to attempt to rescue her. Full of regret for giving his daughter to the Aureans, he'd accepted immediately.

Which was how Alexandra ended up here, guiding half a dozen Inophean sailors down a lugelike tunnel into the depths of the dragon's lair. What she was doing was reckless, for if they succeeded in extracting Elodie, the dragon would be very, very angry. But Alexandra could no longer sit idly by, not when her own daughter had been brave enough to speak up, to try to do *something* rather than squeeze her eyes shut at the injustice and pretend it wasn't happening.

The men secured their ropes and slid down, one by one. The tunnel ran vertically, its sides slick and smooth. The only interruptions to the glassy stone were patches of yellow mushrooms. This had been one of Alexandra's mother's favorite harvesting spots. Alexandra still remembered the first time she'd been allowed in a harness and lowered down into the tunnel to pick the feathery lemon-cap mushrooms. She'd been nine years old, Cora's age.

Lord Bayford was the last down the ropes. When he reached the bottom, he tugged several times to indicate to Alexandra that he'd landed safely.

This was as far as Alexandra went, though. Her strength was in navigating these winding mountain paths, not in rescue missions and fighting dragons. She would wait here at the top of the ropes for the Inopheans to retrieve Princess Elodie. If they did not return by sundown—or if she was ever in danger herself—she was to flee. That was the only condition Lord Bayford imposed on letting her guide them. He said he couldn't be the reason another family was torn apart, after he had ripped asunder his own.

"Godspeed," Alexandra said quietly down the tunnel, knowing her words would carry enough to reach them.

Then she settled under an overhang of rock to pray for their safe return, and to pray forgiveness from the Aurean people, for whatever her actions here might bring upon them.

ELODIE

ELODIE SCALED DOWN the anthodite cave walls as carefully as possible, her torn-up hands and weak ankle and general exhaustion threatening to give way and hurl her noisily to her death below, either by the violence of impact from the fall or by notifying the dragon of her return. She had to use another scrap of her dress to wrap around her hands and feet as protection against the sharp flowers, and the pain of the petals even through the fabric almost caused her to lose her grip at least half a dozen times. When she finally dropped down to the cave floor, her fingers and the soles of her feet cramped into stiff, useless claws, and the cloth wrapped around them was stained with blood.

She wished she had some glowworms with her, but in her rush to follow the swallow to the anthodite cave the first time, she hadn't brought any. So she'd have to make sure her wounds were clotted and wouldn't reopen before she could move on. If she was bleeding, she would be an olfactory beacon to the dragon. Elodie pressed the fabric to the myriad tiny cuts, dabbing away extra blood and encouraging her skin to hurry in sealing the wounds.

It took much longer than she would have liked. But only when she was sure she was no longer bleeding did she begin to make her way toward Father and his men. It would do no one any good if she led the dragon straight to them.

If the dragon hadn't already found them.

Elodie hurried through the swallows' music cave and back into the labyrinth. She'd committed to memory the twists and turns from here to the Safe Cave, but she had never taken the paths to the tunnels where Father had entered. Thank the heavens for all the years of solving and creating mazes for Floria.

She took several turns that ended in collapsed passageways, but she could envision the Safe Cave map in her head, and she knew how to backtrack through a maze to find alternate routes. Soon, Elodie was deep inside the labyrinth again and close enough to hear Father's men. As far as she could tell, she was crawling in a series of low-ceilinged tunnels that passed above the caves they were in. Every so often, there were small holes in the porous lava rock that allowed her to look down into the chambers below. She couldn't see them yet, though, so she must still be a short distance away.

The sailors spoke too loudly, their voices reverberating through the maze like bright red flags for the dragon.

Hush, you fools! Elodie wanted to scream at them. But of course she couldn't, lest she alert the beast to her own location, as well.

"What is this?" one of the sailors asked. His voice was brusque; she recognized the accent as belonging to Anto, the strongest of the *Deomelas* crew.

"Looks like a melted shield and helmet," another answered, the tremble in his voice palpable even from where Elodie was, several chambers away. It sounded like Gaumiot, Elodie's favorite sailor. "We're not the first men to come down here. Perhaps they were hunting the dragon."

"What sort of imbecile would do such a thing?" Anto asked.

"There are legends about dragon's blood," said Jordú, whose voice was deeper than the others'.

"Will it turn my lizard into a beast?" Gaumiot guffawed, the bawdy joke tamping down on his nerves.

"Mythological nonsense," Father said. "And keep your voices down. We don't want the dragon to know we're here."

Both Elodie and the Inopheans made progress. Soon she reached the tunnel above them, and she could see them through several pinprick holes in the rock. The sailors had awkwardly donned armor; they were accustomed to loose clothing that allowed them movement aboard a ship. Now they were stiff in chain mail and metal plates. Where had they gotten the armor? Had they pilfered it from Aurean knights?

But before Elodie could whisper to her father, she heard the worst possible noise: leather scraping against rock.

"DEV ADERRUT?"

Oh god. The dragon!

It lunged into the sailors' cave so rapidly its movement was a blur of dark scales and a trail of flame. It snatched Gaumiot before he could even scream. Metal screeched as Gaumiot's armor was torn apart, accompanied by the sickening sound of flesh ripping and bone breaking, wet and soft and hard and rigid at the same time.

Elodie jerked back into the far wall of her overhead tunnel in horror. Gaumiot had spent hours regaling Floria with tales of his adventures on the waters. He'd tended to Lady Bayford during her early bouts of seasickness.

And now he was gone.

"Run, Lieutenant Ravella!" Father shouted toward the cave from which they'd come.

The royal envoy had led them here?

But there was no time for Elodie to dwell on that fact. Below her, Lord Bayford and the other five sailors drew their swords. They were a half dozen humans against a ferocious, ancient monster that had survived much worse than this small expedition. Elodie wanted to draw her knees to her chest and bury her face and stuff her ears full of wax until it was over.

But she couldn't tear her eyes away from her father. The sailors protected him, pushing him behind them as they let out a wild battle cry and charged, slashing at different parts of the dragon. One went for its right wing. Another for its chest. One to its tail, and another, Anto, directly at its head.

He was the next to die. The dragon spewed a jet of fire as Anto raised his sword. The blade melted instantaneously onto his charring skin, and he shrieked as his red-hot armor fused onto his torso and legs, all while flames devoured his hair and face.

No! Oh god, Anto . . .

The dragon's tail whipped against the sailors closest to it, flinging them into the cave wall. Their armor hit with the awful clang of steel on stone, and their bodies crumpled as they fell to the ground.

"This is for Elodie!" the sailor at the dragon's chest cried. He raised his sword to run through the beast's heart. But the dragon swung its head down, mouth open, fangs bared. It crunched through the sailor's bones as if they were mere twigs. Then it spat him out, its reptilian tongue flickering, as if it could not bear the taste of anything but royal blood.

Elodie heaved, only barely holding back her vomit.

Father brandished his sword and took a tentative step forward.

No, stay back! Elodie wanted to cry out. But she dared not draw the dragon's attention to where she hid.

In all the commotion, Jordú, the last sailor, had somehow managed to scramble up onto the dragon's back. He stabbed at it, and the dragon cried out as dark violet blood began to seep from the wound. Jordú flung himself flat against its spine and began to lap at the blood as if it were the fountain of youth.

"Ignoramus!" The dragon snarled. It bucked its reptilian body, and Jordú bounced into the air. The dragon shifted so that the top of one of its serrated wings was waiting to catch him.

The wing impaled Jordú, its sharp point piercing straight through the back of his skull and out through the mouth that had so greedily drunk the dragon's blood only seconds ago. It shook him off its back, the body smacking into the cave floor like a rag doll.

Elodie could only stare, numb with shock at the carnage.

And Father was the only one left.

The dragon readied to strike. But then it stopped midpounce, already arced above him, and sniffed.

"Erru nilas. Dakh novsif. Nykovenirra zi veru manirru se fe nyta."

"Wh-what did you say?" Father stood immobile in his shock that the dragon could speak.

"She's of your blood. How fascinating. I've never met the kind of monster who would sell his own young."

"I—I had good reason!" Father's sword arm dropped as he tried to explain. "It was for my people. I thought . . ."

Anger and dismay curdled Elodie's stomach. She bit back tears and began to back slowly out of her tunnel.

"Dakarr re. Audirru onne vokha dikorrai. Tell her. She hears every word you speak."

"She's near?"

"I can smell her. Watching us. Watching *you.*"

Elodie froze. Fear dribbled down her spine like a snail's trail. "She's still alive?" Father cried. "Elodie? Elodie!"

She didn't respond. How could he have done this to her? Why was he even here?

"Elly, my love, I didn't know! They offered a fortune, enough to save our people a hundred times over. And I thought the dragon was only a legend, a . . . a metaphor! Aurea is shrouded in secrecy. I did not know until the ceremony that the dragon was real, I swear!"

Elodie squeezed her eyes closed and didn't wipe away the tear that escaped. Deep down, she'd always known her father was a bit of a fool, but she'd willfully ignored it, as one does for those they love best.

It had always been her mother, and then Elodie herself, who had to deal with Father's bad decisions. That's why her mother always rode out with him to visit the tenants; it was to fix any problems or mix-ups he'd caused. Elodie remembered how Father chatted jovially with husbands, bringing them smiles and lots of words and reassuring pats on the back. But it was Mother who led the wives into the kitchens where they actually resolved the real issues the families faced: weevils spoiling the flour, coyotes eating the chickens, too many mouths to feed and never enough food or water. Elodie's mother, who knew every soul in the duchy and what resources they possessed, would thoughtfully arrange for a barter of mending the neighbor's clothes for fertilized eggs, or suggest that the youngest two children volunteer at a different tenant's mill in exchange for grain.

After her mother died, Elodie took on that role. But she'd simply picked up where her mother left off, deliberately not questioning why Father wasn't the one doing the work. It was just the way the work was divided—he was the one who could talk a fish into a tree, and she was the one who would physically coax it out to save its life.

But that had come back to haunt her now. Father might not have sold her to Prince Henry maliciously, but he hadn't thought it through.

"*Dakarr re kuirre.* Tell her to come out."

"Wherever you are, Elodie, don't give up."

"*DAKARR RE KUIRRE!*" The dragon snatched Father from the ground. He stabbed at it, jabbing up under a scale, and the dragon roared and shook him. His sword, tipped in violet blood, fell with a clatter to the ground.

Elodie clapped her hand over her mouth to stop from making a sound. She was furious at him. Beyond furious. But she didn't want him hurt. She would never, ever want that.

With the dragon holding her father aloft, his face was close to the small holes in the tunnel where she was watching him from above. His red-rimmed eyes met hers.

Forgive me? they seemed to ask, glazed with tears.

She didn't move for a moment.

Then she nodded. He may have been a foolish man, but he'd loved her as best he could. And she loved him, too, despite his flaws. It was his fault she was in these caves, desperately fighting for her life.

But now he was facing his own death, and she would not send him to his end without her love. She blew him a sad kiss, weighted with everything she could not say.

"The ship is still in the harbor, waiting for you!" Father shouted, making sure to yell downward, rather than up where she actually was. "Elodie, if you can hear me, run! There is another way in and out of these caves, we left ropes for you—"

"NY!" the dragon roared, filling the cave with smoke and flame.

Father! she screamed inside.

But on the outside, she was silent. He'd come into the dragon's lair to rescue her, and she would not let his death mean nothing.

He shrieked as the dragon roasted him alive. The sharpness of his terror and pain pierced like a blade through Elodie's heart, reverberating through her bones. She collapsed onto the tunnel floor, face and hands pressed to the pinprick holes through which she could see nothing but fire and smoke.

But the rock heated like magma and she jerked back, gasping at the burns already blistering on her skin. She couldn't stay here. Father had sacrificed himself for her. She had to escape, and she had to go now.

I love you, Father.

Tears streaked down Elodie's cheeks as she crawled as fast as she could on raw hands and knees through the tunnel toward where Father and the sailors had entered the caves.

It wasn't far before her tunnel opened up taller, then ended abruptly, intersecting the long vertical chute down which the Inopheans had come. The ropes were still dangling there, and the familiarity of the rope—she'd climbed one aboard the ship only days before—gave Elodie the swell of confidence she needed.

She leapt across the chute and grabbed at the rope. Her feet slipped on the smooth, wet surface of the rock, but her fingers wrapped around the rough fibers of the rope and latched on, jerking her shoulders in their sockets but thankfully not out again.

It would have been easier if someone above could haul her up. But if that had ever been the plan, Elodie was alone now, since Father had yelled for Lieutenant Ravella to flee. Elodie had to climb using pure arm strength, since the walls of the chute were too slick to find purchase with her feet.

One torn-up hand over the other, then again and again. Never had she been so glad for all the time in her youth climbing trees.

"Kho zedrae!"

The dragon shot in from the other caves into the chamber below her. "Your father has vexed me, and my patience wears thin!" A thick cloud of sulfuric yellow smoke bloomed up the chute.

It burned Elodie's eyes and throat. She coughed, the caustic gas filling her lungs, sharp like thousands of needles with every breath she wheezed.

But she would not quit. Not now. She could see the waning daylight above her. Hand over hand, hand over hand—

The dragon growled. Unable to squeeze up into the narrow shaft after her, it shot flames and its sticky, flammable brown residue onto the rope, lighting it all on fire.

Like a fuse, the flame consumed the rough fibers and raced up toward Elodie. She had only seconds before it reached her, before she wouldn't be able to hold on, before she'd let go and fall into the waiting jaws of the dragon.

Who will save you? the peasant girl had asked.

"I will save myself!" Elodie cried.

She hauled herself the last two yards, faster than she'd ever climbed before. Just as the flames reached her section of rope, she lunged for the rock at the top of the chute. One of her hands slipped, and she screamed.

But her other fingers clenched around the ledge. She swung her first hand back up and clamped on to the lip of rock. She pulled herself up with the last of the strength in her shaking arms.

The flames devoured the remnant of the rope, and it plum-

meted down the dark chute. Perched above, Elodie watched as
the rope traced a fiery path down what would have been her fate
had she been a heartbeat slower.

"*Kuirra kir ni, zedrae. Nykrerr errai sarif.*"

I am coming for you, princess. Do not think you are safe.

ELODIE

LODIE RAN TOWARD the horses her father and the sailors had left tethered to the pine trees. Her gait was uneven, her sprained ankle awkward, and all her muscles on the edge of complete collapse. The dragon couldn't come up the narrow chute, but it wouldn't take long for it to exit the caves a different way. Elodie had only moments to decide which horse would serve her best; she untied the smallest one, a piebald mare, and clambered onto its saddle.

She had to get to the harbor. Unlike when she was underground, the path was clearer here—down the switchbacks of Mount Khaevis, past the palace in all its ill-gotten gold glory, then through the orchards and fields of aurum wheat and barley toward the briny smell of the sea. But just because the way was clear did not mean it would be easy.

There would be Aurean knights near the palace. And a dragon in pursuit. She would have to set sail immediately and hope the fog would keep them shrouded from the dragon as they raced out to sea.

The odds were emphatically against her.

But she had to try.

"Hya!" Elodie nudged the horse with her heel, and it took off down the mountain. The sun had dipped below the horizon now, and she shivered in her thin, torn dress. Banks of fog spilled over the summit like the froth of a rabid beast, and wolves howled too close for Elodie's liking.

Suddenly, the purpling sky darkened as a silhouette blocked the rising moon. Then just as quickly, hot orange and blue blazed above, casting a fiery glow on Mount Khaevis. The dragon roared, its anger carried by flames.

"KHO ZEDRAE!"

Elodie yanked the horse off the trail and into the woods. They wove through gnarled old trees and through the craggy terrain. She ducked beneath pines and spruces, sending pine cones scattering across the rocks. They leapt over boulders and creeks and thick shrubs of spiny gorse. They sent small avalanches of gravel careening off the mountainside as they changed direction again and again.

But no matter how deep into the mountain Elodie rode, the dragon's wings only beat louder, closer.

The horse's hooves are too loud, she realized. Elodie tugged on the reins and brought the horse to an abrupt stop. "Thank you for your help," she said. "But I have to continue on my own now."

She slid off the saddle, then smacked the horse on the rump. It turned and ran back up the mountain, galloping to rejoin its brethren tied by the cave entrance.

Elodie shoved her way through tangles of thorns. The shrubs grew thick and nearly to the height of some trees, creating a needle-sharp warren in which she could hide. *From one labyrinth to another.*

She wriggled her way deeper and deeper into the thorns.

Their chartreuse flowers gave off a scent like mothballs and mildewed socks, which made Elodie light-headed and nauseous. But perhaps it would also provide cover from the dragon. She hoped it wouldn't be able to sniff out her blood over the pungent stench of the bushes.

"*Akrerra audirrai kho,* Elodie. *Kuirr* or else you will be to blame for what comes next."

I know you can hear me, she translated to herself as she cowered, unmoving, in the thorns. *Come out, or else you'll be to blame for what comes next.*

Elodie shuddered.

The dragon's shadow covered the portion of the woods where she hid, and the beating of its wings sounded as if thunder were crashing directly above her. More fire streaked across the sky, painting dusk in violent streaks of yellow and red.

It roared again, and this time, it launched flames at the copse of trees where Elodie had dismounted her horse, just north of her thorny shelter. The heat of the fire hit like a sonic wave, engulfing the chill of the fog in a single, decisive blow. The force of it shoved Elodie into the thorns, her skin pierced in a dozen different places. If the dragon couldn't smell her blood before, it would be able to soon, now that her blood flowed freely.

Farther up the mountain, a horse whinnied.

"*Zedrae!*" The dragon whirled in the sky and dove down toward the sound of the horse.

It thinks I'm up there, near the horse! For a moment, she was relieved. But then she feared for the horse. *Please don't hurt it,* she prayed as she scrambled out of the bushes.

In her rush, the thorns left long gashes everywhere skin was exposed, and she half limped, half sprinted away from the encroaching flames. With the dragon's attention elsewhere, she ran back to the dirt road and crossed to the other side, putting as much space as possible between herself and the last place she'd hidden.

Here, there were no hedges of thorn bushes. In fact, there was hardly any vegetation at all. But there was a veritable battlefield of downed trees, their trunks charred to black from ancient lightning strikes—or perhaps dragon attacks—and Elodie hoped they were too far burned to catch fire again. She ducked into the clusters of fallen trunks, got down on her hands and knees, and crawled into an overhang of scorched wood. There she crumbled bits of burned bark into ash and smeared it all over her skin to disguise the smell of her blood. She winced as the ash touched her wounds, but infection was the least of her worries today.

A short distance away, the dragon bellowed, likely having discovered that the horse was a riderless decoy. It doubled back, down the mountain to where Elodie had been. Its wings pounded a rhythm in the sky, shaking Mount Khaevis and reverberating through the rocks and into Elodie's bones.

She curled herself into a ball and squeezed her eyes shut. Any second now, the dragon would rain fire down upon her, and she would end up just like these dead trees under which she hid.

It swooped above her, whipping the wind like a hurricane. Twigs and small rocks flew everywhere, pelting her body like scattershot. Branches tore off trees. Several of the charred trunks lifted off the ground and slammed into the mountainside, splintering themselves into shrapnel.

But then the dragon shot past Elodie's hideout of dead trees, down the mountain and toward the palace, spitting sparks as it screamed, "*Vorra kho tke raz. Vorra kho tke trivi. Vis kir vis, sanae kir res!*"

Elodie's eyes widened as she peeked out of her charred shelter of trees.

"I want my share of the bargain. I want my share of the harvest. Life for life, blood for fire!"

The dragon was charging toward the castle, and beyond that lay the farms and villages. Elodie burst from her hiding place.

"Oh god, what have I unleashed?"

FLORIA

FLORIA LOOKED ON sadly as the footman hoisted her packed trunk onto the top of the carriage. "Must we leave so soon?" she asked no one in particular.

Lady Bayford, who had been standing nearby—supervising every inch the servants moved their belongings—answered as if the question had been directed to her. "The wedding is over. Your father is concluding his business with Aurea as we speak. There is nothing left here for us."

But Floria begged to differ. The golden palace was a fairy tale come to life. She'd danced with an earl and a count, and eaten delicacies she could only dream about: sweet dates stuffed with peppery Aurean sheep's milk cheese, roasted pheasant with sangberry jam, whole mountain carp baked in parchment, and miniature silver pear tarts in cages of filigreed sugar. Not to mention the wedding cake inspired by Elodie's wedding gown. The last thing Floria wanted to do was leave the magic of this kingdom behind and return to dry, dull Inophe.

"I wish we could stay here forever," Floria said.

"No, you don't," Lady Bayford snapped.

Floria glared. "Why have you been so awful during this trip? I know you don't like being away from the world you know, but couldn't you have relaxed, just for a week, and let Elodie enjoy her wedding? And let *me* enjoy being in this castle? I don't *want* to go home to our hard, boring life!"

But Floria's chest suddenly ached like a blunt knife was twisting in her heart. Despite how incredible Aurea was, the real reason she didn't want to leave was that Elodie wasn't coming back with them. She was a princess henceforward, and while Floria would always be her sister, Elodie's family was Prince Henry, Queen Isabelle, and King Rodrick now.

And the moment Floria stepped foot on *Deomelas* and Captain Croat set sail, the goodbye would be real. Even though she hadn't seen Elodie since early on in the wedding reception, Floria could still pretend that Elodie would come into her room at any moment, that Floria could help her sister brush her hair before bed, that they could sneak out together onto the battlements to look at the stars or the beautiful torchlight on the mountainside.

"Why can't Father arrange for me to marry that earl I danced with last night?" Floria said. "He was only a few years older than I."

"Don't be ridiculous," Lady Bayford said. "You are still a child."

"I am not! I started my monthlies."

"And yet you don't have the sense not to speak of such private matters in front of others." Her stepmother gave an emphatic sideways glance at the footmen who were securing the trunks onto the carriage. "Besides, I am not allowing another of my daughters to live in a place like this—"

"Daughter?" Floria cried. "You are not my mother!"

Lady Bayford stood with her mouth hanging open, for once without a ready retort or complaint.

Floria almost felt bad. Almost.

She was feeling too much right now, and perhaps it was wrong to direct the outpouring of emotion at Lady Bayford, but she was the only one present to receive it.

"My mother would have been happy for Elodie marrying Henry. But you . . . You pointed out every tiny, imagined flaw and tried to convince her to call off the marriage, and when she didn't, you feigned a headache and left! No real mother would leave her daughter's wedding reception. No real mother would—"

A booming roar and explosion of flames filled the sky. *"Vorra kho tke raz. Vorra kho tke trivi. Vis kir vis, sanae kir res!"* The deep, inhuman voice sounded like smoke and firestorms and avalanches combined.

Lady Bayford threw her arms around Floria, curving over her to protect her.

"What's happening?" Floria screamed as she huddled against her stepmother. "What *is* that?"

"It's the dragon," Lady Bayford said, cradling Floria tighter.

"What dragon?"

"The one that Elodie—"

Another shower of fire fell from the sky. "I am *khaevis*. Hear me now! I want my *zedrae* by tomorrow's moon. Or else the bargain is forfeit, and Aurea shall pay!"

It circled the palace, the shadow of its wicked wings and talons sharp on the golden walls. It blew fire and made what ought to be night as bright as day.

Sparks alighted on the Aurean flags on the tops of the towers, and the crimson and gold banners lit ablaze. Another jet of fire chased the guards on the battlements from their posts, the flames catching on their clothes and licking at the fabric trapped inside their armor, burning them as they screamed and hurled themselves against the tiles and castle walls to put out the pain.

"I AM *KHAEVIS!*" the dragon roared even louder. "By tomorrow's moon! Promise!"

"What is it saying?" Floria shouted, tears of terror streaming down her cheeks as she buried her face against Lady Bayford. "What does it mean? What does it have to do with Elodie?"

"Sh-she . . ."

"She what?" Floria looked up, eyes wild. "Tell me, please. She what?"

The flames in the sky reflected in her stepmother's eyes, as if the hells had already consumed them all. "The bargain . . . it was for Elodie's life."

"What?" Floria clutched Lady Bayford's gown, the gray cloth the only thing keeping her upright.

"Aurea is not the utopia it seems," Lady Bayford whispered, her entire body shaking. "They feed their princesses to the beast."

"No . . ." Floria gasped.

Lady Bayford couldn't stop her own tears as she nodded. But then she looked up at the furious dragon and at the carriage loaded with their trunks. "If the monster is here looking for Elodie, though, it means your father succeeded. We must get to the harbor to meet them."

"Them? You mean Father rescued Elodie?"

"It's the only way I can interpret the dragon's wrath . . . But we must go, Floria. We must be on *Deomelas* and away from here before tomorrow's moon, before the dragon unleashes its punishment on all who remain in the kingdom."

ISABELLE

QUEEN ISABELLE WATCHED the sky turn from the lavender gray of gloaming to the orange of dragon's fury. Behind her, King Rodrick sat on the ground behind a leather armchair, arms wrapped around his knees, head buried under a bearskin, rocking back and forth, back and forth, crying softly.

"Shh, Rodrick. It will be all right." She went to his side and kissed him gently through the bearskin. "Whatever is happening, do not fret. Henry and I shall take care of it. I promise."

Henry burst into the chambers. "Mother, have you seen—"

"Yes. What has transpired?"

Henry glanced in the direction of the whimpering. "Father?"

"The noise . . . the dragon . . . it's triggered a bad episode," Isabelle said. "The royal physician is on his way."

Rodrick collapsed into fits of panic whenever the threat of the monster loomed—be it the night before each of Henry's weddings or just waking from nightmares in which Rodrick relived the memories of princesses he had married when he was younger, and the ceremonies tossing them to their doom. He had managed to survive long enough to see the kingdom safe until Isabelle gave birth to their first son, which happened like clockwork nine months after consummation of the marriage, as it always had for the royal family for eight hundred years. But as soon as baby Jacob was born, the mental fortress Rodrick had built collapsed.

Isabelle did not blame Rodrick for his disquiet; the trauma he'd endured could raze even the strongest of kings. But she also knew there was nothing she could do for Rodrick other than give him space to vent his fears, and call upon the doctor to administer a calming elixir.

What she *could* do, however, was reign over the kingdom. It was why she had been in charge of the weddings and harvest ceremonies ever since Jacob was born.

A brief flicker of pain seized her as she thought of that son, who had been betrothed before he could even walk, and married to princesses again and again throughout his childhood, in order to feed the dragon. Jacob, who fled Aurea when he turned fifteen because he could not stand to be a part of their necessary tradition. He'd stowed away on a trading ship, and she had never heard from him again.

Two days ago, she had lamented that her once cherubic Henry had grown hard with the responsibilities of Aurea. But now she understood that it was better that Henry's heart was made of cold iron.

"Tell me what has transpired," she asked him again.

"The fool Bayford attempted to rescue his daughter," Henry said. "As far as my soldiers can tell, he failed, but somehow, Elodie still escaped. I told you that woman was trouble. I knew she'd upend our way of life."

Isabelle swallowed the *I told you so* and pressed on to what truly mattered in the moment. "We need to capture Elodie and redeliver her to the dragon. We cannot risk it taking its anger out on us, or on our people."

Henry nodded curtly. "But how do you propose we catch a princess who has already proven herself wily enough to escape an inescapable dragon?"

The queen pressed her fingers to her temples as she thought. Meanwhile, the royal physician rushed in and headed straight to the corner, where he gave Rodrick an elixir that would soothe his nerves and make his mind a fuzzier, more carefree place. If only Isabelle could go there, too.

But she couldn't. When she married Rodrick, she swore an oath to do everything she could to protect and provide for the people of Aurea. And the entire country depended on her and Henry now.

She kissed her husband's hand as the doctor led him sleepily to his bed.

Then she turned back to her son.

"How does one catch the slipperiest of mountain carp?" Isabelle asked.

"With hand-selected bait, a wide net that can be tightened, and patience," Henry said.

Queen Isabelle pursed her lips but nodded. "Precisely. Then let us find our bait."

ALEXANDRA

ALEXANDRA AND HER horse tore into the courtyard of her farmstead.

Her husband, John, and Cora sprinted out of the cottage at the sound of hooves pounding.

"Mama, you're safe!"

John hurried to help Alexandra from the saddle. "Where have you been? We've been sick with worry!" His gaze alternated between his wife and the orange-dark sky. From the way he stared at her, Alexandra knew she must look as terrified as she felt.

"Are you all right?" Cora quivered. "I—I saw the dragon. It never comes out to where the people live! Why did it fly over the castle and our villages? I was scared but couldn't find you, and Father did not know where you had gone and I thought . . . I— I thought . . ." She burst into sobs.

Alexandra rushed to her and gathered Cora to her bosom. "I'm here, sweet pea. Don't worry, I'm here."

"But where were you?" John asked again.

"Foraging for mushrooms," Alexandra said weakly. "'Tis the season for lemon caps."

"On Mount Khaevis?" he cried. "You were picking mushrooms on Mount Khaevis during the harvest ceremonies, the one week of the year when the dragon is active, and all are forbidden on the mountain, other than the royal family and the knights of Aurea?"

"Yes?"

"Alexandra, what were you thinking?" he said.

But even though John had taken her at face value, Cora knew instinctively where she'd been. Her daughter looked up from their embrace and said, "Mama? Did you save Princess Elodie?"

The hope in Cora's eyes was too much, and Alexandra had to turn away. "I don't know, sweet pea. I don't know what I've done. But grab the bags we packed. It's time to go."

ELODIE

ELODIE STAGGERED ALONG the switchbacks. The dragon had finally disappeared as night settled in, and she picked her way slowly down the mountain.

She didn't know what she was going to do. Father was dead. Floria and Lady Bayford were waiting for her at the harbor. And if Elodie left, the dragon might kill every soul in Aurea in retribution.

"Damn you, Father." She kicked at a stone and sent it skidding down the dirt path. If he hadn't arranged her marriage with Henry, if he hadn't blindly waved off the dragon part of the deal as hyperbole, she wouldn't be here in this impossible situation.

But then tears began to fall as she lurched onward. "Damn you, Father!" He had been a fool, but he was *her* fool. She could still see him in her memory through the pinprick holes of the lava tube. She would never get to hug the daft man again.

Elodie passed a large, flat boulder. It was covered with lichen, and fatigue washed over her.

I'll just sit for a minute, she thought as she lowered herself on shaking legs onto the soft seat. Above her, the pinecones of a tall evergreen dripped water on her, and even though it probably left streaks through the dirt and ash on her face, it was the closest to a bath she'd had in days, and she basked in the feel of the droplets on her skin.

"That's the first thing I'll do when I'm aboard the ship," she said. "A hot bath. I'll ask the cook to heat a cauldron of water, and then we'll pour the steaming water into the copper tub in Lady Bayford's cabin and I'll sink into it, head and all, and scrub away every last bit of ceremonial paint and cave dust and dried blood and dead skin." Elodie sighed. For a brief moment, she allowed herself to believe that she was through the hardest part of this nightmare. She was going to be safe and clean, and she would happily live the rest of her days as a poor spinster on drought-ridden Inophe. She never needed to see another gilded thing again.

A melody of trumpets jarred her from her daydream. Hoof-beats sounded on the switchbacks below.

What in the hells—

The flickering glow of torches appeared like a grim miasma, rising up from the winding path. Elodie watched with growing horror as the light came closer, climbing up the mountainside.

The torches illuminated the dreaded crimson-and-gold banner of Aurea.

Merdú! Elodie jumped off the boulder and ducked behind it.

The horses came swiftly. First the flagbearer, then a string of knights dressed in the embroidered uniform of the Imperial Guard. Next was Queen Isabelle and Henry. And hogtied to his saddle was a slight girl in black braids—

Floria!

Elodie leapt out from behind the boulder as the retinue charged past. Henry's head whipped around as he caught sight of her, and he smiled cruelly. But then he rode on without stopping, and because they were on horseback and she on an injured foot, they were out of sight before she could even begin to run after them.

Where were they taking Flor? And what were they planning to do with her? Anger and fear roiled in Elodie's belly, even more so than when she herself had been thrown to the dragon. This was Floria, her baby sister!

Below, more hoofbeats sounded. Elodie would not let this opportunity gallop by. She spun around, taking in her surroundings as well as the moon would let her see, and seized on a heavy fallen branch, nearly two-thirds her size.

Elodie readied herself. One good wallop and she could unseat the rider, then steal the horse.

The pounding of hooves came closer. From the uneven gait, either the horse was injured, or whoever was riding was not very good at it. Elodie frowned. All knights would ride horses like extensions of their own bodies. So if it wasn't a knight, who could it be? A straggling trumpeter or flagbearer?

At least they would be easier to overpower than a knight. Elodie steadied her branch, bringing it back to swing.

As the horse turned the bend, the moon shone on a familiar silver cape lined with desert fox fur.

Elodie dropped the branch. "Lucinda?"

Lady Bayford startled and jerked on the reins, sending the horse into temporary confusion. "Who goes there?" She fumbled under her cloak and produced a dagger, clumsily wielded. Elodie could have disarmed her with a simple tap of the tree branch.

"It's me, Elodie," she said, approaching slowly with hands raised.

"Elodie?" Her stepmother squinted. "You look . . ."

"Terrible?" Elodie said.

Lady Bayford had never been good at compliments, so she just nodded.

But this was no time for pointing out her stepmother's flaws. In fact, Lady Bayford was the one person Elodie wanted to see right now.

"Your father, he—"

"My father is dead," Elodie said gently.

Lady Bayford's face crumpled and her body went slack. Elodie caught her as she slid out of the saddle.

Her stepmother clung to Elodie, and it was the most comforting feeling Elodie had felt in days, for Lady Bayford smelled of fussy citrus soap and stiffly starched gray wool, things Elodie had once loathed and now held tight for their familiarity, their sense of security and home.

"I'm sorry," Elodie said. "Father died bravely. I spoke to him before . . . the end. He said to tell you he loved you." He hadn't actually said that, but it was a kindness to say so now. Lady Bayford's breath hitched, but then she nodded bravely into Elodie's shoulder before pulling herself back.

"Floria . . ." Lady Bayford said.

"I saw her. She was tied on to Henry's saddle. Where are they taking her?"

"To the caves, in your place."

Elodie's stomach plummeted to the bottom of the gorge. "But she's not an Aurean princess. That's not what the dragon wants."

"Henry would have forced Floria to marry him if he could, but since you're still alive, he technically already has a wife. So they are using Floria to buy some time while they . . ."

"While they what?"

Lady Bayford took a shuddering breath before she continued. "While they hunt you to give you back to the dragon. And then . . ." She glanced over her shoulder back at the palace below. "Tomorrow there will be another wedding. A woman and her family just arrived today. She is supposed to be the third princess." Lady Bayford winced and clutched her side.

"You're injured!" Elodie lifted her stepmother's cloak to reveal blood soaking through the fabric.

"I tried to stop them from taking Floria. We were going to the harbor—your father gave us instructions to wait there—but then Henry and his knights came and abducted Floria." Lady Bayford reached for her horse. "I have to go. You go to the ship, be safe. I have to save my other daughter."

She said the word "daughter" so simply, without any guile, and Elodie suddenly wondered whether she'd had Lady Bayford wrong all these years. Unable to have children of her own, had Lady Bayford always loved Elodie and Floria, first as their governess, then later, as their stepmother? Lady Bayford complained and fretted constantly, but perhaps that was how she showed she cared. She was a mother hen clucking over each member of her brood, paying attention to every little detail in an attempt to improve it and give her family the best life she could.

But Elodie had never given her a chance to live up to Elodie's idealized version of her mother.

Yet, right here, risking her life, Lady Bayford was trying again.

Elodie softened. "You're injured, Lady Bayford. I'll go."

"You've been through too much. And I owe this to you."

Elodie shook her head. "No . . . You've been a good mother to us, even when we were not generous in our assessment of you. You owe us nothing. I could never forgive myself if I lost Father, Floria, and you on the same night. I need to do this."

Lady Bayford gasped. "Oh, heavens above! I understand their plan now. Floria is the cheese, Elodie. They are counting on you to come after her like a mouse, to lure you back into the dragon's lair. They don't have to hunt you down, because *you* will go to *them*. They'll trap you and then the dragon will kill you, and I can't let you—"

"You can and you will," Elodie said, taking Lady Bayford's hand and squeezing it gently. "I have the caves memorized. I can do this. But what *you* can do is have the ship ready to set sail. If I take this horse, can you get to the harbor?"

"I can do anything for you and Floria." She took off her beloved cloak and draped it around Elodie. "And I believe in you."

Elodie leaned in and kissed Lady Bayford on the cheek. "Then go. And we will meet you there."

HENRY

Prince Henry cringed at the wriggling, squealing mass in the saddle before him. Elodie may have been frightened when they brought her to Mount Khaevis two nights ago, but she was at least dignified in her fear. Her younger sister, however, had no such poise. Floria writhed and shrieked and kept shifting the balance on the saddle, creating a great deal more work for Henry to control the horse.

"Settle down," he snapped as Floria bucked while he navigated them up a hairpin turn on the switchback.

"I will *not* settle down!" she screeched. "Let me go you awful, repulsive ogre!"

"I cannot and shall not do any such thing and you know it," Henry said. "Besides, if anyone is to blame, it is your sister."

"How dare you put the blame on Elodie!" Floria tried to kick him, which was a futile effort, given that her ankles were bound and hanging off one side of the saddle. She only managed a weak sideswipe of the air.

"As princess, Elodie swore to protect Aurea," Henry said.

"The harvest ceremony is a regrettable but necessary part of those duties."

"Regrettable? You call feeding innocent women to a dragon *regrettable?*" Floria unleashed a stream of insults Henry didn't think a thirteen-year-old, let alone a relatively highborn one, would be capable of.

This is why I could not choose Elodie as the princess I kept, he thought. The Bayford women were too spirited. No doubt that Elodie, had she become the future queen, would have tried to put a stop to the harvest ceremonies.

And to what end? Henry wasn't lying when he told Floria that the sacrifices were a necessity. If there were a better solution, one of his ancestors would have figured it out in the past eight hundred years. But the kingdom's unworkable dilemma remained what it was.

Henry also understood that the only way for him to one day rule Aurea—and continue its peace and prosperity—was to maintain an icy disregard for the lives of the women he sacrificed. If he let himself even think of them as people, he might falter in his duty. One need only look at his father, ostensibly the king but in reality, a broken, sniveling mess who could barely hold himself together long enough to crown each new princess before he collapsed into his own mind. And then there was Henry's brother, Jacob, who had listened too closely to King Rodrick's regrets. It had made Jacob weak, and because of that, he'd slipped away from Aurea a coward, stowing away on a trade ship like a common rat rather than royalty.

But Henry was iron-willed like his mother. Queen Isabelle also understood that although the Aurean tradition was cruel, it was inescapable. Good leaders shouldered distasteful burdens in order to provide for their kingdom. Henry had been "marrying"—and thereby creating—princesses since he was five years old, when Jacob left. The annual harvest ceremonies were thus as much a part of Henry's life as sangberries and aurum wheat.

"You may not believe me," Henry said to Floria, "but if there were any other way, we would take it. But there isn't. The dragon demands three sacrifices of royal blood every year or else it will destroy this entire kingdom. There is no compromise. Would you let Elodie bear the guilt of tens of thousands of lives lost, because she was too selfish to give hers in exchange?"

Floria stilled. Henry rode with his back straighter, feeling vindicated at having given her pause.

In front of him, the retinue of knights and his mother slowed their horses' pace. They were approaching the gorge.

It was eerie being here without the usual gathering of masked, hooded men and their spear torches. The solemn ceremony lent an air of sanctity to the sacrifices. Being at the edge of the gorge with only a handful of others felt almost as if they were sneaking around and committing a crime.

Queen Isabelle dismounted her mare. "Bring the girl."

The knights hurried to follow orders, untying Floria from Henry's saddle. Floria immediately resumed punching and kicking. Henry was certain she would have tried biting if the guards weren't all clad in chain mail beneath their velvet tunics.

He grabbed her and twisted her arm behind her. Floria screamed.

"You can go with dignity," he said. "Or I can haul you onto that bridge and toss you in, like I did to your sister."

Floria's eyes bulged. "You didn't."

"I did. And I shan't hesitate to do the same to you."

She turned to Queen Isabelle. "Please, Your Majesty. Don't do this."

The queen would not meet Floria's gaze. "I wish there were another way, child." Then she waved her hand at Henry to get on with it.

"Are you going to walk onto the bridge of your own accord?" Henry asked Floria. "Or must I carry you like a hog on slaughter day?"

Floria thrashed against him, although she could not fight much, since he still had her arm twisted. "Let go of me, you brute!"

"Very well, a hog on slaughter day it is," he said, hoisting the slight girl over his shoulder. A nauseating swell of déjà vu blossomed in his stomach, but he quelled it by freezing out the memory of doing this same thing to Elodie and dozens before her.

What is one more life, if we can preserve thousands? he reminded himself. Other kings did far worse, fighting wars and sending millions to their deaths in order to keep their countries safe. Aurea accomplished the same goal with only three deaths a year. This harvest would require four—Floria as bait to lure Elodie back—but it was still insignificant compared to the cost of failure.

He marched down the stone bridge, into the cold wall of fog. Floria pummeled her fists against his back and kneed his chest, but her blows were nothing against his armor but a dull clang of metal.

When he reached the lowest point on the bridge, though, he paused. Perhaps it was because Floria was so young. Perhaps it was because, unlike the women he married, she hadn't gotten to enjoy a wedding day full of bliss, the one gift Aurea could give the princesses before they took the women's lives.

"Make a wish," he said to Floria in an attempt to do her at

least one small honor. "If it is within my power to grant it, I promise you, I shall."

"I wish for Elodie to live. And I hope the dragon torches you and your entire family," Floria snarled.

Henry shuddered. Then he took a breath to steel himself and threw her into the abyss.

ELODIE

LODIE AND HER horse hid in a copse of trees as Prince Henry and Queen Isabelle's cortege rode by, back down the mountain. They no longer had Floria with them. As soon as they passed and were far enough not to hear the hooves of Elodie's horse, she raced up the way they'd come.

She stopped only for a minute at the top of the chute that Father and his knights had originally descended. Elodie thought about going back into the caves that way. But if she wanted to find Floria, the best place to start would be the gorge, the most likely spot where Henry and Isabelle would throw her sister in. Elodie flinched at the image of poor, innocent Floria hurled to the dragon. Elodie would have taken her place a thousand times if she could have.

But what was done was done, and Elodie had to find a way to solve it.

She was about to climb back onto her horse when a coil of rope caught her eye. It must have been one of the spares for her father's sailors, because it had already been secured to a nearby tree but remained unused. Elodie grabbed it and threw it down the chute, letting it unspool. This rope would serve as her backup plan. She didn't know where Floria would be in the labyrinth, but Elodie did know that any maze was easier to solve if there were multiple exits. That's how she used to design the beginner mazes for Floria, when Flor was very little. More than one way out meant more ways to succeed.

Elodie checked once more that the rope was secured. Then she jumped back onto her horse and galloped to the gorge where this had all begun.

Without the torches of the sacrificial ceremony, the stone bridge was nearly invisible in the thick fog. But Elodie would know where it was even without moonlight. Partially because she'd had memory-enhancing Aurean beer coursing through her veins on the night of the ceremony. But mostly because one never forgets the moment when her husband throws her into a dragon's lair.

"Hold on, Flor! I'm coming!"

The quickest path was straight down. Elodie could scale the walls. Or she could jump.

The latter option was risky. But her arms and legs were exhausted from all the climbing she'd already done, and if she fell from the sides of the gorge while attempting to climb, she'd likely slam off the rock faces and break bones. Or die.

And unlike the last time, when Henry had thrown her off the bridge like jetsam tossed overboard at sea, Elodie knew what lay at the bottom of this gorge: a thick trampoline of spongy moss. If she jumped and curled up into a tight ball, she might be able to land without much impact.

Elodie leapt off the bridge.

She brought her knees into her chest and tucked her head. Her arms wrapped around her legs, making her as compact as possible. Her stomach somersaulted as she careened down, down, down in freefall.

And then she hit moss. The first bounce was violent, all her organs rattling in the cage of her bones. But the second and third bounces were softer, until Elodie rolled to a stop on the bed of moss.

She unfurled quickly, rising to her feet in a defensive posture. Elodie surveyed her surroundings, confirming it was as she remembered. One tunnel to the right, which led to the original swallows' cave. Another, shorter passageway on the left, which led to the chamber where Elodie had been herded, and where the blond princess before her had met her end.

But there must be another way to the Safe Cave, for it was unlikely that all those princesses—whose names were carved into the wall—had taken the route Elodie had, through that impossibly narrow fissure, twisting and turning sideways until it spit her out into the glowworms' colony.

With no sign of the dragon, Elodie had time to examine the rest of the walls of the gorge. While she did so, she picked up the whalebone corset she'd discarded two days ago and fashioned it into a proper splint for her ankle.

Elodie noticed again the V carved into the wall. It was above a small alcove about a yard off the ground. She had been too panicked—and chased by a dragon—to see the path during the previous times she'd been here.

THIS WAY.

~V

"I hate you, but I'm also glad for you," Elodie muttered.

She hauled herself up the short distance into the alcove. It was a tunnel about five feet high, and from the looks of its direction, it would lead to the Safe Cave.

But Elodie didn't follow it immediately. Instead, she stayed put, listening for Floria. She could be anywhere in this labyrinth, but if Elodie could hear her, perhaps she'd be able to discern a general direction.

But there was only a sinister silence. No sound of Floria. No unearthly muttering from the dragon. Only the distant *plink plink plink* of water dripping off stalactites.

Please let Flor be all right . . .

She's fine, Elodie tried to convince herself. Floria was sent down here as a lure to bring Elodie to the dragon. Floria was not the sacrifice.

Would that stop the dragon from eating her, though? Or killing her as it had Father and the sailors—

Elodie clenched her fists to squeeze out the memories of her father's last moments.

Flor is fine, she reiterated to calm herself. Elodie forced her brain to look at the situation logically.

The dragon had proved itself to be a patient, calculating beast. The sailors had meant nothing to it, but Floria was more valuable.

If the dragon wanted princess blood, it would wait for Elodie to come.

Yes, that makes sense, Elodie thought. She ran through her logic twice more to make sure it was sound and not merely wishful thinking. Her conclusions seemed to hold up.

That did not guarantee that Floria was uninjured. And she was certainly scared. But it would be better for Elodie to have a plan. Charging in without one would only get them both killed. That was, unfortunately, what had happened to Father and his men. Elodie needed to slow down and strategize if she was going to save Flor.

I know these caves, Elodie thought. *I know the layout. I know where there are resources I can use. I can do this.*

Frightening, but not impossible, their mother would say.

And I believe in you, Lady Bayford had said.

Elodie nodded, as if both of her mothers were there. And then Elodie plunged into the tunnel toward the Safe Cave.

FLORIA

FLORIA REMEMBERED HITTING the bottom of the gorge and slamming into the moss, her right arm shattering. She remembered the awful sound of scaly leather against rock, and the smoky voice that preceded it, rumbling through the caves asking, "Is that you, *zedrae*?"

She remembered a loud sniff, followed by an angry snarl at the discovery that she wasn't Elodie.

And then the harsh cloud of yellow gas, fumes like sulfur that stung her eyes and pricked like needles in her nose, in her throat, in her lungs. Everything went yellowish-black, and she remembered nothing after that.

She woke on a tall stone platform in the center of a vast quartz cave. The air here was close—humid and too warm. She knew she was inside the mountain, and yet there was light here, a soft blue glow unlike sunlight or moonlight or any other light she'd ever seen.

"Where am I?" Floria tried to prop herself up onto her elbow, then immediately cried out in pain and collapsed. She'd forgotten that she'd broken her right arm when Prince Henry threw her into the gorge. She would never mistake wealth and a hand-some face for chivalry again.

If she had the luxury of a future.

When the stabbing pain in her arm receded to a constant throbbing, Floria pushed herself up to sitting with her good arm. Her body complained even at that and she groaned.

But then her mouth dropped open as she took in the rest of the cave. The blue light she'd noticed before glowed from pockets in the craggy ceilings and reflected off the quartz walls, which were studded with shimmering rubies and diamonds and sapphires. But the gems did not occur naturally; it was as if they had been embedded there, and Floria wondered if jewels were also part of the price Aurea paid to the dragon.

The blue glow also came from recessed parts in the granite walls, and in divots in the ground. Sometimes it seemed as if the source of the light was moving, a pattern of gentle, undulating waves.

What is it?

But she couldn't get closer to see, because she was trapped. Floria lay on a wide, broken stalagmite ten feet high and maybe eight feet in diameter, surrounded by a vast green pond. Essentially, she was stuck on a prison tower in the middle of a moat. The pond connected to a deep subterranean river, although the water remained stagnant, thick with algae and the smell of decay.

Crumbling dragon statues jutted out of the river, made of the same violet-gray granite as the mountain. Some of the statues were fierce with bared fangs. Others glared with jaws open as if spewing fire. The one closest to Floria loomed out of the pond and over her like a reptilian sentinel, all ridged stone but for its yellowing teeth made from the tusks of two dozen elephants. There were a few dragon statues that seemed quiet and wise, but most were primed for battle. What they had in common was they were all ancient, missing ears or teeth or parts of wings.

What really caught Floria's eye besides the gems and blue glow, though, were the gold coins. On the far side of the cave, there was a flat expanse of them, not a pile, as she would have imagined a dragon's hoard (in myths and legends, the dragon's treasure was always found in heaps inside its lair). There must have been thousands of coins, each as big as her palm. Floria shivered; it reminded her of the gold tiles on the floor of the Aurean throne room.

One of the dragon statues stared at her with intense violet eyes. Then it blinked.

Floria screamed.

The statue moved.

Except it wasn't a statue at all, it was alive.

"*Oniserrai su re, kev nyerrai zedrae,*" it rasped.

"Wh-what?"

"You smell like her, except you are not a princess," it said, seemingly annoyed at having to repeat itself, even though she hadn't been able to understand it before.

"I smell like Elodie?" Floria whispered, huddling into as small a form as she could make herself. The dragon was enormous, each dark gray scale like one of the heavy shields carried by knights. Its fangs glowed ominously in the light, and dried blood caked the rim of its mouth. The biting odor of sulfur still clung to its hot breath.

"*Idif sanae. Idif innavo. Thoserra kokarre.*"

Floria didn't know what the dragon had said, but its tongue had flickered, snakelike, and licked at the air. Savored it.

"Are you g-going to eat me?"

"Not yet."

"But you will?"

The dragon only showed its teeth in what might have been an amused smile or a threat, but regardless, the result was the same. Floria wet herself.

Its nostrils flared. Could it smell her shame?

"If you're going to eat me, just do it now. Quickly, please!"

The dragon lunged at Floria. She shrieked, expecting to be impaled by those awful fangs. But instead, it knocked her off the stone platform and into the green pool below.

She flailed in the pond, the temperature disconcertingly hot. She swallowed water and algae before bursting to the surface, gasping for air. Floria had never learned to swim—no Inophean could in that parched land where lakes and rivers were as much legend as dragons—and she thrashed against the river plants plastered on her body, which seemed hellbent on dragging her down to drown.

Smoke plumed from the dragon's nostrils as it watched her, its prey, flounder.

The third time after she went under and then came spluttering up, the dragon asked, "Have you finished washing yourself now?"

Washing! Is that why it had knocked her into the pond? So that when it ate her, it wouldn't have to taste that she'd wet herself?

The dragon opened its jaws, reeking of sulfuric gas and smoke and the iron tang of blood, and Floria squeezed her eyes shut. *Now* this was the end.

But it only snicked the back of her gown with its teeth, as gently as a cat with its own kitten, and lifted her back onto the stone platform unharmed.

Probably to preserve her to get Elodie to come. Floria slumped like a soggy cake in the middle of a platter.

The dragon watched her with its violet eyes, gold slits glinting at their center.

Please save me, Elodie, Floria thought, at the same time thinking, *Stay away, El.*

She wanted both equally, and yet knew in her gut that she could have neither.

ELODIE

ELODIE STUDIED THE map on the Safe Cave wall. There was a large space in the center marked with a skull and crossbones. It was fed by several tunnels.

"I suspect that's the dragon's lair."

If that was right, then the chances were high that was where it was keeping Floria. Elodie had previously explored much of the map and even other parts that weren't documented here. While many of the chambers were small enough to make it difficult for the dragon to maneuver inside, the skull and crossbones cave at the heart of the labyrinth was drawn big enough that it would likely be the most easily defensible spot. The dragon would want to keep its prize—Flor—in a place where it could move and strike with ease. Elodie tapped the center of the map. She would need to devise a plan for how to get there, and how to distract the dragon so it wasn't home when Elodie arrived.

As she thought through different options, she also updated the map with the new information she'd gained since she was last in the Safe Cave, in case it helped future princesses thrown into the gorge. First she drew the path from the top of the anthodite flower cave along the cliff-side ridge, and included a warning: DEAD END.

Then she drew in the chamber where the dragon had murdered Father, the tunnel above it, and the way to the chute that led straight up and outside to a much more manageable part of Mount Khaevis. However, the chute was not scalable without a rope already secured from the top. Elodie stopped to consider how to label it. She decided on a vertical arrow and NEED ROPE.

Probably not helpful, yet it was information, and circumstances *had* allowed Elodie to escape that way once before.

When she was finished, Elodie knew what she was going to do to rescue Floria. At least, she knew how she was going to *get* to Flor, assuming her sister was in the center chamber. Then they'd have to make it to the slippery chute she'd used last time to escape. It was, unfortunately, on the far side of the labyrinth, with plenty of opportunity for the dragon to catch up and torch them. Elodie sent up a small prayer that luck would be on her side once more.

Having light would make it easier to navigate the tunnels. Elodie crawled the short passage to the glowworm colony. "If I survive this, I'm going to find a way to pay homage to you, I swear." She scooped up several handfuls of glowworms and put them into the pockets of Lady Bayford's cloak, creating dim but hands-free lanterns.

When she crawled back to the Safe Cave, she took one more look around to make sure she hadn't forgotten anything crucial. There was the first message from V she'd read. Elodie's own notes on the dragon's language.

And the names of all the princesses who had come before.

She picked up a shard of volcanic glass and carved, bold and deep:

ELODIE & FLORIA

· · ·

ELODIE DID NOT go directly to the dragon's lair. Instead, she snuck through the tunnels that were too small for the monster to follow and returned to the cave where Father had died.

She braced herself for his burned body. But when she stepped inside the cave, there was nothing left to remember him by. The dragon had burned him to ashes.

Elodie choked back a mourning sob. She could not let the dragon hear her. She'd moved as softly as she could to get here, and she was not going to give herself away before she could set her plan in motion and rescue Flor.

An Inophean short sword lay on the stone. Elodie knew it was Inophean because it was plain, unlike the elaborate gold-work of Aurean weapons. The initials R.A.B. were etched into the hilt—Richard Alton Bayford.

Father.

Her knees gave way and she fell to the ground beside his sword.

I am sorry I couldn't save you, she thought.

The truth was, Elodie should never have been in the position of needing to do so. It was only because of her father that she'd been in the caves in the first place.

But he had tried to do the best he could. He'd made a mistake in marrying her to Prince Henry, but he'd paid the ultimate price attempting to fix it.

She swallowed the hard lump in her throat and rubbed away the tears in her eyes. She had to stay on task. If she and Floria got out of here, there would be plenty of time to grieve for Father. And if they didn't, they'd see him soon enough in the heavens.

Elodie picked up the sword. Its tip was covered in dried purple blood.

The dead sailors had also left behind a few things Elodie could use in her plan. There was a longsword, half a melted shield, and a waterskin. She contemplated the armor and chain mail on the knights, but she couldn't stomach removing it from their corpses.

That's all right, what I already have will suffice.

Growing up, Elodie's favorite toys had been the ones she could look inside of to examine how they worked. Some contained complicated watch parts that she enjoyed teasing apart. But the best ones, she'd thought, had straightforward mechanisms that made them run. The elegance of simplicity struck her as not only beautiful, but also wise. The fewer pieces there were, the less likely they were to go wrong.

Which was precisely what she had in mind now. Using a boulder as the fulcrum, Elodie set up a scale of sorts with the knight's longsword as the lever, and the shield fragment hanging on the blade side and the waterskin on the hilt. She used Father's sword to puncture a hole in the waterskin, and it began to slowly drip

Elodie watched to make sure her contraption would hold.

"Kho nekri . . . sakru nitrerraid feka e reka. Nyerraiad khosif. Errud khaevis. Myve khaevis."

She froze as the dragon's voice echoed like a whispered threat

But Elodie would not let it frighten her now. *I'm coming, Flor.* She took her father's sword and began stealthily to make her way to the heart of the caves.

ELODIE

HAVING READ FLORIA many bedtime stories over the years about dragons and other mystical creatures, Elodie thought she'd be prepared for a dragon's lair. But as she snuck to the end of one of the tunnels leading into the cave, the beauty took her by surprise. She had expected something primitive and sinister, perhaps a pit littered with gnawed princess bones and smeared with blood and gore. But instead, stalactites of pure quartz hung from the ceiling like crystal icicles, the walls sparkled pink, green, and blue with precious jewels, and a section of the ground was covered in gleaming gold coins.

True, the gems were probably collected over the centuries from the hems of all the princesses' gowns—Elodie remembered what her own dress had looked like when the priestesses first put it on her—and the coins were the same as the ceremonial one Queen Isabelle had placed in her hand before she was thrown into the gorge. But still, the overall effect was stunning. The royal family might live in a gold castle, but the true ruler of Aurea lived in an underground palace of even greater splendor.

The cave extended beyond what Elodie could see from this vantage point, for the tunnel she was in came at the lair from an angle. She could feel Floria's presence, though, as sisters often could. When they were younger, Elodie would often wake a minute or two before Floria came into her bedroom needing to crawl under the covers with Elodie after a nightmare. Hide-and-seek was nearly impossible, because the sisters always seemed to know where the other would be.

Elodie tightened her grip on her father's sword as she poked her head around the end of the tunnel.

The dragon was right there, glaring at her. She almost cried out but caught herself just in time.

Because its scowl didn't move. Its eyes were vacant sockets. This dragon wasn't alive; it was made of stone, and one of its ears was missing.

Elodie pressed herself back against the tunnel wall, though, as her pulse slammed through her veins. *Please don't let the real dragon smell my adrenaline,* she thought. She was covered in the ash of the dead trees, but still, she attempted to slow her breathing and calm her nerves. She thought of the peace of Inophean sunsets, when the sky turned varying shades of pink on the horizon. She thought of the feeling of swinging through branches, and the victory of making it to the highest boughs. She thought of riding horses with Father, of reading history books with Mother, and even of doing arithmetic with Lady Bayford when she was Miss Lucinda, the governess.

Her heartbeat slowed, and Elodie emerged from the tunnel again, this time prepared for the dragon statue. She was not shocked when another one presented itself—this one with broken wings—and then another lying on its side, one without teeth, and more, like a museum of ancient history documenting dragonkind. In fact, Elodie was grateful for the statues the dragon must have collected from all over the isle, for they provided excellent cover as she made her way into the vast cave.

She crept behind what had once been a fountain of a two-headed stone dragon curled like an enormous letter C. If it had been functioning, the head on the bottom, with its open jaws, would have taken in water, and the head on top would have roared it out. It reminded her of the statues that greeted ships as they entered the Aurean Sea, except those didn't have two heads. She wondered if, in the past, dragons really had had two heads, or if the fountain statue was a result of artistic license, like a representation of the two different seasons of the dragon's personality—angry and spouting fire during harvest season, then docile and underground once its hunger had been appeased.

Or perhaps Elodie was reading too much into it.

Regardless, the interior of the statue was an excellent place to hide and get a better view of the cave. Elodie climbed inside the bottom dragon head's jaws and scaled the body and throat until she was crouching inside the mouth of the top dragon head, Father's sword resting on the forked stone tongue.

From this elevated position, she saw the actual dragon, its large body coiled around a different part of the cave floor covered in gold coins. But instead of its usual dark gray, its scales had an iridescent lavender shine to the edges, and they seemed to grow even more lavender as the dragon cooed over the gold coins.

Coo? Elodie furrowed her brow. But indeed, the dragon seemed almost to be singing a lullaby. Not in the human sense, but there was something undeniably *tender* about the way it gazed upon the coins, its normally harsh voice coming out like soft steam rather than charcoaled smoke.

But then Elodie saw beyond the dragon and gasped. There,

on a rock platform in the middle of a deep green pond, was Floria, hunched over in a wet dress streaked with algae. Her sister seemed smaller than ever, one thin arm cradling the other against her shivering body, her quiet sobs filling the air.

The dragon jerked up and sniffed. Its spine bristled, serrated wings rippling, and its scales changed instantaneously from lavender to predator gray. Oh god, it must have heard Elodie's gasp. She bit her lip and tried in vain to calm her pulse, hoping instead that if the tree ash wasn't enough to mask her smell, then being inside this statue would keep the scent of her blood from escaping.

"Is it you, *zedrae?*" the dragon rasped.

Floria looked up, eyes darting around the cave. She started shaking her head, not sure where Elodie was, but trying to convey a warning all the same.

The dragon turned its head around the cave slowly. Inhaling. Trying to pinpoint Elodie's scent.

Perhaps the ash on her skin and the statue were helping

Don't move, Elodie thought. She breathed as softly as she could. She kept watch on Flor and the dragon. She hardly even allowed herself to blink.

In the distance, the loud clattering of metal on stone sounded, echoing through the tunnels. The dragon whipped its head toward the noise, then bared all its teeth in a ravenous smile. "I have you now, *zedrae.*"

It slithered in a rush out of the cave, down a tunnel toward the far chamber where Elodie's contraption had done its job: with the waterskin empty, balance on the lever had failed, and the shield weighed too heavily, pulling the knight's longsword off the boulder fulcrum and onto the ground with a crash.

Thank you, physics, Elodie thought as she clambered out of the two-headed dragon statue.

Floria jumped to her feet in the center of the platform. "El!"

"I'm going to get you out of here, we don't have long!"

Her father's sword and her sprained ankle made Elodie's gait uneven, though, and she tripped as she ran across the expanse of gold coins. They shifted beneath her feet and as she scrambled to get up. Elodie couldn't find purchase, and she stumbled again, sliding facedown onto the coins.

Or, rather, where the coins *used* to be.

"What *are* those?" Floria whispered, the horror in her tone sending chills up Elodie's spine.

Elodie gagged at what the gold coins had been hiding. What she lay directly upon.

Dozens of cracked eggs, ranging from the size of her fist to twice the size of her head. And inside the eggs were mummified dragon babies. The eggshells were pale purple speckled with gold. The dead babies were dry, flaking gray leather pulled taut over fragile skeletons.

"It's a graveyard," Elodie said, gasping and scrabbling upright to get her face farther away from them.

The dragon's cooing came back to her, as did some of the things it had said when it wasn't hunting Elodie, when it had just been here in its own lair but its voice had carried through the labyrinth. *My babies . . .*

It had been talking to its stillborn young.

Oh, stars . . .

Something inside Elodie broke, like a part of an internal watch mechanism springing loose. The dragon was a vicious beast, but it was also a mother that had lost its family. Its children.

What power could grief wreak? Merely thinking about losing Floria had caused Elodie to boil with such rage, such determination, that she would have charged blindly into a battle against even an army of dragons. And that was only for the *potential* loss of a sister.

What would happen to a mother that had *actually* lost its babies? Not one, but dozens of them?

Elodie had been so busy surviving, she hadn't thought about *why* the dragon did what it did. She'd only assumed it knew no better, that it was driven by pure animal instinct.

But it was clearly intelligent, and now, Elodie also remembered something she'd learned from Princess Eline's blood in the Safe Cave: *The dragon had once had a family, too.*

For the first time, Elodie empathized with the dragon.

"It's been in here all alone for ages," she said, looking around at the crumbling statues. They must have been constructed across hundreds of years by the worshipping Aureans, and collected over that same span of centuries by the dragon to keep itself company.

"What are you talking about?" Floria said.

"The dragon. It's been by itself in these caves for so long. The notes said it had a family once, too. But what happened? How long has this dragon been here all alone?"

"I don't know what notes you're talking about, El, but don't start feeling sorry for it! It *eats* people like us, and it's going to come back any second and do just that if we don't hurry!"

Elodie blinked, and reality slammed back into her.

She scrambled to her feet and ran from the graveyard of dragon babies. But when she got to the shore of the pond, she stopped short. Elodie looked across the expanse of deep, seemingly bottomless green water to Floria on the platform, and back.

"I can't swim," she whispered. And of course, neither could Floria.

The sisters stared at each other. So close, yet impassably far.

And then a voice hot with fire rasped through the tunnels, accompanied by the angry scrape of leather on stone. *"Ni reka. Nytuirrai se, akrerrit. Fy nitrerra ni e re.* I am coming to claim what is owed. Your blood and your sister's are mine."

ELODIE

E LODIE LOOKED AT Floria, communicating in that brief glance
not to leave the stone platform. Not that Flor could, given
that she couldn't swim, either. But still, it was worth conveying
the message, because with what was about to happen . . . well,
Elodie needed to make sure her sister stayed put and didn't try
anything rash.

The harshness of leather rushing and scraping against rock
echoed through the tunnels. Elodie ran to hide in the shadows of
one of the many statues near the tunnel from which the dragon
would emerge, making sure she'd be able to position herself between Floria and the dragon. It had gone that way to chase after
the noise of Elodie's contraption rigged from the sword, shield,
and waterskin. Based on the sounds of its angry movements, it
was returning through the same tunnel.

She held Father's sword steady and took in a steeling breath.
The dragon was close now. Elodie could feel the vibration of its
scales on the rocks.

The dragon charged into its lair, smoke already billowing
from its nostrils, fangs bared.

The first thing it saw, however, was the uncovered eggs and its desiccated, stillborn babies exposed.

"DEV ADERRUT!" It came to a sudden halt on the hoard of coins.

Elodie sprang from behind the statue and pointed the sword directly at one of the dragon's violet eyes.

"Kho aderrit," she said. *I dared.*

It snorted, and a plume of fresh smoke puffed from its nose. It glared at the sword pointed at its eye. *"Voro nyothyrrud kho. Sodo fierrad raenif."*

That won't kill me, you know. It will only make me angry.

Elodie knew she was taking a risk. But she had a plan, and that required maneuvering both herself and the dragon to where she wanted them to be. She needed to buy some time to do it.

Elodie advanced a step, the tip of the sword forcing the dragon back a few feet. She moved a little to her right. The dragon, a hunter even when it had a blade pointed at it, followed her shift in position. Elodie just needed to keep repeating the movement, a hundred small steps and pivots along the riverbank, to have a chance at saving herself and Flor. To distract the dragon from what she was doing, she would need to keep talking.

"Vis kir vis, sanae kir res," Elodie said. "Life for life, blood for fire. The meaning of the first part is clear—if the kingdom sacrifices lives to you, you will spare the lives of the rest of Aurea."

"Did you only come to that conclusion now?" the dragon growled. "How disappointing."

"No. That part was obvious. But 'blood for fire' . . ." She recalled what it had said when she was in the cave of mushrooms and icicles. *Nyonnedrae. Verif drae. Syrrif drae. Drae suverru.* The dragon didn't want just any royal spawn to eat. It wanted the right one. The cunning one. The princess who survives.

There was a purpose to the sacrifice beyond the bloody symbolism. The dragon had told her it had been waiting for her for a very long time. Elodie was smart and resourceful. She was a survivor.

She had a role to play in the dragon's grander plans.

"Blood for fire . . ." Elodie glanced at the split eggs and all the stillborn babies. "You think our blood will bring back dragons, don't you?"

The dragon flinched under her mocking tone but did not move more than that while she had a sword at its eye. "Not *think*. I *know. Sanae kir res.* Those were the last words my mother spoke to me. The blood of The One shall herald the beginning of the next generation of dragons."

Elodie shifted a few more feet and made as if she were going to jab at the dragon's eye. "Selfish. You would kill so many just because you're lonely? You are cruel and heartless." She said it all in Khaevis Ventvis.

"Do not befoul my language by speaking such terrible lies!" the dragon spat, sparks leaping from its mouth. "It is *humans* who are cruel and heartless! It is the fault of *humans* that I am all alone!"

The dragon rushed at Elodie, teeth slashing through her dress and into the skin of her chest. At the same time, she plunged her father's sword into its eye.

Except it didn't go in. The beast's eyeball was hard as marble. Elodie's blade sliced only the surface and skimmed off. *Merdú!* But then the blade found purchase in the soft folds in the corner of the dragon's eye.

The momentum of the attack threw Elodie against the monster, so her wounded chest hugged its cheek, the dragon's purple blood now spilling like violet-black tears.

It shrieked, the sound high-pitched and piercing like a thousand spears against glass, and in its pain, it flung Elodie to the opposite bank of the river. She landed roughly in the mud, the jolt knocking the sword from her grip.

"Elodie!" Floria screamed.

There was blood all over Elodie's chest and dress. A purple haze formed a corona in her vision, the threat of a concussion or shock about to overtake her. She had only enough wits to drag herself and the sword out of the reach of the river before violet clouded everything she saw.

"Retaza!" a small voice whimpered. It came from the mouth of a dragon, a young one. "Retaza, my belly aches."

A full-grown dragon with lavender scales lay next to the little one. They were on the shore of a subterranean river.

It was the same cave Elodie was in now, except there were no dragon statues. No gold coins. Only a river and a baby and its mother.

Retaza. Mother.

Was this . . . a memory?

Elodie's mind was in the scene, but she was not. Rather, she seemed to be hearing and seeing through the perspective of—

The dragon! Its blood was all over her. And now she was experiencing one of its memories, just like the visions of princesses past.

But this was from a long, long time ago. This dragon was only a baby then. How long ago? A millennium?

Let the story unfold, Elodie thought.

She stopped asking questions and allowed the blood memory to engulf her. The sounds and thoughts in Khaevis Ventvis no

longer sounded sharp and ominous, but instead soothing and familiar, as they would to dragon ears.

*The mother dragon opened heavy-lidded eyes. It seemed to take her
effort.*

"*Retaza, my belly aches,*" *the little dragon said again.*

"*Rest, kho aikoro.*"

"*But I'm hungry. I want more meat.*"

"*There is no more.*"

"*I only got to eat a little,*" *the young dragon whined.*

The mother surged upright, her golden pupils wild. "*It was already
too much! The princess Victoria poisoned her own blood. I did not know
until it was too late. I should not have given her arm to you . . .*"

*The little dragon whimpered, curling against the throbbing in her
stomach.*

*Why could they not live together in peace, the dragons and the hu-
mans who had recently arrived on the isle? Why were they trying to
force the dragons from the isle that had been their home for a thousand
years?*

*But then the small dragon remembered that the humans did not
even know she existed. Her mother had kept her hidden away, for as
soon as the new arrivals saw her mother, they had immediately decided
that she was evil. Simply because they could not understand any creature that did not look like them.*

*Her mother was trying to keep her safe. She had survived the sol-
diers sent by the king and queen, but now, if there had been poison in
the princess's blood . . .*

*Is that why her mother lay on the banks of the river, hardly moving?
The little dragon had consumed only a few bites of the princess, but her
mother had eaten the rest.*

"*Retaza?*" *the young dragon said, barely audible for the trembling
in her little voice.* "*Are we going to die?*"

"Ny," her mother said, wheezing at the same time that fire flamed from her nostrils. She staggered to her feet, but the gold in her eyes was clear. "I will not let you die. I. Will. Not."

The dragon roared in the cave. Not in the past, but now. Elodie bolted upright, the memory vanishing as she blinked at the prowling dragon, clotting purple blood crusted around its injured eye.

Elodie gripped the handle of her father's sword tightly and scrambled to her feet, readying the blade for another attack.

And yet it was no longer as easy to wish the dragon ill, now that she'd seen it as a baby, with a mother. And its own babies . . . even though the mummified fetuses were horrific to look at, they were still innocent lives that had done no wrong upon the world.

"What happened to your mother?" Elodie asked.

The dragon, which was stalking toward her, stopped. "*Kho retaza?* How do you know about my mother?"

Elodie touched the drying purple blood on her sword.

The dragon growled deep in its throat. "No one has ever walked my memories before. They are *mine!*"

Right. Elodie may have felt some empathy for the dragon because she'd seen part of history through its eyes. But that didn't mean the *dragon* felt any differently about *Elodie*. In fact, sharing the memory was probably akin to stealing treasure from the deepest, most private chamber of its lair.

She had to return to her plan for saving herself and Floria. Elodie glanced at the platform of stone to confirm that her sister was still safe. She was.

So now Elodie just had to maneuver the dragon a little farther away . . .

"I am sorry," Elodie said. "I didn't mean to invade your privacy by seeing the vision of your mother. But Victoria—"

"Victoria murdered my *retaza*," the dragon hissed, spewing smoke and ash.

"I'm sorry," Elodie said again, and she meant it. She had lost her mother, too.

"Humans are never sorry!" the dragon roared while it advanced toward Elodie. "As my mother lay dying, she reminded me of the bargain the first royal family had made. She made me promise I would remember how Victoria tricked and killed her. Then my mother prophesied that revenge would come one day, that a princess's blood would give birth to a new generation of dragons. The One who survives. *Sanae kir res.*"

Elodie still didn't understand why the dragon was trying to kill her if it wanted a princess to survive. Or maybe they had different definitions, and what Elodie had done—escaped, fought back—meant she had already survived. But that was not enough for her; she wanted full survival.

She glanced at their position in the cave. They were almost where she wanted them. And Floria was watching, quiet but alert, far enough away now.

"And you believed your mother's deathbed delirium?" Elodie asked. *Just a few more yards . . .*

"It was *not* delirium," the dragon rasped. "You humans with your small minds cannot comprehend how the world truly works. My mother *knew* what was to come. She knew I would live, but Victoria's poison ensured there would be no more dragons thereafter."

"I see," Elodie said, shifting them the last few yards she needed. "So you exacted your revenge year after year, holding tight to your mother's prophecy."

"*Ed, zedrae.* The world craves balance, and some day, a princess's blood will right the wrongs of the first. *Vis kir vis. Sanae kir res.*"

Elodie thought again of the color of the dragon's scales when it was cooing to its dead children. The color of its mother in the memory. And the color of Elodie's own gown. The priestesses had chanted a song in the dragon's language, but they had long forgotten the meaning of the words. Is that what had happened with the color of the dress, as well?

Perhaps the first priestesses—the ones of Victoria's era—had known that lavender was the color of a dragon's scales when it was in the role of a mother, and the color of a dragon who yearns for a child of its own. And if the prophecy was correct, then one of the princess sacrifices would be the key to *this* dragon becoming a mother again.

If that was the case, the dragon was right that humans were the ones who were cruel. They were terrible even to their own kind, dressing their princesses as symbols of fertility to the creature to which they would be sacrificed.

But it did not change the fact that Elodie was pitted against this dragon, and only one of them could win. And now she had the dragon where she wanted it.

"Vorra kho tke raz!" The dragon shot a plume of flame at Elodie. The fire swallowed her arm, accompanied by the dragon's sticky, flammable tar, which spattered on her hair and lit it on fire. The fur trim of Lady Bayford's cloak burst into flames, too, and searing heat engulfed Elodie. The pain turned her vision into nothing but white stars.

The river . . .

She couldn't see. She couldn't swim. But the only hope she had was to put out the flames, so she threw herself into the water.

It snuffed out the fire immediately. In shock, Elodie opened her eyes underwater, watching as her singed hair floated around her. The skin on her arm was red and raw, the charred sword clutched in her fist.

Everything moved as if time had slowed down, and the colors were all more saturated. Lady Bayford's cloak billowed in the deep green water. The agony of the burns delivered itself in ponderous bursts, flares of searing pain drawn out to torture her. And blue glowworms drifted out of the cloak's pocket, as if saying farewell since they were no longer useful as a lantern—

Wait! Elodie's mind snapped back into real time. The glowworms could heal. She snatched at them and tried to put them on her burned skin, but because they were underwater, the helpful worms couldn't stay and just kept floating away . . .

Her lungs burned. She needed to kick to the surface soon or drown. The white stars in her vision returned, and Elodie knew she had mere seconds left if she wanted to live, if she wanted to save Floria.

Elodie grabbed handfuls of glowworms and stuffed them into her mouth, swallowing them whole. Her reasoning was, like the dragon mother's deathbed prophecy, half delirious. Elodie hoped the other half was astute.

Instinct made her legs kick, and she exploded through the surface of the river. A few more glowworms floated there and she scooped them toward her body, silently entreating them to stay.

"Elodie!" Floria screamed.

She looked up just in time to see the dragon plunging into the river after her. The water surged up and carried her closer to shore, though, and her feet brushed the rocky riverbed.

"*Senir vo errut ni desto,* Elodie. *Nykomarr.* This was always your destiny, Elodie. Do not fight it."

"I don't believe in destiny," she said, wincing with every

movement as she flailed and tried not to drown. "I believe in making my own future."

"So trite. I expected more from you." The dragon narrowed its eyes, then dipped its mouth down into the river. Bubbles began to rise, and the water churned.

Then it began to boil. The dragon was blowing fire into the river, and the scalding water came in waves against Elodie's already burned body. She screamed as the waves shoved her toward shore, and she scrabbled up the sloped riverbed, hot water in her nose, her mouth, her lungs.

The dragon stalked toward her, sloshing through the boiling river and coming ashore.

Elodie coughed up the water. She couldn't succumb now, she had to check her surroundings.

She was not too far off from her original plan. She hacked up some more water, then got up and ran limping to where she needed to be, dragging her father's sword with her.

"I won't give in to you," she said. "If you want my blood, you're going to have to come and get it. Just like your mother did to Victoria."

"Elodie, no!" Floria cried.

Floria's call distracted the dragon just enough for Elodie to get in front of the two-headed dragon fountain. "Come on!" she taunted. She would be merciless in her barbs, because it was the only way to make sure her plan worked. "What are you waiting for? Permission from your *retaza*? The one who left you here all alone? Permission from the dead babies you collect like morbid dolls? I am tired of this game, too. BURN ME, BITCH!"

Apoplectic, the dragon's eyes turned into pure, molten gold, and it unleashed a roar of fire as scorching and furious as a thousand hells.

She threw herself out of the way. The flames hit the two-headed fountain, into the open mouths, blasting through the C-curve of the statue, then back out the other stone jaws like a boomerang. Fire exploded straight back at the dragon, and globs of its own sticky tar flung into its face, onto its neck, torso, and wings, and also burst into flame.

The dragon roared. It thrashed on the cave floor, its wings smashing statues, its tail slamming into the walls and dislodging centuries of emeralds and rubies and sapphires in a shower of color like sadistic confetti.

It got to its feet and tried to beat the flames out with its wings. But the sticky tar covered its body and would not be snuffed so easily, and instead, the motion lifted the dragon into the air. It slammed into the ceiling like a gargantuan fireball. Crystal stalactites shattered and crashed down.

The dragon smashed back onto the ground and rammed into Floria's platform. The column of rock beneath it splintered at the impact, and the entire structure began to crumble.

"Elodie!"

"Floria!"

The dragon howled and rolled itself into the river.

Elodie ran as fast as she could toward her sister.

The platform collapsed, and Floria tumbled down with it.

KHAEVIS

S HE SLAMMED DEEP into the river.
   It was nothing but agony.
Every cell, writhing.
Every thought, despair.

*I am burning and dying and losing my connection to my babies,
leaving them all alone as I have been alone all my life. I am burning and
dying and it is the fault of the unlikely princess, the one who survived,
the one who was supposed to bring on the next era of great dragons but
who is instead the one to end us all . . .*

This is not how it was supposed to transpire.

This was not how the great legends of the dragons ended.

Alone

    alone

        alone . . .

But the river extinguished the fire. And although gravely injured, khaevis began to make the hazy journey back from pain
to awareness—

If I am dying, I do not have to die alone. I can take her with me.

Elodie.

Vis kir vis. Sanae kir res.

If I cannot have the latter, then I shall make my own new bargain:
Neither of us shall live without the other.

Khaevis closed her eyes. She thought a final farewell to her babies.

Then she flexed her talons underwater and prepared to rise one last time.

ELODIE

A S THE ROCKY platform broke apart, it became an avalanche, flying across the pond, onto the shore. Sharp shards battered and sliced Floria, and when they all hit the ground, the avalanche buried her beneath it.

Elodie threw aside her sword and began heaving away rocks. The glowworms were doing what they could for the burns on her skin, but her arm still screamed in pain, and tears streamed down her face from both agony and fear for her sister.

"Flor, can you hear me?"

No answer.

Elodie hauled rock after rock, driven by the very adrenaline the dragon so prized. Pain became a mere backdrop, a buzz that she knew she'd have to pay for later, but for now, could not afford to give attention.

"Flor, say something, please!"

The stones seemed to grow heavier. Elodie kept digging, kept lifting, but she hadn't slept in so long, hadn't eaten enough. She'd fought too much. She had almost nothing left.

A pile of rocks and gems avalanched and buried the hole Elodie had made.

"No!" she cried.

And then . . .

"El?" Barely a whisper.

"Flor! Flor, I hear you! I'm going to get you out!" Elodie jammed her hands into the newly fallen rock and dug harder and faster, flinging emeralds and rubies aside as if they were worth nothing, for to her, it was true. The only thing worth saving here was Floria.

Finally, she saw her sister's arm, bent at an awkward angle. The shards of rock around her were covered in blood. Elodie cleared a path, hurling rocks away until she'd made a hole big enough to see Floria's battered face.

"Oh, Flor!"

Her sister smiled weakly. "This really isn't how I imagined your honeymoon."

Elodie laughed and cried at the same time. She heaved more rocks out of the way until there was enough space to extract Floria.

She couldn't pull on Flor's broken arm, though.

"I'm going to have to pull you up by your armpits," Elodie said.

Floria nodded and tried her best to shift her position to enable it.

Elodie squatted and reached down, sliding her elbows underneath her sister's arms.

"This might hurt a bit when I move you."

"I can handle it," Floria said.

"On the count of one, two, three!" Elodie yanked her sister out.

Floria screamed. But it wasn't because of her arm. "Elodie, watch out!"

In a torrential wave of water, the dragon rose from the river. Its burned scales sloughed away like it was shedding, and in their place was raw, pale purple skin. *"Mirr dek kirrai zi!"*

The dragon struck at the broken platform with all its force. Elodie grabbed Floria, and they rolled off just in time.

"Run!" she yelled at Floria.

Elodie lunged for her sword, grabbing it by the hilt.

The dragon charged at Elodie again, all finesse in its attack gone in the face of its fury. As it rushed toward her, she dodged, tucking herself into a ball and rolling along the shards of rock and quartz.

She sprang back to her feet. The dragon shrieked its high-pitched, horrible metal-on-glass scream, and Elodie instinctively threw her hands over her ears.

It whipped around. *"Mirr dek kirrai zi . . ."* it snarled again. *Look at what you've done.*

Elodie's eyes widened as the dragon rose up and loomed above her like a sword-winged cobra. Its purple skin glistened with droplets of river water.

Unarmored! she realized. Without scales, the dragon's skin was exposed, as fragile as an embryo's. Elodie tightened her hold on the sword.

The dragon shrieked again and spat fire. Then it slammed down on top of Elodie.

She speared her sword straight into the dragon's armorless skin. She felt it impale vulnerable flesh and embed into the soft, pulsating muscle of the dragon's heart. Dark violet blood gushed from its chest.

The dragon's eyes bulged. But then they narrowed as it focused on Elodie, who still held on to the sword.

"If I die, I shall take you with me!" it roared in Khaevis Vent-vis as its front claw smashed into Elodie from behind, crushing her against its chest. One of its talons pierced straight through her back.

Through *her* heart.

"Oh . . ." Elodie gasped.

She'd always imagined she would be more eloquent in her dying moments. That she would be old and elegant, surrounded by children and grandchildren in a room bursting with love.

But instead, there was a dank, hot dragon's lair, and Elodie had only enough breath for a single "oh."

How unfortunate, she thought wryly. The fear of death dissipated, this close to the end.

Crimson blood spurted from Elodie's body, mingling in the deep violet pool of the dragon's own mortal wound.

"Elodie!" Flor screamed. She hadn't fled. Of course she hadn't.

But Elodie could see nothing now but blood, red and violet, and raw dragon skin. In the end, this is all they were, souls temporarily given flesh, fighting for the right to live, to be mothers and daughters, sisters and friends, for however brief a flash of time until their souls departed again. Perhaps the dragons were terrible. Perhaps humans were. Or perhaps they were all the same, only doing the best they could in an imperfect world.

With the last of her strength, Elodie withdrew her sword from the dragon's breast. "I am sorry," she whispered. "And I forgive you."

The dragon's eyes met hers for a moment, and a large purple tear fell down its scarred face.

Then it crumpled backward, slamming onto the cave floor, and Elodie went with it, pinned by its talon on top of the dragon's chest in a final, fatal embrace.

FLORIA

FLORIA RAN CRYING and screaming toward Elodie. She climbed the dragon's still-warm body, grabbed its massive claw, and tried to pull it out.

But the talon had punctured straight through her sister, who lay facedown in a hot pool of dark violet blood mingled with red. Steam rose off the surface and Floria gagged at the miasma of sticky iron tang that rose from it.

"You can't die, you can't die," she sobbed as she crouched down at Elodie's head to try a different approach. She took her sister by the shoulders and pushed upward, wincing through the sharp pain in her own broken arm, until she could lift Elodie's body off the talon.

She could not carry Elodie and had to lay her down on the dragon, still in the pool of blood. Then suddenly, blue slugs began to fall like a hailstorm from the roof of the cave, bringing with them the glowing blue light she'd seen earlier. "What's happening?"

They landed on Floria's face and on Elodie's prone body. They wiggled all over Floria's neck and seemed intent on migrating into the open gash on Elodie's chest. "Get away, you disgusting little maggots!" Floria swiped them off Elodie. "She's not dead! She's not, she's not!"

But no one could survive a dragon's talon skewered through their heart, and Floria collapsed into hysterical tears over her sister. She covered the hole in her sister's chest to protect her from the worms.

"I love you, El. We were supposed to see each other grow up and married off to kind husbands, to write each other letters every week and visit every summer with our children. We were supposed to be best friends and I was going to send you new recipes from wherever I lived, and you were going to send me new mazes to solve. But now that's never going to happen," Floria sobbed. "And I hate this stupid dragon labyrinth! I never want to see another maze again!"

Her sister had been the very first face Floria saw when she was born. Not her mother or the midwife, but Elodie. Father said that's why they'd always been so close. As soon as Floria came out of the womb, Elodie smiled at her and said, "Mine."

Now, Floria cried so hard her vision blurred. There was nothing but the infinite shadow of a future without Elodie. The dragon had said its mother knew things, and Flor understood how that could be so. With Elodie lifeless beneath her, Floria knew how bleak the rest of her own life would be. No matter how the sun shone, there would always be a cloud in its path, a gray gloom to remind her that she was alone in the world. That the other half she'd always thought she'd have—Elodie—was gone.

Floria wailed, eyes squeezed shut and face pressed against her sister's chest.

She cried a never-ending river of tears, losing track of time. She cried until her throat was raw, until her heart felt like stone, until she had wrung herself out and there was nothing left, not even the will to walk out of these now-dragonless caves and live, to claim the life her sister had saved for her.

When the tears finally ran out, though, Floria forced open her swollen eyes.

Everything glowed blue.

Which was so cruel! Elodie had always said that blue was the color of hope. And there was nothing good here, nothing to hope for, nothing but foul slugs crawling all over the back of Floria's neck, and that abominable blue glow coming from the hole in Elodie's chest, and—

Flor jolted upright.

Why was El's chest glowing? Floria had covered it with her own body, so the glowworms couldn't wriggle inside.

But the blood on Elodie's chest was dried. The skin was scarred but healing. Floria's jaw hung open.

"The hole . . . what happened to the hole the dragon's talon ripped open?"

It was closed.

How is that possible?

Floria ran her fingers gingerly over where the gaping wound had been not long ago.

The glowworms left shimmering trails of blue mucus on Elodie's skin. It reminded Flor of the thick ointment Lady Bayford used to rub on El's abrasions whenever she skinned her knees falling out of trees.

Could it be—?

Floria picked a glowworm off the back of her own neck and placed it on a laceration on her arm. The strange, leechlike creature immediately began squirming over it and releasing iridescent blue slime.

The skin around the cut rippled, ever so slightly, as if waking from slumber and stretching. To Floria's astonishment, the redness of the wound faded to dark pink, then light pink, and then the cut began to close.

"Unbelievable . . ." she whispered.

"What's unbelievable?" Elodie said drowsily.

Flor gasped and dropped her arm. The glowworm stayed securely adhered to her skin, continuing with its work.

"El . . . did you . . . Oh god, tell me I wasn't hearing things! Did you say something?"

Elodie's eyelids opened slowly. Her irises looked purple in the glowworms' blue light. It almost seemed as if the pupil glimmered gold.

She blinked, and the illusion disappeared. She looked at Floria. "What happened?"

Fresh tears streamed down Flor's face. "I don't know! I— I thought you were dead."

Elodie winced, touched her chest, and lay back down with eyes closed. "I think I *was*."

"Then how—?"

"I have no idea." But then she opened her eyes and looked at Floria. The corner of Elodie's mouth curled up in a hint of a smile.

"It worked," she said, awestruck.

"What did?" Floria asked.

Elodie reached up and plucked a blue glowworm off Flor's face. "I swallowed a bunch of them when I was underwater. As insurance."

Floria gasped as she understood. "So when the dragon speared you with its talon, you were able to heal from the inside."

Elodie nodded. "But I'm still surprised it worked so well, and that quickly."

But then Floria furrowed her brow.

"What's wrong?" Elodie asked, propping herself up on her elbows slowly. Even though the gaping wound was closed, there was still probably healing going on in her organs and bones, not to mention the glowworms now diligently working on the burns on her body.

With shaking hands, Flor pointed at the pool of blood they were sitting in. "The dragon's blood . . . some of it might have gotten into you." She proceeded to tell Elodie what her eyes had looked like when they first opened.

Elodie paled.

But then she touched her chest and closed her eyes, as if she were listening to her heart. Or perhaps she was listening to something even deeper inside.

A smile slowly spread across her face.

"If that's true," Elodie said, "then I have an idea."

Floria grinned, partially out of relief, and partially in anticipation.

She loved when her sister had ideas.

LUCINDA

LUCINDA GREETED EACH refugee at the harbor and welcomed them onto the ship *Deomelas*, which would take them away from Aurea. Alexandra and her husband and daughter stood on the other side of the line, sharing hugs with their fellow citizens who had decided to leave the country. It was Alexandra and Cora who had asked Lucinda if she would be willing to help them. Then it was they who'd spread the word that there was a berth on the *Deomelas* for anyone who could no longer support a kingdom that prospered on the blood of innocents.

Yet even as Lucinda watched the solemn procession of these noble people who would leave their near utopia behind on principle, she also watched the horizon for the two she most wanted on this ship—her daughters. No matter that she had not borne them herself, Elodie and Floria were hers, and all that she was was theirs. Love was not tied to birth; it was forged through shared experience and suffering, from a desire to give, even if nothing was offered in return.

Please, please be safe. Please come, and we will sail away, and no matter what happens, we will be together, and that will be enough.

"Lady Bayford?" little Cora asked. The concern in her down-turned eyes suggested she'd been calling Lucinda's name for a while. "Are you all right?"

Lucinda gave her a sad smile. "Not yet, dear. But I hope I shall be."

Just then, hoofbeats pounded on the road to the harbor. Lucinda's stomach flipped, unsure whether it ought to be excited for the possibility of her daughters, or whether it ought to be sick at the likelihood that it would be an Aurean knight with a gloating message that Elodie and Floria were dead, and that Lucinda was ordered to depart immediately—with no husband, no children, and an empty heart.

Cora took her hand and squeezed, as if she knew Lucinda needed it. Cora did not let go.

The sound of the hooves grew nearer, and soon the horse crested the hill and the rider became visible.

The *riders*.

"Elodie! Floria!" Lucinda ran down the dock toward them. Never in her life had she run before, because it was undignified and she looked like a newborn desert goat still unsure of its limbs, but Lucinda did not care right now. The only thing that mattered was getting to her girls as fast as she could, to sweep them into her arms, to promise them she would never let them down ever again.

They met where the dirt road curved into the harbor, and Lucinda flung herself at Elodie and Floria as soon as they dismounted.

"I thought I had lost you," she murmured into their hair as she held them close.

"You will never lose us," Elodie said. "I know we have some old wounds to close, but one thing I can promise: Whether we are beside you or on the other side of the world, you'll never lose us again."

Lucinda looked anxiously up at the sky and at Mount Khaevis.

"The dragon isn't coming," Elodie said. "We're safe."

"I'm sorry for how we treated you," Floria said. "El told me you tried to come after me yourself. Thank you . . . Mama."

Mama. Lucinda started to cry. Not Stepmother. *Mama.*

"No, no, it was my fault," Lucinda sniffled. "I'm sorry."

The three stayed intertwined for minutes more.

Finally, Lucinda broke their embrace. "The two of you weren't too heavy for the horse?"

Elodie smiled. "*That's* what you want to know? Not 'How did you defeat the dragon?' "

Lucinda flushed. "Well, yes, that, too. I'm just in a bit of shock and my mind isn't prioritizing its questions in the right order."

Floria threw her uninjured arm around Lucinda again, and Lucinda melted at the touch she'd yearned for all these years. It was all she had ever wanted.

In the distance, music floated on the wind from the gold castle. It was the same song Lucinda had heard when they first arrived on Aurea. The same as when she discovered what Elodie's wedding would mean.

Elodie's head was tilted toward the palace, too. "I thought the third wedding wasn't supposed to be until tomorrow."

"They moved it up because they were afraid of the dragon," Lucinda said. But she wanted to spare Elodie from reliving her own awful wedding. "Come on board," she said to both her daughters. "We will get a doctor for Floria's arm and your other injuries. And you can tell me all about how you escaped."

"Actually . . ." Elodie said, ear still cocked toward the music. "Floria will have to tell you. I have one more thing I have to do." She turned to leave.

"But we're ready to set sail." Lucinda knit her brows. "Where are you going?"

"To crash a royal wedding."

Lucinda blinked in confusion. But then she smiled, amusement arriving with understanding.

"You're going to crash a wedding looking like that?" She gestured at Elodie's tattered, burned, and bloody clothes and the ash and old paint smeared all over her. "Not if you are going to represent the House of Bayford, you're not."

Elodie laughed again and hugged her. "Now that's the mother I know and love."

Lucinda smirked. "Come with me then and we'll get you cleaned up. I know just the dress you ought to wear."

ELODIE

THE THIRD ROYAL wedding was underway when Elodie stepped onto the palace terrace. She wore an Inophean wedding gown, the one Lady Bayford had originally made for Elodie's wedding day, until the Aurean seamstresses took that honor away. But Elodie saw now how perfect Lady Bayford's design was. The dress had a pale gray corset overlaid with delicate gold lace, and sleeves of the same lace that elegantly covered shoulder to wrist. The skirt was composed of layers of black and white tulle, which Lady Bayford had scrimped and saved for years to buy. And underneath the skirt, Elodie wore silver breeches. Lady Bayford had included it in the design, in case the bride felt the need to climb a tree or ride a horse on her wedding day.

At first no one noticed Elodie, for she was just a late guest at the back of the audience, presumably about to find an empty seat in the last row of chairs. In front, Henry stood under the same golden pavilion where he'd married Elodie only two nights prior. In her place was another young woman in a tightly cinched gown of blood red. She had dark brown skin and long black hair that fell in gentle waves all the way down to the small of her back. She wore gold combs with the pattern of dragon's scales, and an awfully familiar pendant around her neck.

They will be safe in the imperial vault, Henry had said. Apparently to be given to the next bride.

The guests who had not noticed Elodie began to pay attention, however, when she did not sit down and instead began walking down the aisle in the middle of the ceremony. It started as just a whispering in the back rows as she walked slowly—regally—past them, then became a ripple that tumbled forward.

As the tide of whispers reached the pavilion, Elodie bent down and rolled a palm-sized ceremonial gold coin down the aisle.

It stopped at Henry's boot. He looked down, vexed at the interruption, until he noticed what had hit him.

The coin had landed with the image of three princesses faceup.

"I do believe that belongs to you," Elodie said.

Henry startled and looked up. His gaze met Elodie's at the same time that Queen Isabelle rose from her throne. It took the tattooed priestess and the soon-to-be princess a moment longer to catch on that something was amiss. Finally, King Rodrick saw what was happening. He leapt up from his throne.

"You're alive!" he cried.

Queen Isabelle narrowed her eyes at Elodie. "What are you doing here?"

"I declare this wedding over," Elodie said.

"What?" The bride-to-be frowned. From the front row, a man who was likely her father jumped up and shouted, "Who the hells are *you*?"

"I," Elodie said, "am Prince Henry's wife."

"Lies," the father of the bride said. "My daughter is to be the princess."

"I'm sorry, but that will not be possible," Elodie said. "Henry married me two nights ago. You can ask him yourself if it's true."

The man, his daughter, and every wedding guest whipped their heads toward Henry, whose face had turned an unattractive shade of puce.

"Elodie," Henry said, his tone cloying, like too much honey on toast. "I have been so worried for you. We didn't know where you went. I haven't slept at all since—"

"Since you tried to kill my sister?"

The crowd began to murmur. They were accustomed to bride sacrifices, but this was a new twist.

Queen Isabelle pushed past the priestess, Henry, and the bride-to-be to the front of the pavilion, hands balled into fists as if she meant to defend the ceremony, even if it meant a brawl with her former—technically current—daughter-in-law.

"How are you even here?" she spat. "You should have been . . ." The queen glanced at the bewildered girl at the altar and did not finish her sentence.

But Elodie had no qualms about finishing for her. "I should have been eaten by the dragon? The one you tried to feed me to, twice? The one the royal family has been sacrificing princesses to for eight centuries?"

The bride-to-be squealed.

Elodie looked at her kindly. "You look beautiful tonight. Perfect. But if I can give you any advice from one woman to another—you don't want to go through with this. Get away from here, as far as you can go. Now."

"I—I don't believe you," she said.

"I wouldn't have, either, in your position. But let me ask you

this: Did Henry lodge your family in a beautiful, ten-story-tall
tower of gold? Did he give you those hair combs with a note that
he hoped you'd wear them on your wedding day? Did he kneel
before you on the battlements, give you that necklace around
your throat, and ask you to marry him? Did he claim that, despite the fact that the marriage was already arranged, he was
truly in love with you?"

The princess-to-be's eyes bulged. But then she gathered the
red fabric of her skirts and ran.

Elodie turned back to the royal family. "As for the dragon, I
slayed her."

The queen blinked at Elodie. And then Queen Isabelle started
laughing. "You, vanquish the dragon? No one has been able to
touch that monster for eight hundred years, and I'm to believe
that you, a wisp of a woman from a no-name duchy, actually
slayed it?"

"Yes. And then I saved her." Elodie took a step forward and
raised her arms.

Attached to the gold lace of her sleeves, a sheer, lavender
capelet unfurled. At Elodie's request, Lady Bayford had fashioned it from the last remnants of the gown the priestesses had
dressed Elodie in.

Now, with Elodie's arms held proud, the capelet fluttered in
the breeze.

Like wings.

And then, in the near distance, came the beating of actual
wings like a war drum. The air vibrated with the pulse of it.

The sky shifted from an ordinary indigo blue to a fierce,
glowing one.

"What is—" Prince Henry began.

The dragon dove down from the clouds and into view, her

chest glowing bright blue from the glowworms Elodie had heaped inside the dragon to heal her heart.

The wedding guests screamed and fled.

Only Queen Isabelle, King Rodrick, Prince Henry, and Elodie remained on the terrace.

"Thoserra rekirre ferek?" the dragon asked.

"No, don't burn them yet," Elodie said.

"Impossible," Henry said. "How are you controlling it?"

"I'm not," Elodie said. "She is here because we are kin." Elodie reached for her shoulder and tore off a gold lace sleeve.

At first glance, there was just soft skin, the burns healed. But then Elodie turned her arm and the moonlight hit it at a different angle.

Instead of human skin, a shimmer of gold, shield-shaped scales shone in the light.

"Sanae kir res," Elodie said. "We shared our blood, the dragon and I, and from that merging of power, a new generation will rise."

"No," the queen uttered.

"I'm afraid so." Elodie's eyes flashed violet.

The golden scales glittered once more, then cascaded down her arm, up her neck, and over the rest of her skin. A blinding gold light engulfed her and grew, emanating larger and brighter.

And then the Elodie of the past was gone, and in her place, stood a dragon thrice the size of the princess she'd been a moment before.

"Movdarr ferek dek neresurruk!" the older, larger dragon rasped. "Show them what they deserve."

"Ny," the gold dragon said, her voice husky with fire and smoke and power, but still decidedly Elodie. "I will not be the one to sentence them. I will let them choose."

"I—I don't understand," Henry whispered. But it was unclear whether he couldn't comprehend Elodie's transformation or if he simply didn't understand why she wouldn't kill him right away.

She decided to answer the latter. "Despite the suffering you have wrought upon others, I cannot know all the ways in which you, yourselves, have suffered in inheriting your kingdom's bloody legacy. So I offer you a choice: Accept your end now, or abdicate, leave Aurea, and never return."

Henry sniveled, then turned and ran.

But King Rodrick bowed to Elodie, his entire body relaxing, as if in relief. "It is finally over."

When he rose, he extended his hand to Queen Isabelle.

She took it without hesitation and together, they stepped forward.

Elodie nodded her golden head once at them, and then to the dragon.

She did not watch the king and queen's end. But as Elodie unfurled her wings and leapt off the palace rooftop, she let out a long, weary exhale and echoed the sentiment.

"Thank the skies. It is finally over."

FLORIA

J UST AS FLORIA finished telling Lady Bayford and the passengers
the tale of her time in the dragon's cave, the gold palace of
Aurea was lit aflame.

Everyone gasped and ran to the railing of the *Deomelas*.
Everyone but Flor.

Seeing her standing back, Cora—the girl who had helped or-
ganize the refugees—asked, "What does it mean?"

"It means Elodie succeeded in what she meant to do," Floria
said. "The royal family is no more, and the dragon is no longer a
threat."

Alexandra Ravella, the former royal envoy and Cora's mother,
left the railing and joined them. "Then people may return home.
Aurea is safe now, and the odious practice of sacrificing princesses is over."

Floria nodded. "Anyone who wishes to may disembark."

Lady Bayford came to her side. "But anyone who still wishes
to set sail with us may. Inophe may not be as prosperous as
Aurea, but it is a land with a good heart, and we welcome you."

"What should we do?" Cora's father asked. "We know the land and the people here."

"On the other hand," Alexandra said, "my role in Aurea's tainted past will always be too clear to me."

Floria watched as both parents turned to Cora, waiting for her to weigh in. Flor's respect for them swelled immensely.

"I think I should like to see the world," Cora said. "If that's all right?"

Alexandra and her husband nodded, their eyes glistening as they scooped Cora into a hug. "Yes, that's more than all right. We will start anew."

Floria swiped away tears of her own, suddenly missing Father.

Lady Bayford wrapped her arm around Floria. "And what will you choose to do, my love?"

Floria leaned into Lady Bayford's warm bosom, not wanting to leave the security of the woman who had been there her entire life. But at the same time, she looked at the castle at the base of Mount Khaevis and the smoldering plume of smoke where Elodie was also marking a new start.

"The hardest part of a mother's job is letting go of her babies," Lady Bayford said, stroking Floria's hair. "As much as I want to keep you under my wing forever, if you want to fly, you should fly."

"But I don't want to leave you by yourself."

"I won't be." Lady Bayford smiled. "I am mother of this new brood." She spread her arms as if to encompass Cora and Alexandra and the refugees who were settling in for the journey to Inophe. "And as Elodie said, whether you are beside me or on the other side of the globe, I will still be in your heart. You cannot get rid of me that easily."

Floria laughed and hugged her. "I will miss you."

"Come visit Inophe from time to time," Lady Bayford said, "and bring me samples of all the delicacies you encounter on your travels."

"I will. I promise."

Then Flor disembarked the ship, leading those who had decided to stay to shore, back to Aurea.

EPILOGUE

AWEEK LATER, ELODIE stood in human form on the peak of Mount Khaevis as the sun rose. From here, she could see the melted rooftop of the palace, where her husband of mere days had abdicated and fled. Where Queen Isabelle had taken King Rodrick's hand in their final moment and accepted their fate solemnly.

And where Elodie had decided how to chart the future.

Floria stepped up beside her. "What next, Your Majesty?"

The title sounded surreal, yet right at the same time. For Elodie had always known her life would require her to lead a people. It just hadn't turned out as she expected.

In her youth, she'd believed that good leaders sacrificed everything for their citizens. And she'd been willing to do so, regardless of how backbreaking the work or how heavy the burden of trying to keep a citizenry alive in a harsh land. But then Henry offered marriage, and she thought she'd found an easy solution to all of Inophe's problems.

Yet, as with all stories people tell themselves, the truth is rarely found in the first version, or even the second or third. No, the truth is buried deep inside the storyteller, and only when she is ready for it—no matter how difficult it may be—will the truth reveal itself. Most people never find it.

But the brave do.

Elodie looked out at the mountain again. The answer, she knew now, was not found in grand gestures, but in the daily small decisions. In taking care of not only her people but herself at the same time.

"Everything will change for Aurea," Elodie said as she turned to Floria. "The people no longer have to fear the dragon, and I want them to enjoy not only prosperity, but also peace and security and joy.

"I'm going to be a different kind of ruler than they are accustomed to. I want to know my subjects, just like I knew the people of Inophe. I want to understand their needs and their desires, what they treasure and what they still dream of. And I will heed not only my own counsel, but theirs as well, for I freely admit that I still have much to learn."

The sun glinted on Elodie's arm. Floria touched it gently, where it was shifting back and forth from human skin to golden dragon scales. "And what about this? Are you going to try to hide it?"

Elodie shook her head. "No. This new kingdom will be transparent. I will not hide from my people, and we will no longer hide Aurea from the world. Some may be scared of me at first— and some may choose to leave—but ultimately, I will show them the beauty of what dragons can be. However, there will be a lot of work to do."

"I'll be right here to help you."

"I know." Elodie contemplated the violet-gray peaks and valleys of the mountain, the expanses of silver pear orchards, and the vast fields of golden wheat. Beyond that were the villages with their thatched roofs, the peasants with their harvest songs, and the sailors on the trading ships, ready to bring Aurea to the world, and the world to Aurea.

Then the dragon flew into view, rising from the horizon and cutting majestically across the sky.

"Do we know her name?" Floria asked.

"Dragons don't have names," Elodie said. "But she says we can call her Retaza."

"Retaza," Flor murmured. "That's lovely. What does it mean?"

"Mother," Elodie said, smiling, just as the sunlight hit the dragon's scales. They glinted lavender, iridescent at the edges.

The scales on Elodie's own arms undulated in response, and the tingle of power and magic sparked across her skin. The air around her felt charged, too, and it smelled of ancient forests and amber and musk, but also of flower buds and fresh rain and new beginnings.

She inhaled deeply. And then she let the change wash over her, basking in the warmth of the golden light, the domino shift of skin to scales, and the electrifying strength that rippled through every inch of who she was and who she ever would be.

As the transformation completed, Retaza flew up to meet them.

"Your Majesty," she said in Khaevis Ventvis, bowing her reptilian head.

"Retaza," Elodie said. *"Erra mirvu rukhif mirre ni."* Speaking the language with a dragon's tongue felt so right, as if all the awkward gaffes of Elodie's past were simply because she'd been in the wrong skin. *"Dakh vivorru novif makho?"*

"Aezorru. Akorru santerif onne divkor. Kodu ni sanae. Farris errut verif."

"Hey, don't leave me out of the conversation," Floria said.

Elodie smiled. "I'm sorry. I was asking about the new egg. It's glowing and growing stronger with each day. Retaza flatters me and claims it was my blood that revived the race of dragons."

"*Sanae kir res,*" Retaza said.

"It goes both ways." Elodie stretched and let her gold scales ripple under the sun's radiance. "This is because of you. *Sanae kir res.*"

"You're preening," Floria teased.

Elodie laughed. "Perhaps a little. But how about we put this magic to some use?"

Her sister bounced on her toes. "I thought you'd never ask." Flor scrambled onto Elodie's golden back and settled against the soft nape of her neck, holding tight.

"Ready?" Elodie asked.

"I'm always ready."

Retaza led the way.

And then Elodie leapt off the top of Mount Khaevis.

At first they plummeted

    Down

        Down

           Down . . .

But then Elodie unfurled her wings and smiled.

She was a queen.

A dragon.

But most of all, she was herself.

And she soared.

ACKNOWLEDGMENTS

W OW, WHAT A wild ride this has been. There aren't enough thanks in the world to express my gratitude to my publisher and the team at Netflix for this incredible journey. From writing the book to visiting the film set to collaborating with so many brilliant minds . . . Just WOW.

Thank you to everyone at Random House Worlds. My editor, Elizabeth Schaefer, is a shining light and pure joy to work with. Thank you also to my publisher, Scott Shannon, publishing director Keith Clayton (who has excellent taste in coffee), Alex Larned, Jocelyn Kiker, Faren Bachelis, Lara Kennedy, Julia Henderson, Frieda Duggan, Lydia Estrada, Elizabeth Rendfleisch, Cassie Gonzales, David Moench, Jordan Pace, Adaobi Maduka, Ashleigh Heaton, Tori Henson, Sabrina Shen, Lisa Keller, Megan Tripp, Maya Fenter, Matt Schwartz, Catherine Bucaria, Abby Oladipo, Molly Lo Re, Rob Guzman, Ellen Folan, Brittanie Black, and Elizabeth Fabian for all your incredible enthusiasm and support for my story.

To the wonderful filmmaking team: Joe Lawson, Cindy Chang, Nick Nesbitt, Emily Wolfe, Veronica Hidalgo, and Sam

Hayes at Netflix; director Juan Carlos Fresnadillo; screenwriter Dan Mazeau; Jeff Kirschenbaum and everyone at Roth Kirschenbaum Films; and publicists Nicola Graydon Harris and Robin McMullan. Thank you for bringing me into the process of making the *Damsel* movie.

To Millie Bobby Brown, Robin Wright, Angela Bassett, Nick Robinson, Ray Winstone, Brooke Carter, Shohreh Aghdashloo, and the rest of the cast—I am in awe of your talent. It's an honor to create art alongside you.

To my brilliant, indefatigable agent, Thao Le—you make magic happen. Thank you a thousand times, and a thousand times more.

Thank you to Tom Stripling for introducing me to Ursula Le Guin's "The Ones Who Walk Away from Omelas." Thank you to Reese Skye for creating the dragon's language, Khaevis Ventvis. And thank you to Joanna Phoenix for your insightful feedback on my characters.

And as always, thank you to my loyal readers, and all the booksellers, librarians, and social media bookworms who champion my novels. I could not do this without you!

AUTHOR'S NOTE ON THE DRAGON LANGUAGE

ALTHOUGH IT MIGHT seem random at first, Khaevis Ventvis is actually a fully functioning language invented for the world of *Damsel*. In the following pages, you'll find the phonology, grammar, syntax, and vocabulary for Khaevis Ventvis as might have been formed over millennia by powerful, legendary creatures that at the same time live in a rather limited world.

I cannot take credit for this language; it was created by my daughter, Reese Skye, a linguistic phenom and grammar enthusiast who has taught herself Spanish and Japanese, with French on the horizon. As I write this Author's Note, Reese is thirteen years old (the same age, incidentally, that J.R.R. Tolkien was when he invented what many consider his first constructed language, Nevbosh). I am terribly fortunate that Reese was willing to invent this language and explain it to me.

The first consideration in creating Khaevis Ventvis was figuring out what mattered to dragons: What does a dragon's world look like? What are its priorities? And what, on the other hand, does it pay little regard to?

For example, the name of the language itself is derived from the words "dragon" (*khae:* sky; *vis:* power) and "language" (*vent:* wind; *vis:* power). The reasoning is that dragons would not think of themselves as "dragons," which would've been the label given them by humans (a decidedly lesser species). Rather, dragons would think of themselves as the power of the sky, and the breath and words that came out of their mouths as the power of the wind.

Aurea is a Europe-inspired world, and hence, Khaevis Ventvis is modeled on the grammatical structure of romance languages like Spanish and Italian, with many roots hailing from Latin. However, the dragons' grammatical structure is simpler than that of human language, by virtue of having a less complex society.

For example, Spanish provides for both an informal and formal "you" pronoun. However, dragons are so powerful they would only ever speak to peers or those below them. Therefore, there is no need for a formal "you" pronoun.

Example: *(Ni) tvorriv za ka.* You had run away.

Similarly, there is no subjunctive mood, as dragons possess enough strength that they have little use for grammar constructs that are used only in situations of uncertainty. The conditional form *does* exist; note, however, that the first-person conjugation is rarely used, as dragons tend to take decisive action and get the results they seek. Nevertheless, the conditional form is useful with regard to nondragon actors.

Example: *(Khono) tvorraia se, kev erraia sokhif.* We would run, but we're tired.

FOR THOSE INTERESTED in delving deeper into the language, the following appendices contain highlights of Khaevis Ventvis:

Appendix A: Primer on Khaevis Ventvis Phonology and Pronunciation

Appendix B: Overview of Khaevis Ventvis Grammar and Syntax

Appendix C: Khaevis Ventvis–English Dictionary, Abridged

Appendix D: English–Khaevis Ventvis Dictionary, Abridged

Never-ending thanks, again, to Reese Skye for this incredible language, which continues to grow outside the pages of this novel. Any mistakes in this book (translations, explanations, etc.) are mine alone.

APPENDIX A

Primer on Khaevis Ventvis Phonology and Pronunciation

Khaevis Ventvis is a syllable-timed language, meaning that each syllable takes approximately the same amount of time to pronounce (as opposed to stress-timed languages, in which unstressed syllables are shorter). Every vowel in Khaevis Ventvis is pronounced separately; there are no combinations. For example, the word *khaevis* (dragon) would be pronounced as *xa.e.vi:s*.

Written	International Phonetic Alphabet	Examples* * Pronunciation examples from wikipedia.org/ wiki/Help:IPA/English
a	ɑː	palm, bra
e	ɛ	dress, prestige, length
i	iː	fleece, pedigree, idea
o	oʊ	goat
u	uː	goose, cruel
r	ɾ	caro, bravo, *partir* (like single r in Spanish)
k	k	kind, sky, crack
d	d	dye, cad, ladder

v	v	vie, leave
s	s	sigh, mass
t	t	tie, sty, cat, latter
f	f	find, leaf
n	n	nigh, snide, can
th	ð	thy, breathe, father
kh	x	loch, Chanukah
z	z	zoo, has
y	aɪ	price, pie
m	m	my, smile, cam

APPENDIX B

Overview of Khaevis Ventvis Grammar and Syntax

Meaning

Dragon: *Khaevis* (*khae:* sky; *vis:* power)

Language: *Ventvis* (*vent:* wind; *vis:* power)

Note: The name for the dragon language is Khaevis Ventvis, as this is how the dragons would have thought of it themselves—that is, the way they speak their power.

Syntax

Subject-Verb-Object (SVO) language: Khaevis Ventvis generally follows accepted English syntactic rules.

Grammar

ADJECTIVES

Adjectives generally end in *-if.* They go before the modified noun.

The prefix *san-* is added before an adjective to increase (big to bigger, etc.).

ARTICLES

Khaevis Ventvis does not use articles (a, an, the).

PRONOUNS

Subjective pronouns are implied in the verb conjugation; they don't have to be explicitly stated. For example, "I run" is said as *Tvorra* rather than *Kho tvorra*.

Objective pronouns, however, are placed in the object position. For example, *Kuirr tu kho* means "Come to me."

-las is added to the ends of independent pronouns when they're possessive (mine, yours, etc.). Dependent possessive pronouns (my, your, etc.) use the Khaevis Ventvis pronouns and are placed in the same positions as adjectives. For example, *Kho tke raz* means "My share of the bargain."

English	Khaevis Ventvis
I	kho
you	ni
he	fe
she	re
gender neutral	ve
we	khono
they	ferek

NOUNS

The same form is used for both singular and plural nouns. For example, *khaevis* means both "dragon" and "dragons."

VERBS

Verbs in Khaevis Ventvis are highly regular and always end in *-rre*.

The root is found by dropping the *-e* at the end of the infinitive.

The prefix *ny-* is added to negate verbs (Example: *savarrud:* they will save; *nysavarrud:* they won't save).

The following table illustrates how to conjugate Khaevis Ventvis verbs.

To Run—*Tvorre*

	Present	Past	Future	Conditional*
English example	*I run*	*I ran*	*I will run*	*I would run*
Kho (I)	tvorra	tvorrit	tvorrad	tvorra se
Ni (you)	tvorrai	tvorriv	tvorraid	tvorrai se
Fe/re/ve (he/she/ gender-neutral)	tvorru	tvorrut	tvorrud	tvorru se
Khono (we)	tvorraia	tvorrutiv	tvorraiad	tvorraia se
Ferek (they)	tvorruk	tvorrukut	tvorrukud	tvorruk se
	Present Perfect	**Past Perfect**	**Imperative**	
English example	*I have run*	*I had run*	*Run!*	
Kho (I)	tvorra zi	tvorrit za	tvorr (root)	
Ni (you)	tvorrai zi	tvorriv za	tvorr	
Fe/re/ve (he/she/ gender-neutral)	tvorru zi	tvorrut za	tvorr	
Khono (we)	tvorraia zi	tvorritiv za	tvorr	
Ferek (they)	tvorruk zi	tvorrukut za	tvorr	

* The conditional tense is primarily used in connection with the actions of others. Since dragons are such powerful beings, they rarely experience uncertainty in their actions. (Example: "The princess would run if she could. But I will catch her.") There-fore, the first person conjugation of the conditional tense is rarely used. Likewise, the subjunctive mood and corresponding conjugations do not exist in Khaevis Ventvis.

APPENDIX C

Khaevis Ventvis–English Dictionary, Abridged

Conjunctions	
Khaevis Ventvis	**English**
a	with
e	and
em	or
er	on/in
kev	but
kir	for
kod*	because
nisi	unless
su	like
te	so
tu	to
u*	of

* *Kodu:* "because of" or "thanks to" (combines the words for "because" and "of")

Question Words

Khaevis Ventvis	English
dakh	how
dakhi	how much
dek	what
den	when
der	where
det	why
dev	who

Verbs

Khaevis Ventvis	English
aderre	to dare
aezorre	to glow
aikurre	to love
akorre	to grow
akrerre	to know
andikorre	to predict/foretell
annurre	to pay
audirre	to hear/listen
austirre	to drink
dakarre	to tell
demerre	to allow/let
dikorre	to speak/say/talk
ensentirre	to feel (emotional)
erre*	to be/there is _____
esverre	to wait
faserre	to make (someone do)
fierre	to become

* For phrases like "How are you?" the verb *vivorre* is used in place of "to be." For example, "How are you?" becomes *Dakh vivorrai?*

frakarre	to smell
irre	to go
kesarre	to hide
kirre	to do
kokarre	to taste
komarre	to fight
komerre	to eat
kosentirre	to feel (physical)
kosirre	to understand
kovenirre	to meet
krerre	to believe / think
kuarre	to ask
kuirre	to come / to come out
manirre	to sell
menirre	to remember
minarre	to finish
mirre	to see / watch
mothyrre	to die
movdarre	to show
mukurre	to face
neresurre	to deserve
nitrerre	to have
nitrerre (ki)	to have (to)
nokherre	to sleep
nytuirre	to follow
oniserre	to smell (like something)
othyrre	to kill
rekirre	to burn
resirre	to breathe fire
resorre	to warm / heat
rykarre	to give
sanaerre	to bleed

savarre	to save
severre	to persist
sitarre	to wake up
suverre	to survive
tennerre	to keep
thoserre	to be able to
tiskirre	to grieve
traerre	to bring
tuirre	to lead
tvorre	to run
utirre	to use
vasarre	to happen
vinirre	to fly
visirre	to fall
vivorre*	to live
vorre	to want

* For phrases like "How are you?" the verb *vivorre* is used in place of "to be." For example, "How are you?" becomes *Dakh vivorrai?*

Adjectives

Khaevis Ventvis	English
demif	disappointing
diunif	long
dymerrif	delicious
idif	same
iokif	amusing
khosif	alone
kosorrif	welcome
kurrif	dark
novif	new
novsif	fascinating/interesting

nyrenif	empty
nyrokzif	bad
nyrukhif	unhappy
nytaif	small/young
nyterif	weak
raenif	angry
renif	full
rokzif	good
rukhif	happy
sarif	safe
sokhif	tired
synif	useless
syrrif	clever
ta	so/such
taif	big
terif	strong
verif	right/correct/true

Nouns

Khaevis Ventvis	English
adroka	belly/stomach
ae	here
aikoro	love
antrov	cave
avor	dread
dekris	down
desto	fate/destiny
divkor	day
drae	person/one
evoro	escape
fama	name

farris	story
feka	brother
fenekri	son
ferdivkor	today
ferkorrikh	tonight
ferrae	scream
fetaza	father
innavo	bravery / courage
invika	isle / island
ira	path / way
irae	chase
khae	sky
khaevis	dragon
korrikh	night
kurrae	dark
makho	egg
mivden	pardon
nekri	baby
nydrae	no one / nobody
nynnavo	cowardice / coward
nyta	child / young
omvra	shadow
onnedrae	any(one) / everyone
orro	treasure
raz	bargain / agreement
reka	sister
renekri	daughter
res	fire
retaza	mother
rykae	sacrifice / gift
sanae	blood
saro	safety

syne	waste/pity/shame
terin	end
timavor	fear
tke	part/share
trivi	harvest
varae	choice
veru	monster
vin	bird
vis	life/power
vokha	word
vor	hope
zedrae	princess

Miscellaneous

Khaevis Ventvis	English
ante	before
dekonne	whatever
diunif aeva	while/long time
ed	yes
etia	again/also/too
fy	now
kir rever	in return
kosor	welcome (home)
kyve	less
mirvu	very
myve	more
ny	no
onne	every
sakru	soon
senir	always
sodo	just/only

sy	until then / later
syne	waste / pity / shame
tein	last
vo	this
voro	that

APPENDIX D

English–Khaevis Ventvis Dictionary, Abridged

Conjunctions	
English	**Khaevis Ventvis**
and	e
because*	kod
but	kev
for	kir
like	su
of*	u
on/in	er
or	em
so	te
to	tu
unless	nisi
with	a

* *Kodu:* "because of" or "thanks to" (combines the words for "because" and "of")

Question Words

English	Khaevis Ventvis
how	dakh
how much	dakhi
what	dek
when	den
where	der
who	dev
why	det

Verbs

English	Khaevis Ventvis
to allow/let	demerre
to ask	kuarre
to be*/there is _____	erre
to be able to	thoserre
to become	fierre
to believe/think	krerre
to bleed	sanaerre
to breathe fire	resirre
to bring	traerre
to burn	rekirre
to come/to come out	kuirre
to dare	aderre
to deserve	neresurre
to die	mothyrre
to do	kirre
to drink	austirre
to eat	komerre

* For phrases like "How are you?" the verb *vivorre* is used in place of "to be." For example, "How are you?" becomes *Dakh vivorrai?*

to face	mukurre
to fall	visirre
to feel (emotional)	ensentirre
to feel (physical)	kosentirre
to fight	komarre
to finish	minarre
to fly	vinirre
to follow	nytuirre
to give	rykarre
to glow	aczorre
to go	irre
to grieve	tiskirre
to grow	akorre
to happen	vasarre
to have	nitrerre
to have (to)	nitrerre (ki)
to hear/listen	audirre
to hide	kesarre
to keep	tennerre
to kill	othyrre
to know	akrerre
to lead	tuirre
to live*	vivorre
to love	aikurre
to make (someone do)	faserre
to meet	kovenirre
to pay	annurre
to persist	severre
to predict/foretell	andikorre
to remember	menirre

* For phrases like "How are you?" the verb *vivorre* is used in place of "to be." For example, "How are you?" becomes *Dakh vivorrai?*

to save	savarre
to see / watch	mirre
to sell	manirre
to show	movdarre
to sleep	nokherre
to smell	frakarre
to smell (like something)	oniserre
to speak / say / talk	dikorre
to survive	suverre
to run	tvorre
to taste	kokarre
to tell	dakarre
to understand	kosirre
to use	utirre
to wait	esverre
to wake up	sitarre
to want	vorre
to warm / heat	resorre

Adjectives

English	Khaevis Ventvis
alone	khosif
amusing	iokif
angry	raenif
bad	nyrokzif
big	taif
clever	syrrif
dark	kurrif
delicious	dymerrif
disappointing	demif
empty	nyrenif

fascinating/interesting	novsif
full	renif
good	rokzif
happy	rukhif
long	diunif
new	novif
right/correct (same as *true*)	verif
safe	sarif
same	idif
small/young	nytaif
so (same as *such*)	ta
strong	terif
such (same as *so*)	ta
tired	sokhif
true (same as *right/correct*)	verif
unhappy	nyrukhif
useless	synif
weak	nyterif
welcome	kosorrif

Nouns

English	Khaevis Ventvis
any(one)	onnedrae
baby	nekri
bargain/agreement	raz
belly/stomach	adroka
bird	vin
blood	sanae
bravery/courage	innavo
brother	feka
cave	antrov

chase	irae
child/young	nyta
choice	varae
cowardice/coward	nynnavo
dark	kurrae
daughter	renekri
day	divkor
down	dekris
dragon	khaevis
dread	avor
egg	makho
end	terin
escape	evoro
everyone	onnedrae
fate/destiny	desto
father	fetaza
fear	timavor
fire	res
gift (same as *sacrifice*)	rykae
harvest	trivi
here	ae
hope	vor
isle/island	invika
life (same as *power*)	vis
love	aikoro
monster	veru
mother	retaza
name	fama
night	korrikh
no one/nobody	nydrae
pardon	mivden
part/share	tke

path/way	ira
person/one	drae
pity (same as *shame*/*waste*)	syne
power	vis
princess	zedrae
sacrifice (same as *gift*)	rykae
safety	saro
scream	ferrae
shadow	omvra
sister	reka
shame (same as *pity*/*waste*)	syne
sky	khae
son	fenekri
story	farris
today	ferdivkor
tonight	ferkorrikh
treasure	orro
waste (same as *pity*/*shame*)	syne
word	vokha

Miscellaneous

English	Khaevis Ventvis
again/also/too	etia
always	senir
before	ante
every	onne
in return	kir rever
just/only	sodo
last	tein
less	kyve
more	myve

no	ny
now	fy
soon	sakru
that	voro
this	vo
until then/later	sy
very	mirvu
welcome (home)	kosor
whatever	dekonne
while/long time	diunif aeva
yes	ed

PHOTO: © ERIN ASHFORD

Evelyn Skye is the *New York Times* bestselling author of six novels, including the forthcoming *The Hundred Loves of Juliet*. A graduate of Stanford University and Harvard Law School, Skye lives in the San Francisco Bay Area with her husband and daughter, Reese, who created the dragon language in the *Damsel* novel.

evelynskye.com
Instagram: @evelyn_skye

ABOUT THE TYPE

This book was set in Dante, a typeface designed by Giovanni Mardersteig (1892–1977). Conceived as a private type for the Officina Bodoni in Verona, Italy, Dante was originally cut only for hand composition by Charles Malin, the famous Parisian punch cutter, between 1946 and 1952. Its first use was in an edition of Boccaccio's *Trattatello in laude di Dante* that appeared in 1954. The Monotype Corporation's version of Dante followed in 1957. Though modeled on the Aldine type used for Pietro Cardinal Bembo's treatise *De Aetna* in 1495, Dante is a thoroughly modern interpretation of that venerable face.